"You know, daughter," [...]
weeks like this and I think w[...]
we need."

"I know," Kate agreed. "It has been wonderful.
The Indians have cooperated so well, and we have
drawings of the villages and families in their tepees." She held up a couple of the sketches. "And I
just love these drawings of the children."

"Here come some more," P.G. said, pointing to
four horsemen approaching the wagon. "No doubt,
they'll be wanting their pictures drawn."

Kate laughed. "You can't say we haven't been
getting cooperation from them, can you?"

"Well, we can't turn them down," P.G. said. He
looked around. "Now, what happened to those
charcoal sticks?"

"Oh, I put them in the wagon," Kate said. "I'll get
them."

Kate climbed up onto the wagon, opened the
canvas cover, and went inside. The canvas allowed
only a shaded light through. She began looking
through the blankets, papers, baskets, and other
paraphernalia.

"I said I put them in here, and I know I did," she
called out to her father. "But I tell you, I can't find
them."

She felt the wagon tip as someone climbed on.

"You don't have to come up here, Father. I'll find
them."

The curtain parted, and Kate looked around.
There, grinning obscenely, was the painted face of a
Sioux warrior. . . .

Ralph Compton's

Clarion's Call

A Novel by Robert Vaughan

A SIGNET BOOK

SIGNET
Published by New American Library, a division of
Penguin Putnam Inc., 375 Hudson Street,
New York, New York 10014, U.S.A.
Penguin Books Ltd, 27 Wrights Lane,
London W8 5TZ, England
Penguin Books Australia Ltd,
Ringwood, Victoria, Australia
Penguin Books Canada Ltd, 10 Alcorn Avenue,
Toronto, Ontario, Canada M4V 3B2
Penguin Books (N.Z.) Ltd, 182–190 Wairau Road,
Auckland 10, New Zealand

Penguin Books Ltd, Registered Offices:
Harmondsworth, Middlesex, England

First published by Signet, an imprint of New American Library,
a division of Penguin Putnam Inc.

First Printing, May 2001
10 9 8 7 6 5 4 3 2 1

PUBLISHER'S NOTE
This is a work of fiction. Names, characters, places, and incidents either are
the product of the author's imagination or are used fictitiously, and any
resemblance to actual persons, living or dead, events, or locales is entirely
coincidental.

Chapter One

Lieutenant Colonel George Armstrong Custer, in full-dress uniform, sat uncomfortably in a cane-back chair in the waiting room outside the presidential chambers. Laying one leg across his knee, he began to playfully toss his hat onto his boot. He did this a few times, grew bored with it, then changed positions, sticking his legs out in front of him to relieve the soreness in his back.

Although the president's appointments secretary was busy at his desk, he glanced over at Custer, casting a look of disapproval at the man who had been waiting here for over four hours. The man was persistent, the secretary would have give him that. This was Custer's third day of waiting, in vain, for an audience with President Grant.

Custer got up from his chair and walked over to stare through the window. On the lawn outside, groundskeepers were hard at work, and he could hear the whirr of a half-dozen lawnmowers being pushed to cut the early spring grass.

Behind him the door opened, and he looked around to see two officious-looking civilians enter.

"Hello, Mr. Kennedy. Is the president busy?" one of them asked.

"Just a moment, Senator, and I will announce you," the president's secretary said.

Custer watched as Kennedy disappeared through the door leading to Grant's office. A moment later he returned.

"You two gentlemen may go right in," he said.

Thanking him, the two civilians started through the door. "Mr. President," Custer heard one of them say, just as the door closed behind them.

Custer walked back over to the secretary's desk. "Mr. Kennedy, this is my third day, and I have been waiting here for four hours," he said. "You tell me that the president is too busy to see me, yet these men come in and are granted an immediate audience."

Kennedy put down his pen and pinched the bridge of his nose. He drew a deep breath, as if he were about to jump into a stream of cold water. "I'm sorry, Colonel," he said. "But surely you must realize by now that the president has no wish to see you."

"Has he told you why?"

"He hasn't come right out and said it, but I know

he found your intemperate comments with regard to his brother and certain members of his Cabinet most disquieting."

"All right, if I can't see him, then at least get him to say that he refuses to meet with me, so I can leave Washington and rejoin my regiment."

"He won't do that, either," Kennedy said. "I asked him if I couldn't just tell you that he won't meet you so you wouldn't have to stay around waiting for him. He says that he will meet with you, but in his own time."

"In his own time?"

"I'm afraid so."

"I have no more time," Custer said. "My regiment will soon be taking to the field, and I must be there when they march."

"I'm sorry, Colonel. There is really nothing I can do," the secretary said.

Custer looked at the door that led to the president's office. He took a couple of steps toward it, then raised his hand as if to open it.

"Colonel?" Kennedy said, rising from his chair.

For one moment Custer considered pushing the door open and barging into Grant's office. Grant would hear him out. Custer would make him listen.

"General Custer, please," Kennedy said, taking a hesitant step toward him. In an attempt to be more conciliatory, Kennedy had used Custer's brevet title. Although Custer's actual command rank was lieutenant colonel, the fact that he had been breveted a major general during the war entitled him to the courtesy of being addressed as general.

Custer paused, ran his hand through his reddish-blond hair, then sighed.

"Mr. Kennedy, have you a pen and paper?"

"Yes, of course," Kennedy answered, opening the drawer to his desk. He handed Custer a sheet of paper, a pen, and an ink bottle.

"Thank you," Custer said. He walked over to a side table, sat down, and began to write.

To His Exc'y the President,   *May 1, 1876*

Today, for the third time, I have sought an interview with the President, not to solicit a favor, except to be granted a brief hearing, but to remove from his mind certain unjust impressions concerning myself which I have reason to believe are entertained against me. I desire this opportunity simply as a matter of justice; and I regret that the President has declined to give me an opportunity to submit to him a brief statement which justice to him, as well as to me, demanded.

Resp'y submitted:

G. A. Custer
Lt. Col Seventh Cav.
Bvt. Maj. Gen. U.S.A.

New York, May 1

The name Kate McKenzie was one that any reader of the society columns of New York newspapers would recognize, for as the daughter of a celebrated artist, she was a frequent guest of the city's most elite *affaires sociales*. She was twenty-two years old, of medium height, slender, with hair the color of burnished copper. Her emerald eyes were dusted with flecks of gold, which in a certain light seemed to match her hair. She had a fine, fair complexion, though she did have a tendency to freckle when exposed to the sun.

Kate wasn't exposed to the sun at this moment. Rather, she was standing under the golden glow of the chandeliers and gas-jet lamps of the New York Art League's gallery foyer. The league was sponsoring a showing of her father's work, and she was acting as one of the hostesses.

The fame and reputation of Kate's father, P. G. McKenzie, did not end on this side of the Atlantic. He had shown in Paris, London, and Vienna, and was nearly as highly acclaimed in Europe as he was in America.

P. G. McKenzie counted among his friends such men as Renoir, Monet, and Albert Sisley. He had studied in Paris under Eugene Isabey, but was not unduly influenced by his teacher's academic romanticism. P.G.'s unique style was best explained by a noted art critic of the *New York Tribune*, in a glowing account of P.G.'s work, *Train Shed*:

> *It gives one a remarkable feeling of presence in the interior of a train shed. This is accomplished in part by a brilliant use of diffuse light, but also by the optically perfect perspective of his subject. Atmosphere is captured in a bold and imaginative way. McKenzie is a major artist with an exquisite feel for form, and it is most noteworthy to discover that P. G. McKenzie is constantly growing as an artist. A new spirit and vitality has appeared in his paintings. He has developed an eye for the variations of light and color that breathe life into his work.*

When Kate read the last comment, she and her father held a small, private celebration. Such a statement, they both knew, was a compliment to Kate's own dexterity with the brush.

P. G. McKenzie was suffering from rheumatoid arthritis. Because of that, he had trained Kate to take over much of his work. She was nearly equal to him in skill, and she now made many of the preliminary drawings as well as some of the finished work. The new vitality the art critic had noticed in P. G. McKenzie's work was in fact the result of Kate's own technique.

It wasn't simply vanity that caused P. G. McKenzie to keep secret his arthritis. It was to protect a dream. For years, he had nurtured the ambition to go west and paint the American Indian in his natural habitat. Kate had been a part of that dream for so long that she felt a compulsion just as strong as her father's. Thus, when the New York Art League commissioned P. G. McKenzie to do a series of paintings that would accurately portray life among the Plains Indians, she was as delighted as her father.

They both knew that the commission would be in jeopardy if the Art League knew of P.G.'s affliction, so they kept it, and Kate's involvement in his work, a closely guarded secret.

Despite their caution, the project was almost jeopardized by another matter beyond their control. The Indians were beginning to make trouble in the Black Hills, and the Department of Interior refused to grant permission for P.G. and Kate to undertake the assignment.

But P.G. had one last card to play. President Grant was a great fan of P.G.'s work, and had hung what was possibly P.G.'s most famous painting, *Toward Higher Office*, in the White House. The work depicted President Lincoln lying on the bed after having been shot, surrounded by those who made up the deathwatch. Above Lincoln, painted in glowing color, was his soul being transported to heaven by a host of angels.

The president responded to P.G.'s personal appeal, and overrode the Department of Interior with a presidential letter, authorizing P.G. and Kate free access to any and all Indian lands.

"Please be aware," Grant cautioned in his letter of permission, "that this just clears you with regard to the Department of the Interior. Your actual clearance, once you are in the Dakota Territory, will depend upon the capacity of the military authorities to guarantee your safety."

Now, as Kate circled the gallery, her smiles to the patrons reflected both her contentment in the current show's success, and her eagerness to see a bold new frontier.

Chicago, May 5

The train shed smelled of coal smoke, steam, and teeming humanity, with a note of sausages, cabbage, and various other cooking odors thrown in. In addition to the aromas, the depot was a symphony of sound: steel rolling on steel, whistles, clanging bells, chugging pistons, venting steam, rattling cars, shouted orders, and the cacophony of hundreds of individual conversations.

Although he was wearing a brown tweed jacket, tan trousers, a red vest and bow tie, and a brown derby, the man who stepped down from the train in Chicago projected a military bearing. Brevet Major General George A. Custer picked up his carpetbag, then started up the platform toward the depot shed. There, he would be able to ascertain which track the train for St. Paul would be using, as well as when it would be leaving.

He was intercepted by an army lieutenant who stepped up to him and saluted crisply.

"General Custer?"

Custer returned the salute. "I didn't think anyone would recognize me in mufti," he said. "What can I do for you, Lieutenant?"

"I'm sorry, sir," the lieutenant said, "but I must place you under arrest."

"What?" Custer gasped in shock. "Did you say you were placing me under arrest?"

"I'm afraid so, sir," the lieutenant replied uncomfortably.

"Upon what charge?"

"Absent without orders, sir."

"That's nonsense. I am on leave, and I am, even now, returning to Fort Lincoln."

"According to the charges, sir, you left Washington without first calling upon the president," the lieutenant said.

"I left Washington without calling on the president?" Custer blustered. Then he thought of the three long days he had sat in the anteroom, begging for an appointment, and, suddenly it became funny to him. "I'll be damned." He laughed. "Who would've thought an old maid like Grant would have something like that in him?"

"I beg your pardon, sir?"

Custer's eyes narrowed. "Lieutenant, you don't have it in mind to put me in jail, do you?"

"No, sir. General Sheridan has asked that I bring you straight to him."

Custer breathed a sigh of relief. "Good." He had served with Sheridan during the war, and Sheridan had long been his friend and sponsor "Very well. Lead on, Macduff."

"What in the hell got into you, Custer?" Sheridan asked. "I mean, what in heaven's name made you think you could say such things about the president and get away with it?"

"General, I didn't volunteer to testify before the Clymer Committee, I was subpoenaed," Custer said.

"But the testimony you gave . . . accusing Secretary Belknap of selling Indian agencies, even suggesting that the president's own brother was involved."

"I said no more than what is being said about them all over the West, General. The only thing is, I had the courage to say it before a congressional committee."

"There is no proof of these accusations. All you did was repeat hearsay," Sheridan said. "God's whiskers, man, what you did is little better than repeating malicious gossip!"

Sheridan, who was considerably shorter than average men, managed to project a rather notable presence with his closely cropped gray hair and a dark, sweeping, walrus-style mustache. Getting up from his desk, he walked over to look at his wall map. He had no reason to study it; it was merely a way of gathering his thoughts. Custer knew enough to be quiet during this prolonged pause. Finally, Sheridan turned to him. "I got you out of trouble once before, Custer. You may recall, you had been suspended for one year without pay, and I brought you back to active service."

"Yes, sir, I do recall," Custer said. "And you have my undying gratitude for that."

Sheridan turned away from the map and glared at Custer. "Yes, Armstrong, I can see how much gratitude you have shown."

"Perhaps if we sent a wire to General Sherman?"

"Sherman?" Sheridan exploded. "Sherman and Grant are like this, don't you know that?" Sheridan crossed his fingers to illustrate the point. "Sherman is the one who ordered your arrest."

"But surely he will let me rejoin my regiment in time to accompany them in the field?"

"Sherman wanted you court-martialed and discharged from the service! I managed to talk him into a suspension."

"How long of a suspension?" Custer asked.

"How long? What does it matter?" Sheridan replied in exasperation. "I'm trying to save your career, and all you are worried about is going into the field with your regiment."

"General, if I don't go with my regiment, then I have no career. I can't remain safely back at Fort Lincoln while my regiment is in danger. Is there nothing you can do about it?"

Sheridan took a cigar from its humidor, inhaled it's rich bouquet, then ran his tongue along the side. "There's nothing I can do alone," he said as he struck a match.

"You have an idea?" Custer asked, hopefully.

Sheridan lit his cigar, then answered Custer through puffs of thick smoke. "Perhaps, if you appealed to General Terry. Terry will be in charge of the expedition."

"I'll go see him at once," Custer said, starting toward the door. Then he stopped. "With the general's permission," he added.

Sheridan sighed. "If Terry wants you, have him send the telegram through me. I'll endorse it. But I can't promise you anything, Custer."

"You've come through for me before, Phil," Custer said. "I'm sure you will be able to do so again."

"Don't count on it forever, Armstrong. One of these days you are going to go to the well, and you'll find that it has gone dry," Sheridan said, waving his cigar to make the point.

Chapter Two

Fort Abraham Lincoln, Dakota Territory, May 5, 1876

As the officers of the Seventh Cavalry waited for Major Marcus Reno to arrive, they drank coffee and carried on a spirited conversation about a baseball game contested on the previous day between the Seventh Cavalry and the Sixth Infantry. First Lieutenant Quinn Pendarrow, a tall, well-proportioned, blond-haired, blue-eyed man who was also present, took no part in the conversation. Instead, his interest was held by a letter he had received in the morning's post.

April 28, 1876

Dear Quinn,

    Yours of the 5th, instant in hand, I take pen in hand to answer as quickly as I can. I am happy that you have submitted a letter resigning your commission, even though you expressed some misgivings about having done so. In your letter to me you spoke of such things as loyalty, honor, and duty.

It is those very things I now ask you to consider. What about your loyalty and honor to me? What about your duty to the promise you made, when you said you would resign? By submitting your resignation, have you not fulfilled that loyalty, honor, and duty?

You must understand that, in the confines of an army post, you and your fellow officers lead such narrow lives that you do not even realize what the average person thinks of you. They regard all soldiers as misfits, alcoholics for the most part, men who are unable to hold even the most ordinary positions.

Do you think I want to be married to someone whose station in life is so low? How much nicer will it be for you to work as a sales manager for my father? You will be well paid, we will enjoy the privileges of society, and you will never have to face the possibility of being scalped by some wild savage.

In addition, as soon as we are married, Father has promised to buy a house for us. I'm sure even you would agree that a house in St. Louis will be much better than some drab and dreary officers' quarters on an army post in that godforsaken West you so love.

> *Yours,*
> *Suzie*

"From Miss Parkinson?" Lieutenant Godfrey asked when he saw Quinn so engrossed in his letter.

Quinn folded the letter and put it in his inside tunic pocket. "Yes."

"She must be some girl to get you to give up your commission."

"She is," Quinn said.

"When is the wedding?"

"My resignation takes effect at midnight on the twelfth of May. The wedding will be on the fourth of June."

"Too bad. That means you'll miss our big expedition," Godfrey said.

"Yes, I guess it will."

"The way things look, you and General Custer will both miss it."

"Have you heard anything new? Is there still no change in the general's situation?"

Godfrey shook his head. "I'm afraid not. Apparently he has made an enemy of President Grant himself. Not even Custer's luck can overcome that."

Quinn chuckled. "Leave it to our commander— when he goes out to make an enemy, he goes to the very top."

"That's true enough. Certainly, no one has ever accused Custer of timidity," Godfrey replied, laughing with him.

"Still, it doesn't seem right that the officers and men of the Seventh Cavalry would take to the field without Custer to lead them," Quinn said.

Major Reno, who was the acting commander of the Seventh Cavalry, came into the room just in time to overhear Quinn's comment.

"Mr. Pendarrow, you aren't suggesting that I am incapable of leading this regiment in the field, are you?" Reno asked in a clipped tone.

Seeing Reno, all the officers, including Quinn, stood respectfully.

"I asked you a question, Lieutenant. Do you believe I am incapable of leading the regiment?" Reno repeated, his dark eyes flashing the challenge.

"No, sir, of course I don't believe that," Quinn answered quickly. "It is just that General Custer has been in command of the Seventh ever since I have been here. It is only normal that I would have a difficult time imagining anyone else in that position."

"You don't have to *imagine* me in that position, Lieutenant, for I already *am* in that position," Reno said.

"Yes, sir, of course you are, sir."

"Everyone in the regiment is feeling so sorry for Custer, but remember, he has no one to blame but himself. It is by his excessive personality and hot-headed remarks that he wound up in this fix in the first place. Let that be a lesson to all of you," Reno continued, looking around at each of the assembled men's faces. "An officer on the active rolls has no right to publicly criticize his superiors."

"Interesting observation, Major. Are you not doing the same thing about my brother?" Captain Tom Custer asked coolly.

"I am not, sir. General Custer has been suspended, therefore he is not, at this moment, my superior," Reno replied. "Now, gentlemen, as we personally will have no say in the final disposition of Colonel Custer's situation, I propose that we leave him to his own devices while we set about the business at hand. Lieutenant Varnum, share your information with our fellow officers."

Varnum, the chief of scouts, turned to address the other officers.

"Gentlemen, this morning one of my scouts returned with some excellent intelligence as to the whereabouts of the small group of Indians that has been attacking riverboats, shooting at trains, and setting grass fires on the prairie."

"Who are they, Charley?" Captain Yates asked.

"It is a band of Lakota, led by a warrior named Red Eagle."

"Red Eagle?" Yates shook his head. "I don't think I've ever heard of him."

"He's never given us any trouble before," Varnum said. "Word is, he had himself a vision, and in that vision he becomes a great war leader. Now, he's trying to make the vision come true."

"Doing what? Shooting a few arrows at boats? Setting a few fires?" Tom asked. "Hardly the stuff of a warrior, let alone a chief."

"I intend to go after him," Reno said.

Surprised by the pronouncement, Tom Custer

looked at Reno. "Excuse me, Major, but surely you don't intend to take the field?"

"I surely do. We are charged with bringing in the hostiles, are we not?"

"Yes, sir, but we are only days away from conducting a major operation with General Terry. Are you sure going into the field at this juncture is the wisest course?"

"Captain Custer, I am commanding the Seventh Cavalry now, not your brother," Reno said sharply. "You may have been accustomed to questioning his orders, sir, but you will not question mine. Is that understood?"

"Understood, sir," Tom said, holding his anger in check.

"Good. I'm glad that we understand each other. Now, gentlemen, here's my plan. I want this post to be a beehive of activity for the rest of the day. We are going to be making all preparations to leave tomorrow morning at daybreak. I want the wagons loaded, and I want rations and ammunition issued."

"Excuse me, Major," Captain Benteen said. Though now only a captain, Frederick W. Benteen held the brevet of a full colonel, having occupied that rank during the war. Short and stocky, with long hair the color of shocked wheat, he was the oldest and most experienced officer in the regiment. Using his pipe as a pointer, he indicated the front gate. "I know the Indians who are living just outside our gate are supposed to be friendly, but isn't there a chance that some of them might be equally as friendly to this Indian we're going after . . . what's his name . . . Red Eagle?"

"Oh, I hope so, Benteen. I truly hope so," Reno replied. "Because that is part of my plan. Tomorrow morning at dawn we will throw open the gates and make a big show of sending out the cavalry. We'll have trumpets blowing and flags waving. Then you, Captain Benteen, will take the first battalion, as well as three troops of the second battalion, through the gates, make a big, noisy circle, eventually winding up right back here at the fort."

"That's all, sir?" Benteen asked, a little confused.

"That's your part of the plan," Reno said. He turned toward the door, then called out. "Lieutenant Ford, would you come in, please?"

Lieutenant Ford, who had been waiting just outside the officers' mess, came in when summoned. Lean and balding, Ford was in his late thirties. A cavalry officer in name only, having spent over ten years in one staff assignment after another, he was at the moment the regimental supply officer. The others looked at Ford with curiosity, wondering what role he would have to play in an actual field operation.

"Lieutenant Ford will take one platoon of I Company and leave very early tomorrow morning, while it is still dark."

Tom Custer looked surprised. "You are giving Lieutenant Ford a platoon from my company? Ford is a staff officer, with no experience in the field. What about Lieutenant Pendarrow? Shouldn't he be taking it? After all, he is my executive officer."

"I know Lieutenant Pendarrow's position, thank you very much," Reno replied. "He will be going along. But, as he has already submitted his resignation, I feel that an officer with a somewhat more permanent status should be in command."

"Then give me the platoon," Tom volunteered.

"What's the matter, Captain? Do you fear there may be some glory somewhere, and there be no Custer to take advantage of it?"

"It's not that, Major, and you know it," Tom said bitterly. "I am concerned about putting my men in danger under the command of an inexperienced officer."

"Your concern is noted, Captain, but Lieutenant Ford will be in command," Reno said. He looked over at Quinn. "Mr. Pendarrow, I'm sure I can count on you to put yourself at Mr. Ford's disposal?"

"I'll help Lieutenant Ford in whatever way I can," Quinn said.

"I didn't come into the army yesterday, Mr. Pendarrow," Ford said dryly. "I don't need your help. I won't require anything from you but your compliance with my orders."

"But of course you will have that, sir," Quinn said, bristling at Ford's provocative statement. "As would any officer appointed over me."

"Yes, well, we would expect no less, wouldn't we?" Reno said, then continued. "Lieutenant Ford, have your men leave behind anything that isn't absolutely necessary. I want nothing that will rattle or make noise. The Indians in the village will be sleeping when you leave, and I don't want them to see you go. Slip through their camp as quietly as you can, then head for Snake Head Creek, which is about twenty-five miles southeast. I want you and your platoon there by sunup." Reno consulted his almanac. "The sun rises tomorrow at six-thirty-five. Will you make it?"

"We'll be there, sir," Ford promised.

"Good. Gentlemen, this is a complex operation that depends upon precise coordination and proper execution. Before dawn and under cover of darkness, I will take the fourth battalion down to the base of the bluff, where we will load onto the steamer *Far West*. When Captain Benteen leaves with his troops in the morning, all the Indians will be watching him. That diversion should allow Captain Marsh to get his boat under way without any of the Indians realizing that an entire battalion is aboard."

"What do you have in mind for me?" Tom asked.

"Captain Custer, I am pleased to inform you that you and your battalion will remain behind. You must make it look as if business as usual is going on here."

"I'm to have no role?" Tom asked.

"On the contrary. I've just told you your role. You are to make the Indians think that, except for the ones who left with Captain Benteen, everyone else has remained at the post. As I recall when we started this conversation, you were against this operation anyway, so this particular assignment should suit you well."

Tom glared at Reno, but said nothing.

"Cooke, the map, please."

Captain Cooke, the adjutant, unfolded a map and held it up so everyone could see it. Reno put his finger on the map to illustrate his point.

"Now," he began, "with Benteen riding in a big circle up here, Red Eagle and his men will be forced down this natural draw to the vicinity of Snake Head Creek. He should reach Snake Head Creek here, halfway between Lieutenant Ford's location and the point where Snake Head Creek empties into the Missouri River. I will off-load my battalion where the creek joins the river. Once I get them on shore, we will take up a position along the breaks. Red Eagle will be caught between my battalion and

Lieutenant Ford's platoon. Lieutenant Ford, it will be your job to drive the Indians toward me."

"Yes, sir," Ford said.

"As I told you, this all depends upon precise timing. Which means, Lieutenant Ford, that at exactly nine o'clock tomorrow, you and all your men must start moving along the creek toward my position. At *exactly* nine o'clock, not one minute later. You must be punctual."

Ford nodded.

Reno looked up from the map, his eyes blazing in excitement. "When Red Eagle and his followers meet me, they'll be like sitting ducks. I'll cut them to pieces. Gentlemen, it's about time that the Eastern press learns that our victories over the Indians have been Seventh Cavalry victories . . . not George Armstrong Custer victories. And this will bring home that point."

"Are you looking for a Seventh Cavalry victory, or a Marcus Reno victory?" Tom asked.

"What difference does it make, Captain, if we are successful?" Reno replied.

"Well, if you ask me, I think it's a brilliant plan," Ford said.

"Major, there is one thing that concerns me," Quinn said, pointing to the map. "I have been down Snake Head Creek quite a few times, and I know that it is cut in a dozen or more places by draws, sloughs, and gullies. What would keep the Indians from going up one of those draws and setting up an ambush?"

"Your mission is one of classic cavalry deployment. Shock and speed. Once you get started, you must move forward with all deliberate speed. Do you understand me? All deliberate speed. Stick to that plan, and the Indians won't have time to set up an ambush." Reno turned to Ford. "You do understand that, don't you?"

"Yes, sir, I understand," Ford replied.

"Then, gentlemen, by this time tomorrow we will have a victory to celebrate," Reno said, beaming.

Chapter Three

Early the next morning, because Quinn allowed no lanterns to be lit, his platoon had to ready themselves by the dim light of the stars. Quinn looked over the platoon, inspecting arms and ammunition, examining girths, bits, and bridles, as well as the condition of the horses' hooves.

"Tenshut!" one of the men suddenly called, and everyone came to attention. Quinn turned to see Captain Tom Custer strolling toward them. Tom wasn't wearing a hat, his jacket hung open, and he was stifling a yawn.

"Good morning, Captain," Quinn said as he saluted. "You didn't have to get out of bed."

Tom's return salute was so casual that he was still holding the riding quirt in his hand. "This platoon is from my company. You didn't think I'd let you and your men get away without wishing you good luck, did you?"

"The men and I appreciate your coming down, sir."

"You know, Quinn, you don't have to go out on this scout. I don't care what Reno says, this is still my company. I can send Benny in your place."

Benny was Second Lieutenant Hodgson.

"I'd hate to have to write Miss Sue Parkinson and tell her that her fiancé was scalped by Indians on his very last scout," Tom continued.

"I appreciate your concern, Captain, but until my resignation is official, I am still an officer in the U.S. Cavalry," Quinn said. "I'll do my duty."

Tom nodded his approval. "I figured you would feel that way," he said. "And I would expect no less, but I thought I would give you the opportunity."

"Sir, the platoon is ready," Sergeant Flynn announced, walking up to the two officers.

"Thank you, Sergeant."

Tom looked around. "Where is Lieutenant Ford?" he asked.

"He isn't here."

Tom was surprised. "He hasn't arrived?"

"No, sir. But I'm sure he will be here shortly."

"You don't need to make excuses for him."

"No, sir, I realize that."

Tom pulled out his pocketwatch and examined it. "If he doesn't show up in five minutes, leave without him. I'll take care of Reno."

"Yes, sir."

Quinn's opportunity to lead the platoon was short-lived as they saw Ford running toward the stables across the quadrangle.

"Your command nearly left without you, Lieutenant," Tom admonished.

"The orderly didn't wake me in time."

"Of course it would be the orderly," Tom said with a scornful snort. "Very well, Mr. Ford, the command is yours. You had better get started."

"Yes, sir," Ford replied. "Platoon, to horse. Officers and noncommissioned officers, post," he ordered.

Quinn and the platoon sergeant, Sergeant Flynn, "posted" by taking their places at the head of the platoon.

"Prepare to mount," Ford called. Then, "Mount!"

As one, the men mounted.

"Remember," Tom cautioned, "you must make your departure from here as quietly as possible."

"Yes, sir. Right, by column of twos. Forward, ho!"

At his command, the platoon began moving out at a swift trot, following Lieutenant Ford. Sergeant Flynn rode beside Quinn. As they were only at platoon strength, there was no guidon bearer to hold aloft the battalion colors.

A couple of the post guards opened the gate to allow the riders to exit the fort. One hundred yards later the horsemen were on banks of the wide, shallow Missouri, moving swiftly past the sleeping tepees of the Indians who were camped alongside. Following their orders, the men rode very quietly, the only sound the dull thud and brush of hoofs in the dirt and dry grass, the twist and creak of leather, and the subdued clinks of bit chains.

By dawn, in accordance with Reno's instructions, the platoon was in position on the banks of Snake Head Creek. The horses had been watered, and the men were waiting for their orders. Sergeant Flynn and Trooper Scott were standing on top of the highest knoll, looking toward the east. Though only a private, Scott was the oldest trooper in the platoon. He was also the most experienced, having been a colonel in the Confederate cavalry.

"There," Scott said. "Do you see it?"

"I'll be damned. That's some kind of a trick, all right," Flynn said.

"What is it?" Quinn asked, walking up to see what the two men were doing.

"Trooper Scott was showin' me a trick he learnt durin' the war, 'bout how to see riders up to ten miles away or more," Flynn said.

"That sounds like a pretty good trick," Quinn said. "How does it work?"

"It only works just after sunrise, or just before sunset, when the sun is very low on the horizon," Scott explained. "With the sun at that angle, you can sometimes get a flare from dust, kicked up by a distant body of men. There is just such a flare out there now, about seven or eight miles distant."

Quinn raised his glasses and looked in the direction Scott pointed out. Then he saw it, a tiny glow, far off.

"Yes," he said. "Yes, I see it. Think it's our Indians?"

"Has to be, sir," Flynn replied. "Cap'n Benteen and the cavalry are some west of here. And Major Reno and his men ain't goin' to be doin' no movin' around to speak of."

"Mr. Pendarrow!" Ford called, "what are you doing up there?"

"Sergeant Flynn and Trooper Scott have spotted the Indians, sir," Quinn replied.

"Indians?" Ford hurried up the slope. "Where are they?"

"About eight miles that way, sir," Scott said, pointing.

Ford snorted. "Eight miles? I may not have much field experience, but even I know you can't spot a body of men eight miles away."

"Yes, sir, take a look," Quinn said. He raised his binoculars, then sighed. "No, sir, you won't see them now. The sun has moved."

"The sun has moved? What are you talking about?"

"Tell him, Trooper Scott," Quinn said.

Scott explained his theory.

"That's hogwash, Scott. Mister Pendarrow, get the men mounted. It's time to get started."

"Sir, I volunteer to ride as point man," Scott offered as they started back down the slope.

"We won't be using a point man."

"Beggin' your pardon, sir, we have to use a point man," Sergeant Flynn insisted. "Otherwise we could be riding right into an ambush!"

"We *are* riding into an ambush, Flynn. That's the whole point," Ford said. "An ambush for the Indians." He laughed.

"Sir, with all due respect, the Indians are ahead of us. We have seen them," Scott said. "You have to have someone riding point."

"Trooper, you are forgetting your place?" Ford asked. "You may have been a colonel with the graybacks, but here you are just a private, and you don't presume to tell an officer what to do. When we return to the post, I intend to charge you with insubordination. Lieutenant Pendarrow, is this all the control you have over your men?"

"Sir, I don't think Trooper Scott meant any disrespect," Quinn said. "I think he was just concerned about—"

"Enough!" Ford interrupted in exasperation. "What *is* it with you people? Do none of you understand the term military discipline? Get mounted at once!"

"Yes, sir," Quinn said as he, Scott, and Flynn started toward their horses.

"All right, to horse!" Flynn shouted at the soldiers, some of whom were taking a nap to make up for the sleep they lost that morning.

"Men," Ford said, standing in the stirrups to address the platoon, "we are going to ride up the creek bed. We will start at a canter, continue for ten minutes, then slow to a trot. Above all, keep it closed up, and keep moving!"

"Sir, you don't mean the creek bed, do you?" Quinn asked. "Surely you mean we are going to be riding along the ridgeline, following the creek."

"You heard Major Reno's orders to me, did you not, Lieutenant Pendarrow?" Ford said. "He was most specific. Once we get started, we are to proceed with all deliberate speed. We can move much faster by staying in the creek bed than we can by riding up on the ridgeline where we will constantly be traversing gullies."

"Yes, sir," Quinn replied grimly.

"Forward, ho!" Ford ordered, and the platoon started forward at the canter.

"Sir," Sergeant Flynn said to Quinn a half hour later, "look up ahead. See how the walls close in on the creek bed like that? Once we get in there, it will be too narrow for maneuvering."

"You're right." Quinn called up to Ford riding at the head of the column. "May I recommend that we leave this creek bed and take the high ground, just until we are through that restricted canyon ahead?"

"Our orders are all deliberate speed, Pendarrow," Ford called back over his shoulder. "We will ride through."

"Lieutenant Ford, there must've been some reason why Major Reno sent me on this scout with you. It doesn't take two officers to command one platoon. I can only assume that he intended me to offer you the benefit of my experience in the field," Quinn said, trying to rein in his frustration. "And my recommendation is—"

"I am aware of your recommendation, Mr. Pendarrow," Ford replied. "We will continue as before."

"Yes, sir," Quinn replied, shaking his head.

They were halfway through the narrow canyon, and Quinn was beginning to hope they might make it all the way without incident, when there was a sudden shout, followed by a horse whinnying in pain.

"Rock slide!" someone yelled.

Quinn twisted in his saddle to see hundreds of rocks, many the size of 24-pound cannonballs, sliding down each side of the sheer walls. As they were coming down both sides, he realized at once that it wasn't a natural occurrence.

"Injuns!" another shouted, just before a cloud of arrows rained down on them. Most of the arrows clattered off the steep rocky walls on either side of them, but from the shouts and groans of fear and pain, Quinn knew that at least some of them had found their marks.

"Dismount! Dismount!" Ford ordered.

"Ford, no! We can't dismount! We're in a confined area! We've got to get out of here!" Quinn shouted.

"Goddammit, Pendarrow! Quit questioning my commands!" Ford screamed.

Quinn looked into Ford's eyes and saw absolute panic.

"I said dismount!" Ford ordered again.

The platoon was made up of seasoned cavalrymen who knew that the moment any body of cavalry dismounted, it would lose one-fourth of its effective fighting force because every fourth man was detailed to hold the horses of the other three. More important, they knew that if they dismounted they would be sitting ducks for the Indians up on the ridgeline. But they were, above all, soldiers, and they had been given their orders. Reluctantly, they dismounted.

"Lieutenant, we've got to get the hell out of . . . unh!" That was as far as Sergeant Flynn got before an arrow penetrated his heart.

"Sergeant Flynn!" Quinn shouted.

"Lieutenant Pendarrow, we're getting slaughtered here!" Trooper Scott shouted, and as Quinn looked around he saw in addition to Flynn, at least four more men down.

"Lieutenant Ford, we must remount!" Quinn tried again.

At that moment one of the troopers holding the horses was hit. He was right in front of Ford, and seeing him, Ford's eyes grew wide in terror. In seeing stark death right before his shocked eyes, he realized, finally, that he had made a mistake in dismounting. "Mr. Pendarrow . . . Mr. Pendarrow, the . . . the . . . com . . . command is yours."

"Platoon, mount!" Quinn shouted, without even acknowledging Ford's relinquishment of command.

As Ford attempted to mount, he was brought down, not by an arrow, but by a rifle shot, for now Indians armed with rifles had joined in the fray. Quinn looked at the fallen lieutenant and saw that the bullet had struck him in the forehead, killing him instantly.

"Column of twos, forward at a gallop!" Quinn shouted, leading the men out of the narrow restriction. "Scott!"

"Yes, sir!" Scott was just behind him now.

"When we get to the cross-gully ahead, take the left column into the gully on the left! I'll take the right. As soon you can get out of the gully, circle back and charge the Indians on the ridge!"

"Yes, sir!" Scott replied.

They reached the cross-gully in a hundred yards,

then split into two different directions. Quinn was relieved to see that the gully had shallow sloping sides so that they were able to exit quite easily. Very quickly, they were up on top of the ridge and at the same level as the Indians.

"Now!" Quinn shouted to the men who had come with him. "Skirmish line front! Charge! Charge the bastards!"

At this point the situation changed, and the advantage belonged to the cavalry, for the Indians were not only dismounted, they were surprised by the sudden and unexpected counterattack.

The troopers began firing, and several of the Indians went down. The remaining braves began to run.

"Run them down! Run the bastards down!" Quinn shouted, caught up in the excitement of the battle.

The cavalry, in two elements now, with skirmish lines on top of the walls on either side of the canyon, pursued the Indians on both sides at once. The cavalry charged at a full gallop until, finally, they reached a very deep cross-gully with walls that were much too steep for the horses to go down. Here the Indians managed to slip into crevices and behind rocks as they scrambled down the canyon face to the floor, a hundred feet below.

"Dismount. Continue to fire!" Quinn ordered, and the troopers then hurried to the edge of the cliff, where, taking up the kneeling position, they continued to pour deadly accurate fire on the escaping Indians.

Once on the gully floor, the Indians were able to find draws and off-shoot canyons that allowed many of them to slip away. Then Quinn saw one of them standing defiantly on the far side of the wide, steep gully. He was wearing a full headdress, his face painted red and his arms folded almost defiantly across his bare chest.

From the headdress, the red face, but, mostly from the Indian's demeanor, Quinn realized that this was their chief, Red Eagle.

The soldiers were still firing, though by now all the Indians had managed to scramble safely out of range.

"Cease fire, cease fire! You're wasting ammunition!" Quinn shouted.

The firing fell off raggedly, with the last few shots echoing back from the gully walls. For a long moment Quinn and Red Eagle stared at each other across the wide gully.

Quinn put away his pistol. "Trooper," he said quietly to the soldier nearest him, "let me borrow your carbine."

"If you're thinkin' 'bout that there Injun, Lieutenant, he's too far away for a carbine. Now iffen we had us an infantry rifle, we could fetch him down for sure."

"Let me have it," Quinn repeated. The trooper handed the carbine to him. Quinn flipped up the rear ladder sight and set the elevation.

Red Eagle saw Quinn taking very careful aim, but realizing that he was out of range, refused to move an inch.

Quinn took a deep breath, let half of it out, and squeezed the trigger. The carbine barked, then rocked back against his shoulder. Across the gully a handful of feathers in Red Eagle's headdress flew, scattered from the impact of the passing ball.

"Whooooweee! Did you fellers see that?" the trooper who had loaned his carbine shouted to the others. "The lieutenant clipped that Injun's feathers!"

The cavalrymen on both sides of the creek cheered.

Red Eagle had not moved, even when the bullet had whined so close by his head. Slowly he turned, then disappeared on the other side of a small rise. By now all the Indians were gone, leaving only the sound of a sighing wind.

Quinn looked around at the soldiers who were with him. "Did we lose anyone?" he asked.

"Not since the first volleys, sir," one of the troopers replied.

"Scott? Did you lose anyone else over there?" he called across the creek.

"No, sir," Scott called back.

"Send four men down from your side to recover our killed and wounded. I'll do the same from this side," Quinn shouted across. "We'll regroup back at the gully where we separated!"

"Yes, sir!" Scott replied.

"The rest of you men, stay alert for any return of the Indians, and keep your eyes on your friends below while they are recovering our fallen comrades. We don't want to leave them unprotected."

"What about the dead Injuns, sir?" someone asked.

"What about them?"

"Injuns don't like to leave their dead on the battlefield, but we come up on these heathens so fast they didn't have no choice. Iffen we was to take the bodies with us, it would be bad medicine for 'em."

Quinn thought for a moment. He now had a greatly reduced platoon, deep in Indian territory. If he did take their dead, they would surely find a place to attack again, and it might not turn out as well.

On the other hand, if he left the dead and the Indians took time to recover the bodies, it would give his platoon enough of a head start as to enable them to join up with Major Reno.

"Leave them," he said. "It'll buy us some time."

Chapter Four

St. Paul Minnesota, May 6, 1876

Brigadier General Alfred Terry, his long, narrow face further elongated by the Vandyke beard he wore, listened as Custer made his case.

"General, I beg of you," Custer said. "As an old comrade who faced the Rebels with me, as a friend, as a brother officer—find some way to let me accompany my regiment."

Terry pulled on his beard as Custer continued to plead his case.

"I know my actions were improper," Custer continued. "But please understand, I was guided more by zeal than by rancor. Believe me when I say that I meant no malice toward the personal integrity of the president. I was only doing what I perceived to be my duty in pointing out graft and corruption among the Indian agents."

General Terry shook his head. "Custer, you were the most brilliant cavalry officer of the war. I think everyone agreed with that, even our Confederate adversaries. But ever since the war you have managed to get yourself into one scrape after another. And each time you do so, you make newer, and more powerful enemies. Now you have incurred the wrath of the president of the United States. And not only the president, but General Sherman. Even General Sheridan is about ready to wash his hands of you. How many times can your friends pull you out before the situation becomes hopeless?"

"I'm begging you, Al," Custer said, using Terry's first name in as personal appeal as he could make. His eyes welled, and though he wasn't sobbing aloud, a tear spilled across his ruddy cheeks. "Please, do what you can to help me."

Terry paused for a long, contemplative moment, then sighed. "All right. Send a telegram to the president through military channels. I'll add my endorsement to it."

"What should I say?" Custer asked.

"Be humble, Custer. I know that is difficult for you, but you must be gracious."

Custer nodded. "I'll write it right now," he said. Outside the general's office, Custer commandeered a pen and a sheet of paper from the clerk, then found a spot to compose what, to him, was the most difficult letter he had ever written.

Headquarters Department of Dakota
St. Paul, Minne., May 6, 1876
The Adjutant General
Division of the Missouri, Chicago.
I forward the following:
To His Excellency, The President
(Through Military Channels.)

I have seen your order transmitted through the General of the Army directing that I be not permitted to accompany the expedition to move against the hostile Indians. As my entire regiment forms a part of the expedition and I am the senior officer of the regiment on duty in this department, I respectfully but most earnestly request that while not allowed to go in command of the expedition, I may be permitted to serve with my regiment in the field. I appeal to you as a soldier to spare me the humiliation of seeing my regiment march to meet the enemy and I not share its dangers.

(Signed) G. A. Custer

Custer took the completed telegram into General Terry's office and showed it to him. Terry read it, then nodded.

"That's more like it," he said.

Terry, too, had been writing, and he showed Custer his endorsement.

In forwarding the above I wish to say, expressly, that I have no desire whatever to question the orders of the President or my military superiors. Whether Lieutenant Colonel Custer shall be permitted to accompany the column or not, I shall go in command of it. I do not know the reasons upon

*which the orders given rest; but if these reasons do not for-
bid it, Lieutenant Colonel Custer's services would be very
valuable with his regiment.*

> *(Signed) Alfred H. Terry*
> *Commanding Department*

General Terry went with Custer to the Western
Union office and instructed the telegrapher to inform them of any action, and to include General
Sheridan's approval or disapproval. The next morning, Custer was shown a copy of General Sheridan's
endorsement.

Chicago, Ill., May 7, 1876
Brig. General E. D. Townsend
Washington, D.C.
  *The following dispatch from General Terry is respectfully
forwarded. I am sorry Lieut. Colonel Custer did not mani-
fest as much interest in staying at his post to organize and
get ready his regiment and the expedition as he now does to
accompany it. On a previous occasion in 1868 I asked executive clemency for Colonel Custer to enable him to accompany his regiment against the Indians, and I sincerely hope
that if granted this time it may have sufficient effect to prevent him from again attempting to throw discredit on his
profession and his brother officers.*
> *(Signed) P. H. Sheridan, Lieutenant General*

"It's not exactly a glowing validation, is it?"
Custer asked after reading Sheridan's endorsement.

"Custer, at this point, you should regard any letter that doesn't call for your immediate resignation as a sterling endorsement," Terry said.

"I suppose that's true," Custer said. "Now comes the really hard part—waiting for the reply from Washington. How long do you think it will take?"

"We could hear by tomorrow . . . next week . . . or not at all."

"I'll go crazy, waiting."

Terry looked at Custer. "If you do go crazy, Custer, how shall we know?" he asked.

Custer looked at Terry in confusion for a second, then he burst out laughing so hard that tears came to his eyes. He put his hand on Terry's shoulder.

"Thank you, my friend," he said. "For that laugh, as much as for the endorsement."

"Wait in the hotel, Armstrong. I know it will be difficult, but at this point that's all you can do."

Custer was at breakfast in his hotel the next morning when he saw a sergeant from General Terry's staff come into the dining room. The sergeant stood just inside the door for a moment, and Custer held up his hand.

"Sergeant, I'm Colonel Custer. Are you looking for me?"

"Yes, sir," the sergeant said. He came over to Custer's table and handed him an envelope. "The general just received this a few moments ago. He thought you might like to see it."

With an anxious feeling in his stomach, Custer opened the envelope, then pulled out the message.

Headquarters of the Army
Washington, May 8, 1876
To General A. H. Terry, St. Paul, Minn.

General Sheridan's enclosing yours of yesterday, touching General Custer's urgent request to go under your command with his regiment, has been submitted to the President, who sent me word that if you want General Custer along, he withdraws his objections. Advise Custer to be prudent, not to take along any newspaper men, who always make mischief, and to abstain from personalities in the future.

(Signed) W. T. Sherman
General

"Yahoo!" Custer shouted, jumping up so quickly that his chair fell to the floor with a bang. The other diners in the restaurant, startled by the sudden outburst, halted in mid-conversation and looked over at Custer in puzzlement and curiosity.

"I beg your pardon," Custer said to all of them. "Please forgive my outburst, but I have just received the most wonderful news."

Although none of the diners knew what the news was, they all smiled and nodded at him.

"Sergeant, does the general require anything from me?"

"Yes, sir," the sergeant replied. "He asked me to tell you that he will be taking the train to Bismarck at two o'clock this afternoon, and he invites you accompany him."

"You tell the general that I will be there with bells on!" Custer replied happily.

Kate McKenzie and her father spent a magnificent five days in the spacious comfort of the train's Wagner parlor, in a commodious car equipped with deep plush seats, decorated wood paneling and velvet upholstered walls, fine carpets, and bright kerosene lamps. The nights were passed in a comfortable sleeping car, and all their meals were taken in the dining car.

"Can this be true?" P.G. asked. He was sitting in one of the great chairs of the parlor car, reading a copy of the *Lightning Express News*, a newspaper composed and printed on the train for the passengers.

"What, Father?" Kate asked.

"According to this story, a man named Alexander Graham Bell is working on a device that would send the human voice over a wire. He calls it a telephone, and says it will one day replace the telegraph."

"My," Kate said. "Isn't it amazing what marvelous things men can do now?"

"Yes, it is," P.G. replied. He folded the paper and looked through the windows at the wide open spaces flashing by outside. "This train, for instance. Now, in comfort rivaling that of a person's own living room, one can span the continent from New York to San Francisco in less than two weeks! Why, it wasn't so long ago that it took six months to make that same trip." He was quiet for a moment, and only the rhythmic clacking of the wheels over the track joints intruded. "That's why this mission is so important, Kate. If we don't record life among the Indians as it is now . . . I mean as it really is . . . then their culture will be lost forever. And that would be a sin."

"You don't have to convince me, Father. I'm on your side, remember?"

P.G. held up his hands, now knotted and bent. "You are more than on my side," he said quietly. "You have become my hands . . . my talent . . . my expression. I am so very proud of you."

"Whatever I might be, I owe to you, Father," Kate said. "You taught me everything I know."

"I can't teach talent, my daughter. That has to come from God, and from Him you received a generous share."

"Excuse me, Mr. McKenzie, Miss McKenzie," a

uniformed steward said, approaching their seats. "But your table is ready."

Kate helped her father up, then they started toward the dining car. She was hungry, and the meals had been excellent, but she always approached the trip to the dining car with some trepidation. She opened the rear door of the parlor car and stepped onto the platform. It was as if they had entered another world. The noise was tremendous, and the wind whipped against her dress and hair. The car's normal rocking motion seemed greatly exaggerated back there, and she tightly held on to the railing to keep from being tossed off.

There was a gap between the platforms of the two cars, narrow enough to be stepped across but wide enough that a misstep could drop an unfortunate passenger onto the tracks below. Negotiating that gap was a very frightening experience, and though Kate and her father had already done it many times during the trip, she approached each time with as much caution as she had the first time.

She stood there for a moment, feeling the rhythm of the car and looking down to make sure the heights of the platforms were equal before she made the step. She could see the ties of the railroad bed beneath them rushing by in a blur, evidence of the train's speed.

Kate timed her move, then stepped across, and held her breath until her father had made it across as well. Then they opened the door and stepped into the dining car.

The elegance of the dining car was in keeping with the rest of the train; Kate saw richly paneled walls, plush drapes and upholstery, and vases with fresh flowers on the tables. She and her father were met by a waiter as soon as they stepped inside.

"Your table is ready," the waiter said. "Right this way, please."

Kate and her father sat down and perused a menu that featured blue-winged teal, antelope steaks, roast beef, boiled ham and tongue, broiled chicken, corn on the cob, fresh fruit, hot rolls, and cornbread. Kate ordered boiled ham, and her father took the roast beef.

Two men in military uniforms sat at the very next table to them. One of the two men kept looking over at them, then, when the waiter left, he came over to speak to them.

"Excuse me," he said. "I am Colonel Custer. Are you Mr. P. G. McKenzie, by any chance?"

"Why, yes," P.G. answered. He looked puzzled. "Colonel Custer, I've heard of you, of course. But, I don't believe we have ever met, have we? How is it that you know who I am?"

"I heard you make a speech once when I was in New York," Custer said. "And I have long been an admirer of your work."

"Well, thank you, Colonel," P.G. said, genuinely

flattered by his remark. "And may I present my daughter, Kate."

"It's an honor, Miss McKenzie. Are you two going to San Francisco?"

"No, my dear fellow, we are going to Fort Lincoln."

"Fort Lincoln?" Custer replied in surprise. "Why are you going there?"

"That is only a stopping place," P.G. said. "From Fort Lincoln we are going out into the field to do a series of paintings depicting the American Indian in his natural habitat."

"What?" Custer asked, sputtering in surprise. "Mr. McKenzie, you can't be serious! Don't you realize there is a war going on now?"

"I knew there was some Indian trouble, but I didn't know—"'

"Indian trouble, you call it? Mr. McKenzie, it is considerably more than just trouble. I wouldn't advise you to go through with your plans."

"I'm sorry, sir, but we've come too far to be dissuaded now," P.G. said with the air of one who had heard all this before. "Besides, we have a letter of authorization from the president of the United States."

"You have permission from General Grant to go into the Badlands?"

"We do indeed, sir. Subject, of course, to military approval, which I also have in the form of a letter signed by the commanding officer of the Seventh Cavalry."

"The commanding . . . ? Mr. McKenzie, may I see that letter?"

P.G. handed the letter to Custer. "As you can see, it is signed by Major Marcus Reno."

Custer read the letter, then shook his head.

"You will give the letter back to us, won't you?" Kate asked.

"I'll give it back to you, for all the good it will do," Custer replied.

"What do you mean?"

"Reno was the acting commander when he signed this. I am the commanding officer of the Seventh now."

"Oh." The expression on Kate's face clearly showed disappointment. "Does this mean you won't allow us to come to Fort Lincoln?"

"You may come to Fort Lincoln, where you will be treated by me and my officers as honored guests," Custer said.

"Oh, thank you," Kate replied, smiling broadly at him.

"But as for your plans to venture out into the field . . . I'm afraid that's another matter."

"Perhaps that's a bridge we can cross at a later time," Kate suggested.

"Or, perhaps some alternative solution can be found," Custer replied.

Custer excused himself then and returned to the table with General Terry.

"Do you know those people?" Terry asked as he buttered his roll.

"That's the famous artist P. G. McKenzie and his daughter," Custer said. "They are on their way to Fort Lincoln."

"They are going to Fort Lincoln? See here, Custer, you didn't invite them while you were in New York, did you? Because that is just the kind of thing that keeps you in trouble."

"I didn't invite them," Custer said. "Grant did."

"Grant sent them out here?"

"Not only that, he has authorized them to go out into the Black Hills to paint pictures of the Indians."

"Oh, my," Terry said. "You can't let that happen. You have to stop them."

"Not me, General," Custer replied. "I've been up against Grant once. I don't care to go against him again."

In the mail car, just ahead of the dining car, a postal clerk was working quickly and efficiently, breaking out the mail to be delivered into Dakota Territory. He had been working this route for over two years now, and in that period of time had committed to memory hundreds of names. Though he had never met any of the people, he felt as if he knew them intimately, and he followed their correspondence vicariously, though of course, he never read any of the letters.

One letter today was representative of that. It was from Miss Susan Parkinson, 315 Olive, St. Louis, Missouri, and it was addressed to First Lieutenant Quinn Pendarrow, Seventh U.S. Cavalry, Fort Lincoln, Dakota Territory. The clerk had seen many letters pass back and forth between those two. Knowingly, he held the envelope under his nose and sniffed.

"Oh, my, Miss Parkinson. What did you do, forget the perfume this time?" he asked as he put the envelope in the proper slot.

Chapter Five

Within two days after Custer returned to Fort Lincoln, he hosted a dinner party for several of his officers, including Quinn Pendarrow.

The long dining table was set for fourteen, with enough silver, crystal, and china to do credit to any formal dinner anywhere. Adorning the menu were delicacies recently arrived with Custer: champagne, German chocolates, and tinned brandied peaches. French onion soup and curried lamb would be served for dinner.

Libbie Custer, whose light blue eyes shone brightly with the excitement of the moment, pointed to one of the settings.

"Lieutenant Pendarrow, you will sit there, next to Miss McKenzie."

"But, Libbie, I thought that was my seat," Tom protested.

"Don't be hoggish, Tom, dear," Libbie replied sweetly. "You dine with us practically every evening. It won't hurt you to give up your seat to Lieutenant Pendarrow. Especially as he will be leaving us in a couple of days. Lieutenant Pendarrow, would you please help Miss McKenzie to her seat?"

"Yes, of course," Quinn said.

"Thank you, Lieutenant," Kate said as she was seated.

"I put Lieutenant Pendarrow next to you because we can count on him to behave himself," Libbie explained to Kate.

"Oh?"

"Yes. Our gallant young lieutenant has resigned his commission and is going to St. Louis to be married."

"How wonderful!" Kate effused. "Congratulations, Lieutenant."

"Won't you tell us about your wedding plans, Mr. Pendarrow?" Libbie asked.

Quinn cleared his throat and looked for a long time at his plate. "There, uh, are no wedding plans," he finally said.

The others around the table, even those who had been engaged in their own quiet, private conversations, looked at Quinn in surprise.

"You mean it has been postponed?" Libbie asked.

"Canceled."

Libbie smiled. "Well, I wouldn't worry about it if I were you. All young people get nervous before a wedding. I'm sure the two of you will be married inside of a month."

"One of us already is married," Quinn said. "I received a letter from her yesterday. Miss Parkinson married her father's accountant."

"Oh, Quinn, I'm so sorry," Libbie said quickly. "I know this must be a painful time for you. How unthinking of me to bring it up."

"Please don't feel bad. There is no way you could have known."

The others were quick to express their own sympathy as well and, for a moment, Quinn was very uncomfortable.

"I'm sure that under the circumstances it is all for the better," Quinn said, anxious to move the discussion on to something else.

"No doubt about it," Custer said. "What about your commission? Do you still intend to resign?"

"Unfortunately, General, I have already resigned," Quinn said. "As of midnight tonight, I will be a civilian. I intended to apply to have my commission reinstated, but Captain Cooke informs me that it would take at least six months."

"Yes, I'm afraid that's true," Custer said. "You say you intended. Does that mean you may not apply for reinstatement?" Custer asked.

"It will be difficult, General. If I do apply, I'll have to find a source of employment for the next six months."

"Perhaps something will come up," Custer suggested.

"Will you miss the army?" Kate asked.

"Yes, I'm sure I will," Quinn answered.

Again there was a long, uncomfortable pause, then Tom spoke up. "Oh, say, Autie, what about Bos? Is he coming to join us for the scout?"

"Bos?" Kate asked.

"Boston, our younger brother," Tom said.

"Not only is Boston coming, but young Autie Reed is as well," Custer said. "Autie Reed is my nephew. Named after me, I might add."

"If you don't mind my asking, what sort of name is that?" P. G. McKenzie inquired.

"It's an old and respected—" Custer started, but his explanation was interrupted by a gale of laughter from Tom Custer.

"You may as well tell him the truth, big brother, because if you don't I will," Tom said.

Custer cleared his throat. "It's Armstrong," he said.

"Armstrong?"

"My middle name. As a very young child, I had a difficult time pronouncing it. Armstrong came out as Autie . . . and thus I have been known ever since."

"Well, I like it," Kate said. "I think an unusual name gives one a certain flair."

"Heavens, child, the general certainly doesn't

need an unusual name to have flair," one of the officers remarked, and everyone laughed.

"So, what are we going to do with Bos and Autie when they arrive?" Tom asked.

"Do with them?"

"Yes, when we go on our expedition," Tom clarified.

"Why, he shall do nothing with them," Libbie said. "When you leave for your scout, Bos and Autie will remain here with me."

"Ho, they sure wouldn't care much for that!" Tom said, chuckling. "The only reason they are coming out here is to be able to accompany us on the expedition."

"But, Autie, surely you don't intend to let them accompany you?" Libbie said. "They are both so young."

"I have soldiers in the ranks who are as young as they are," Custer said. "Besides, there will be five members of the family going. Why, it'll be as much a family picnic as it will be a military expedition."

"Five members of your family?" P.G. asked.

"Lieutenant James Calhoun is married to Margaret, our sister," Tom said, speaking of the officer who was sitting next to him.

"I'm a brother-in-law," Lieutenant Calhoun said. "But I am treated more like a brother."

"Oh, what a wonderful thing, to have so many of you in the regiment," Kate said.

"Yes, it is wonderful," Custer said. "And that gives me a marvelous idea. Mr. McKenzie, I would like to request a favor from you."

"Please ask, General," P.G. replied.

"When my brother and nephew arrive, I wonder if you might paint a picture of the five of us."

"Of course. I would be honored to."

"Wonderful. You can get started right away," Custer said.

"Right away?"

"Yes. The sooner the better."

"General, as I say, I would be honored to. But, with your permission, I would prefer to wait until after I have completed my assignment for the New York Art League. That way I can give this portrait all the time it deserves."

"Why, you can give it all the time it deserves anyway," Custer said. "Simply postpone your journey into the field until after you have completed the portrait."

"General, I appreciate your enthusiasm over this portrait. But I really must give first priority to the people who have commissioned me."

"You do know, don't you, Mr. McKenzie, that without General Sheridan's permission, you won't be able to go into the field?" Custer asked.

"Yes, I am aware that I will need the army's full cooperation."

"I know General Sheridan very well," Custer

said. "And I know that he will take a dim view of the idea of any civilians going out into the Indian lands, especially in these trying times. So, if you are waiting for his approval, I think it's only fair to warn you that you'll never get it on your own."

"Do you have some preknowledge to that effect, General?" P.G. asked.

Custer smiled. "Let's say that I know what his reaction will be when I suggest that I will be unable to guarantee your safety."

"Autie," Libbie gasped. "I can't believe you are actually doing this. You are trying to blackmail Mr. McKenzie into doing a painting for you?"

"Now, Libbie, are you telling me that you wouldn't care to have a painting of your Bo and family?"

"Of course I would love to have the painting. But I disapprove of your stooping to these tactics to get it."

"I make no apologies Libbie," Custer said. "I am a military tactician, and as such, I always use whatever method is most effective. If threatening to block Mr. McKenzie access to the field to paint the Indians will get him to delay his mission until he has completed this little task for me, then that's what I'll do. So, what do you say, Mr. McKenzie? Shall I go to General Sheridan as your advocate? Or shall I go to him as your adversary."

"My daughter as well," P.G. said.

"I beg your pardon?" Custer asked, confused by P.G.'s strange answer.

"Kate must receive permission to go to the field as well."

"Surely, Mr. McKenzie, even if I am able to get permission for you, you wouldn't want to subject your daughter to such dangers."

"My daughter goes everywhere I go. She is my eyes, my ears, and more often than not these days, my hands. She must be with me if I am to carry out my assignment."

Custer drummed his fingers on the table for a long moment, studying Kate under the glow of the overhead light.

"I think I can promise you a beautiful painting of you and your brothers," P.G. said. He smiled. "And I'll even throw in a portrait of the lovely Mrs. Custer."

Custer laughed. "I see that you aren't beyond a bit of blackmail as well."

P.G. smiled back at him. "Whatever it takes, General."

"Very well, Mr. McKenzie, your daughter can go into the field with you." He held up his finger. "But you are not to leave the fort until after the Seventh returns from the expedition that is before us."

"And, how long will it be before your expedition returns?" P.G. asked.

"Oh, I expect to make rather quick work of the Indians," Custer said.

"I'm sure you will, General, if Terry will listen to your advice," Lieutenant Calhoun said.

"Terry knows nothing about fighting Indians, and he has admitted as much. Though he will be in overall command, I will be in charge in the field."

"After this, General, you might get your stars back," Quinn suggested.

"Stars be damned," Custer said, stroking his mustache. "After this summer's campaign, Mr. Pendarrow, I will be nominated for president of the United States."

"Autie, are you certain?" Tom asked.

"Tell him, Autie," Libbie said, reaching over to take Custer's hand.

"Not all of my recent trip back east was unpleasant," Custer said. "In New York I met with the Honorable Governor Samuel J. Tilden, as well as several others with whom the governor is allied. The Democrats are certain that Governor Rutherford Hayes will receive the Republican nomination. As Hayes is a former general, Governor Tilden has suggested that my own war record, and, indeed the record I have compiled against the Indians, would serve me in great stead. He intends to put my name before the Democratic presidential convention this summer, and will make the nominating speech himself."

Tom smiled broadly and reached out to take his brother's hand. "Autie," he said in wonder. "You, the president of the United States. What a staggering thought."

"Staggering?" Custer replied. "Well, I'm not sure how I should take that, Tom."

"Wonderful, I meant wonderful," Tom said quickly, and the others laughed when they realized that Custer was teasing his brother.

After dinner, Quinn walked out onto the quadrangle, heading back for his B.O.Q. room. It was the last night he would be able to refer to the room as his own. It would have to be vacated tomorrow, as he would no longer be an army officer on the active rolls.

He thought of Custer's announcement that he would be running for president. Would such a man make a good president? Custer was a vain man, but then, Quinn supposed, it required a tremendous vanity for anyone to consider himself qualified for such a job. Custer was certainly a man of courage. Quinn had never known a more intrepid officer, but with that boldness came a degree of recklessness. Was recklessness a good trait for one who would be president?

Quinn realized that these considerations were not for men like him. He would leave the fate of the presidency in the hands of men who had risen to such positions of power that, in their hands, rested the fate of the nation. For now, it was all Quinn could do to maintain some control over his own destiny. And that destiny, it would appear, no longer included the United States Army.

Quinn took a long, lingering look at the place that had been his home for the last several months. A gentle breeze was blowing from the south, and it carried upon its breath the smell of lye soap from Soapsuds Row. From one of the married N.C.O. houses Quinn could hear the sound of a crying baby. From the nearest barracks he could hear a group of soldiers singing.

Halfway across the parade ground, a soldier appeared, carrying a trumpet. The trumpeter nodded quietly at Quinn, raised the instrument to his lips, and blew air through it a couple of times as if clearing it out. Then he pursed his lips to play, and Quinn stopped to listen to the clear melodious notes.

Taps was the official signal that it was time for everyone to be in bed, and the mournful notes filled the air. Sweeter in sound from the cavalry's trumpet than they ever could be from the infantry's bugle, the music rolled across the flat, open quadrangle, hitting the hills beyond the walls of the fort, then bouncing back a second later as an even more haunting echo.

Of all the military rituals, the playing of taps was

the one that most affected Quinn. He never heard it without feeling a slight chill, and because tonight was the last time he would be hearing it as a member of the military, the chill was even more pronounced.

> Day is done.
> Gone the sun
> From the lake
> From the hill
> From the sky.
> Rest in peace
> Soldier brave,
> God is nigh.

The last note hung in the air for a long, sorrowful moment, and Quinn thought of what he loved about the army: the loyalty of men to their country and their officers, the camaraderie of all members of the Seventh Cavalry, the feeling of belonging. He knew there would never be anything in his life that he could love more than he loved being a member of such an elite band of men.

"Corporal of the guard! Post number six, and all is well!"

The plaintive call from the furthermost guard came drifting across the post.

"Corporal of the guard! Post number five, and all is well!"

The second call was a little closer. They continued down the line until post number two's call, so close that Quinn felt a moment of embarrassment, as if he had intruded upon the quiet, lonely moments that were part of a sentry's privilege and duty.

Slowly, with an ache in his heart for what he was losing, Quinn crossed the dark parade ground to his own quarters.

Chapter Six

A Sioux village

Red Eagle announced his intention to go into the sweat lodge, a tightly sealed tent under which rocks were heated to a very high temperature. When one entered a sweat lodge, one faced a tortuous physical ordeal, for often the temperature would be so high that the skin would burn. Sometimes a person would pass out from the heat. Yet it was considered the single most spiritual act a Sioux could perform. In the sweat lodge those individuals blessed with immense spirituality received messages from the Great Spirit. The sweat lodge was where Red Eagle received the vision telling him that he would be a chieftain, and would participate in a victorious battle against the long knives.

He had recently put that vision to a test, harassing the whites by attacking their boats and trains, and by setting fire to the prairie. He had succeeded in bringing out the army against him, but he could not claim victory in the battle that ensued. He had killed many soldiers, but many warriors had been killed as well.

Later, when the soldier leader fired at him, Red Eagle stood still on the edge of the canyon, challenging fate. If he had misread the vision, he thought, then let him pay for it with his life. If he had read the vision correctly, the soldier leader could do him no evil.

The bullet had cut through the feathers of his war bonnet, but left him unharmed. If he had lost some face with his warriors by not leading them to victory, he regained much of it by facing the bullet without fear.

Now he felt a need to return to the sweat lodge to revisit his vision.

"Perhaps you would not mind sharing your sweat lodge with me?" Sitting Bull asked.

Red Eagle was surprised and flattered by Sitting Bull's request. Though not a war chief, Sitting Bull was the most respected of all the Sioux leaders— greater even than Crazy Horse, Rain in the Face, or Gall. To Red Eagle's sure and certain knowledge, Sitting Bull had never shared a sweat lodge with anyone before, for he was a medicine man who often received visions during such meditations. To request to share the lodge with Red Eagle was the greatest honor he could bestow upon the young man, and it acknowledged Red Eagle as a genuine chieftain.

Red Eagle took great pains in building the lodge, and when it was ready he walked proudly through the village to Sitting Bull's wickiup to inform him. Without a word, Sitting Bull rose from his seat on a mat of soft furs and followed Red Eagle into the lodge.

They sat in silence for a long time, which Red Eagle was certain would be the pattern for their entire stay. But Sitting Bull surprised him again.

"Do you know how I got my name?" Sitting Bull asked.

"No," Red Eagle replied.

"It was my father's name, and he gave it to me for an act of bravery when I was of a very young age. The name was a great gift from my father, for he was given the name by the Great Spirit, and that is the story I will tell you, if you wish to hear."

"I would like very much to hear," Red Eagle replied.

"One night when my father was on a hunting party, a great bull buffalo came slowly toward the hunting camp. The bull made many strange noises from its throat, and the hunters were afraid, but my father was not. My father's name then was Returns Again, and he thought the bull was sent by the Great Spirit to speak to him, so he didn't run from the bull. He went out to listen to what the bull had to say.

" 'What do you wish, messenger of the Great Spirit?' my father asked the buffalo bull.

"The bull slowly moved his head from side to side and continued to speak in buffalo language. Finally, the Great Spirit gave my father the power to understand the language of the buffalo. The bull was saying four names over and over. Four, as you know, is a magic number for the Sioux. Each of the four names had the word Bull as a part, and one of them was Sitting Bull. My father took that to be his name, and now it is mine. Tatanka Iyotake. Sitting Bull."

"That is a good story, Tatanka Iyotake," Red Eagle said. "I am pleased that you told it to me."

"And now, shall I tell you of a vision I have seen?" Sitting Bull asked.

"I would be honored."

"There will be a great battle between the Indians and the soldiers. The Indians will win the battle with a great victory."

"Yes!" Red Eagle said. "Yes, I have seen the same vision!"

"This, I know," Sitting Bull said.

"Who will lead the battle?" Red Eagle asked.

"There will be many leaders," Sitting Bull said. "Crazy Horse. Rain in the Face. Gall. And Red Eagle."

"Red Eagle? Then my vision was not wrong."

"It was not wrong."

"It is a great vision," Red Eagle said.

"I have a song for you," Sitting Bull said. "It has come to me as I sit here. I will sing it for you now."

Sitting Bull began to sing his song, a chant of only four notes, repeated over and over. Red Eagle listened to the words of the song:

> Like the empty sky
> It has no boundaries.
> When you seek to know it
> You cannot see it.
> You cannot hold it,
> But you cannot lose it.
> If you do not understand,
> Then you can understand.
> When you are silent it speaks,
> When you speak it is silent.

Red Eagle did not consciously try to decipher the meaning of the words, but instead let the phrases soothe his mind. Closing his eyes, he rocked back and forth, every fiber of his being in tune with the chant.

Sitting Bull left, but he did not see.

Children played outside the sweat lodge, but he did not hear them.

Steam boiled up from the heated rocks, but he did not feel its sting.

Red Eagle had glimpsed the truth.

Fort Abraham Lincoln

When the bright, crisp notes of reveille reached into every barracks and B.O.Q., Quinn Pendarrow, as he had every morning for the eight years he had been in the military, including his four years at West Point, sprang from his bed. Automatically, he reached for the gold-striped blue trousers, but he stopped just short of pulling them on.

He was no longer in the army.

Putting the uniform trousers down, he walked over to the closet he had built for himself and pulled out a civilian suit. He had never worn this suit, except to try it on when the tailor made it for him. This was the suit he had planned to wear home on the train.

Outside his B.O.Q., the fort awakened to the new day. From the stable came the whinny of horses and the bray of mules. Assembly was played, then he heard the echoing voices of the commanders giving their morning reports, from distant and barely audible to voices that sounded so close it as if he were on the parade ground with them.

"A troop all present and accounted for, sir!"

"B troop all present and accounted for, sir!"

"C troop all present and accounted for, sir!"

The sequential reports continued until every troop and every battalion was heard from.

Quinn walked over to look out onto the quadrangle from his window. A dismounted regimental formation was quite impressive from this angle. This wasn't a perspective he had enjoyed too many times, for he was always a part of the formation.

He watched as Custer took the reports from the battalion commanders, then gave the order to present arms. When arms were presented, Custer did an about-face and, with his saber, rendered a salute. At that moment the signal cannon fired, and, as the trumpeter played "Salute To The Colors," the flag was run up the pole.

Despite himself, Quinn came to attention in his room and rendered a curt salute.

"Order, arms!" Custer called, and Quinn could hear the sounds of carbines being returned to the order arms position.

Custer then dismissed the regiment, and his dismissal was followed almost immediately by the trumpeter playing the "Call to Mess."

Half an hour later, shaved and dressed in mufti, Quinn left the B.O.Q., carrying all his worldly possessions in one suitcase. Having worked up an appetite with his packing, he started toward the Officers' Mess for breakfast. Then he stopped in his tracks.

"Damn," he said aloud. "I can't eat there."

The closest place he knew to get something to eat would be one of the restaurants in Bismarck, three miles away. Like many of the officers in the Seventh,

Quinn had once owned his own horse. But, when he thought he would be going to St. Louis, he sold his personal horse. No longer authorized to draw a mount from the stable, he had no way into town except by way of "shank's mare," as the enlisted men called walking. With a shrug, Quinn hefted his portmanteau and started toward the gate.

He was almost there when an army spring wagon cluttered to a stop beside him.

"You going into town, Lieutenant?" the driver asked. The driver was Trooper Scott.

"It isn't Lieutenant anymore, Scott," Quinn said. "It's just Pendarrow. But yes, I am going into town and, if you are offering it, I would welcome the ride."

"Come on up," Scott invited.

Quinn set his suitcase on the back of the wagon, then climbed onto the seat.

"What are you going into town for?" Quinn asked.

"Why, I'm going to take you, Mr. Pendarrow," Scott replied.

"Are you serious? You got a spring wagon to take me to town? Who authorized it?"

Scott laughed. "If I told you I took it without authorization, what could you do about it? Like you say, you aren't a lieutenant anymore."

"I could refuse to ride," Quinn said. "I don't want to get you into trouble."

"Don't worry about it. I asked Cap'n Custer if I could and he approved it."

"Really? Well, I thank you, Trooper Scott, and next time you see Tom Custer, you can thank him for me."

Scott snapped his reins against the team, and the wagon started forward again. The guard passed them through the gate without saluting. The salute had been so much a part of Quinn's life that he rarely noticed it. But the absence of a salute this time was glaring, and he experienced another twinge of melancholy.

They drove down the road toward Bismarck for a couple of minutes, the only sound the clop of hooves and the rolling of the wagon wheels.

"Mr. Pendarrow, I don't mean to pry, but is it true your girl married someone else?"

Quinn chuckled and shook his head. "Word does get around on an army post, doesn't it? Yes, it's true. Miss Parkinson is now Mrs. Gillespie."

"I'm real sorry about that, sir," Scott said.

"I'm sure I'm not the first soldier who has ever had his heart broken by a young woman. I just wish she had come to this decision before I resigned my commission."

"You'll get your commission back."

"In six months. Too late for this expedition."

"Yes, sir, but missing this particular expedition might not be all that bad a thing."

Quinn looked over at Scott, who didn't look back, but pointedly concentrated on his driving.

"Why do you say that, Scott?"

Scott took off his hat, ran his hand through his hair, then put his hat back on. "Nothing," he said, shaking his head.

"It must be something."

Scott paused for another moment before he answered. "I've got a bad feeling about this scout," he finally said.

"Have you heard something?"

Scott shook his head. "No, sir. But there's something nagging at me. Something I've never felt before."

"You mean, like you might get killed?"

"Yes, sir, only more than that."

Quinn chuckled. "Damn, Scott, how can it be more than that? What's more than getting killed?"

"Getting a lot of us killed," Scott replied.

Quinn could tell that Scott was serious, and he didn't want to make light of the situation any more than he already had. He cleared his throat. "Look, I'm sure every soldier experiences that feeling from time to time."

"That's true. I can remember during the war, just before a battle, men would sometimes share that feeling with me. Generally, nothing ever came from it."

"That ought to be reassuring then."

"It is, most of the time" Scott said. "But from time to time, something did come from their feelings."

"You're a smart man, Scott. Were the percentages of casualties any greater among those who had such feelings, than they were among those who didn't express them?"

"I don't think so, but then you never know, do you? A lot of those who got killed may have had those feelings, but just didn't share them with anyone else."

"Look, I'm not going to tell you that nothing like that will happen during this scout," Quinn said. "But I will say that I don't believe in premonitions. And I'll bet that if truth were known, nine times out of ten when something does happen to someone who has such feelings, it is the result of a self-fulfilling prophecy. They assumed something was going to happen, and that made them less vigilant."

"That could be," Scott admitted.

When they reached Bismarck, Scott stopped in front of the Bismarck Hotel. Quinn hopped down and grabbed his bag.

"Thanks for the ride," he said.

"What are you going to do now?" Scott asked.

"Now? I'm going to get breakfast. First time in six years the army didn't feed me."

Scott laughed. "I mean after that. Are you going to stay around?"

"I don't know. I might check around town to see

what kind of jobs are available. I don't particularly want to go back East, because I want to return to the Seventh when my commission is reactivated."

"Don't blame you for that," Scott said, smiling. "If a fella has to be in the Yankee army . . . the Seventh Cavalry is the place to be. See you around, Mr. Pendarrow." He slapped the reins and the wagon pulled away.

Inside the hotel, Quinn registered, had his suitcase taken up to his room, then went into the adjacent restaurant for breakfast. He was looking for a table when P.G. and Kate McKenzie came into the restaurant just behind him. After greeting one another, they decided to share a table.

"Mr. McKenzie, may I say I've long been an admirer of yours?" Quinn said, once they were seated.

"You know my work?" P.G. asked, a little surprised by Quinn's comment.

"Indeed I do, sir."

"Where have you seen it?"

"I saw a show in New York when I was still a cadet at West Point, and another show in St. Louis when I was at Jefferson Barracks."

"What is your favorite?" Kate asked.

Quinn picked up his coffee cup and held it thoughtfully for a moment. "I'm sure you expect me to say *To a Higher Office*, as that is the best known. But I think my favorite is *Trees in Bloom*."

"Really? Why?" Kate asked.

"I think it's because I know of no other picture that so well conveys the joy, the freshness, or the pleasure of a spring day. And yet, even though the flowers are a part of the painting, I think the shape and molding of the trunks and branches of the tree interest me even more."

"Yes!" Kate said animatedly. She stuck her hand across the table. "Mr. Pendarrow, you are the first person I've ever heard express that opinion, and yet that is exactly the way it is."

"That was the first painting Kate ever assisted me with," P.G. said.

"My assistance was minimal, I assure you," Kate said hurriedly.

"Yes, not like now," P.G. said. He held up his hands and looked at them, and it wasn't until that moment that Quinn saw how gnarled and twisted they really were. Seeing them, Quinn wondered how P. G. McKenzie could paint at all.

Kate reached across the table to cover her father's hands with her own. Quinn was struck by the expression on her face as she looked at her father. It was positively angelic.

"I just do some of the mechanics, Father," she said. "The brilliance and inspiration are yours."

Father and daughter looked at each other with such intensity that it was almost as if they were the only two in the room. Quinn felt privileged at that moment, and yet at the same time, felt almost as if he were intruding.

Finally, as if realizing that he was still at the table, Kate turned toward him.

"So, you are an artist, too?" Quinn asked, more to fill the awkward moment than anything else.

"Yes. I've been studying with Father for many years now."

"And she has surpassed the teacher," P.G. said.

"You must be very proud of her."

"I am."

"Mr. Pendarrow, I believe I heard you say yesterday that you had resigned your commission. Are you out of the army now?" Kate asked.

"I am. Today is my first day as a civilian."

"Does that mean you have no plans for today?"

"Plans? No, I don't have anything in particular planned. Why?"

"Then I wonder if we might hire you."

"Hire me? Hire me to do what?"

"To be my escort."

"I beg your pardon?"

"My job is to do background research for Father, so I thought I might rent a carriage and take a drive in the country around Bismarck. But Father insists that if I do, I should have an escort."

"Your father is right," Quinn said. "And I would be glad to provide that service."

"Wonderful. Then you are hired."

"No," Quinn said.

Kate looked confused. "No? But I thought you just said—"

"I said I would be glad to be your escort," Quinn interrupted. "But I did not say I would accept pay for it."

"Don't be silly, my good man," P.G. said. "Of course you will accept pay for it. I wouldn't expect you to do that without compensation. Besides, as you are out of the army, I'm sure you are in need of employment, are you not?"

"That's true," Quinn said. "But I couldn't live with myself if I accepted money for doing something as simple as this." He looked over at Kate. "Besides, to be in the company of your charming daughter is, in itself, compensation enough."

Kate smiled broadly, and Quinn watched as her dimples displayed themselves prettily. "Oh, my, Mr. Pendarrow, you are quite a charmer," she said.

Chapter Seven

When Trooper Adam Scott returned to the post, he drove to the wagon park. As he was climbing down from the seat to disconnect the wagon, Wagon Master Mug Turner, the civilian in charge of Trains Company came toward him. Trains Company was a support unit for the Seventh Cavalry, consisting of wagons, horses, mules, and pack mules. When the regiment was on the march, the wagons and pack mules made up a train that followed, bringing along all the supplies a large body of men would need on the march. One platoon of soldiers was assigned to the Trains Company, commanded by a sergeant. But as Trains was primarily civilians who either worked for, or were contracted to the cavalry, the individual in charge of the company was generally a civilian.

"Who the hell told you you could have one of my wagons?" Mug Turner growled.

Pointedly, Scott looked at the markings on the side of the wagon. It read, U.S. Army.

"I wasn't aware this was your wagon," Scott replied.

"I'm the wagon master. In a manner of speaking, everything you see here belongs to me." Turner made an expansive wave with his arm.

"Captain Custer gave me permission to use the wagon," Scott said. "I used it to take Mr. Pendarrow into town."

"You should'a let Pendarrow find his own way into town. He's a civilian now."

"You're a civilian, too."

"Don't get smart with me, Trooper. I may not be in the army, but I hold a position with the command authority of captain. I can have you thrown in the stockade before you blink an eye. And, just to prove my point"—Turner took down a large can of grease and held it out toward Scott—"I'm ordering you to take this grease and pack the wheel hubs of all the wagons."

"That's not my job," Scott said. "You want those wheel hubs packed, have your own men do it. I'm going back to duty."

"Come back here, you son of a bitch!" Turner yelled. "I'll have you in irons for this!"

Ignoring his shouts, Scott led the team into the stable.

*　　*　　*

When Tom Custer answered his brother's summons half an hour later, he saw Trooper Scott standing at attention in front of General Custer's desk. Turner was leaning confidently against the wall with his arms folded across his chest, a smug expression on his face.

"You sent for me, General?" Tom asked.

"Wagon Master Turner has come to me with a complaint. Did you give Trooper Scott permission to use a spring wagon to take Mr. Pendarrow into town, this morning?"

"I did."

Custer turned toward his civilian wagon master. "Mr. Turner, I see nothing wrong with providing a departing officer with transportation away from the post," General Custer said. "And as far as I'm concerned, Captain Custer's permission was all the authority Trooper Scott needed."

"He should've come through me, General," Turner replied. "I have an obligation to know the condition of every piece of equipment I'm responsible for. I didn't know but what someone had stolen that wagon."

"You might have suspected that," Tom said. "If you had even known it was gone."

"What do you mean?"

"I mean, Mr. Turner, that you have such a lax attitude with regard to your duties that I don't believe you know at any given time where your wagons are, or what condition they are in. And the same thing goes for your men."

Turner looked at Custer. "General, do I have to stand by and listen to this? I don't care if he is your brother, he doesn't know what he is talking about."

Custer looked at Tom. "Did you inspect the wagon park?"

"I just got through with the inspection, General," Tom answered.

Turner stood up straight and unfolded his arms. "Inspection? What inspection? Hold on here, what are you talking about? Nobody said anything to me about an inspection."

"What did you find?" Custer asked, ignoring Turner's outbreak.

Tom pulled a sheet of paper from his pocket and began reading from it. "Wagon Master Turner fails the inspection in all categories, General. The wagons are not ready for field duty, the harness is in disrepair, the animals have not been properly attended to, the park is filthy, and it looks as if the stalls for the pack animals haven't been mucked in weeks. The men he has, both military and civilian, are the dregs of society. Half were drunk, and all were disrespectful. The only reason I didn't throw any of them in the guardhouse is because I would have to throw all of them in the guardhouse."

"Which is where I got all of them in the first place, General," Turner protested. "You give me the worst of the lot, and expect me to do with them what your own NCOs and officers couldn't do."

"The truth is, General," Tom concluded, "if we were to take to the field tomorrow, we would be better off without Mr. Turner's wagons and mules than we would be with them," Tom concluded.

"Now wait just a minute. What the hell is going on here?" Turner sputtered. "I come in here to bring charges against this soldier. But instead of getting some satisfaction from my complaint, I get this."

"Would you feel comfortable with Bos and Autie Reed working for him?" General Custer asked Tom.

"Are you asking me if I would put the fate of our brother and our nephew in the hands of someone like this?" Tom replied. He looked with disdain at Turner, and shook his head. "Not on your life, General. I would sooner turn them out in Indian country on their own."

"That's what I figured," Custer replied. "We have to put Bos and Autie Reed somewhere, and I planned to put them with Trains. But, as you say, there is no way we can let them fall into the clutches of a man like Turner," General Custer said. He looked at Turner. "Mr. Turner, you are fired. You have fifteen minutes to leave this post."

"Fired?" Turner gasped and sputtered. "What are you talking about? You can't fire me, Colonel," He said resolutely, raising his arms to make his point. "I don't work for you. I work for the United States Army. Only General Sheridan can fire me."

"All right, you aren't fired."

Dropping his arms by his sides, Turner smiled smugly and nodded his head. "I thought you had better sense than to try something like that. Now, about this man Scott—"

Custer interrupted Turner in mid-sentence. "But, as commanding officer, I can keep you off this post, and this I will do. In the meantime, I will send a telegram to General Sheridan, informing him that you are denied access to the post, and to the regimental wagon and mules. If the army wants to continue paying you, even though you are doing nothing to earn it, that is up to the army."

"But . . . but you know General Sheridan won't allow the army to pay me if I do nothing to earn it," Turner protested.

Custer looked up at the clock on the wall of his regimental orderly room. "Mr. Turner, I don't know how much personal property you have to remove, but you now have only fourteen minutes remaining in which to do it. Trooper Scott?"

"Yes, sir?"

"Detail one more soldier to assist you. I want the two of you to draw arms and then escort Mr. Turner from the premises. Make certain that he is gone within . . ."—Custer looked again, at the clock—

"thirteen and one-half minutes. Make certain, also, that he takes no army property with him."

"Yes, sir!" Scott said, a broad smile spreading across his face.

"You'll hear about this, Colonel!" Turner seethed, pointing at General Custer as he hurried from the orderly room. "I guarantee you, you will hear about this."

"I may well hear about it, Turner. But that won't matter to you. You'll be gone."

The return telegram from General Sheridan said exactly what Custer wanted it to say.

> *Mr. Turner is fired. Recommend you hire replacement earliest opportunity.*

With a picnic lunch loaded in the rented buckboard, Quinn and Kate drove through territory that was very familiar to him, but presented exciting new vistas to her.

"Oh, my," she said. "I had no idea it could be so beautiful out here!"

The trail passed through a stand of aspens, across a level bench of land peppered with fluttering yellow, red, and blue wildflowers, and then up a small rise. When they reached the top of the rise, Quinn stopped and set the brake. From this vantage point they could look back on the great sweeping curve of the Missouri River, shining silver in the noonday sun, with the town of Bismarck on one side and Fort Lincoln on the other. At Fort Lincoln the flag caught a breeze, then displayed itself, a bright patch of color against the pale blue sky. Involuntarily, Quinn stood straighter, almost as if he were coming to attention.

"You love it, don't you?"

"Dakota? Yes," Quinn answered. "I like the gray light of early morning when it's quiet. I like it in the middle of the day when wildflowers carpet the plains in every color of the rainbow. I like it in the evening when the clouds are lit from below by the setting sun so that they glow pink and gold against the purple sky. And the stars at night? Why, they sparkle like diamonds on velvet."

Kate laughed softly, and Quinn couldn't help but notice that her laughter was like a wind chime stirred by a breeze.

"If my father and I can only paint the West as beautifully as you describe it, our mission out here will be a success," she said. "It's obvious by the way you put it into words that you love this wild West of yours. But when I said you love it, I was talking about the army."

"Yes," Quinn said. "I liked the army."

"That's not what I said either. I said you *love* it."

Quinn sighed. "I suppose I do, but there's nothing I can do about it now."

"I can't imagine how any woman who claimed to love you could not see what the army means to you. And if she did know, and she really loved you, I can't imagine her asking you to give it up."

Quinn cleared his throat. "Yes, well, it's pretty obvious she didn't really love me, isn't it?"

"Oh, please, forgive me," Kate said, putting her left hand to her lip as if by that action she could call back the words. She put her right hand on Quinn's arm. "I'm sorry, I had no right to say such a thing. I had no right to criticize Miss Parkinson."

Quinn snorted what might have been a self-deprecating laugh. "I have only myself to blame. When you get right down to it, she didn't submit the resignation. I did."

"What do you say we let the whole subject pass?" Kate suggested. "And I'll spread out the cloth and we'll see what the hotel prepared for our lunch."

"Good idea," Quinn said.

The lunch was a bountiful one, consisting of sliced ham, potato salad, deviled eggs, fresh bread, and chocolate cake for dessert.

As they were eating, the sound of a distant bugle call floated to them.

"What is that?" Kate asked.

"It's 'Fatigue Call,'" Quinn said.

"'Fatigue Call'? What an unusual name for a song. What is it for?"

"It tells the men that it's time for them to begin

their afternoon details, stable duty, working on the grounds, that sort of thing," Quinn explained, lacing his hands behind his head, then lying back on the cloth.

"Do you feel guilty loafing around up here when you think you should be doing, what is it . . . stable duty? Oh, that sounds very unpleasant."

"Mucking stalls?"

Kate laughed and made a face. "Mucking stalls? I don't know what that is, but it sounds extremely nasty business."

"Believe me, you don't want to know what it is," Quinn said.

"I can't believe you would miss doing something like that."

Quinn laughed. "Fortunately, Miss McKenzie, officers don't actually perform fatigue call. We tell the sergeants what we want done, the sergeants tell the corporals, the corporals tell the privates, and the privates do it."

"Call me Kate," she said as she lay on her stomach alongside Quinn. "Tell me, Quinn, where would the army be without privates?" she asked.

"The answer is simple. We wouldn't have an army," Quinn replied. "If there is no one for the officers and NCOs to tell what to do . . . what would be the fun of it?" he teased.

Again they laughed, and this time, as they looked at each other, they were suddenly aware of how close they were. By the way each of them was lying, they found that their lips were but a breath apart.

The laughter stopped, and they looked at each other for a long moment. Although it was totally unexpected, Quinn suddenly felt an overpowering desire to kiss Kate. And then, curiously, he realized that her lips were drawing closer to his, almost as if he were willing her to him.

Their lips touched, and because Quinn was lying on his back and Kate was over him, she was not only the initiator of the kiss, she was the sole arbiter of the kiss's parameters.

Kate closed her eyes and drifted with the sensations evoked by the kiss. Suddenly, she realized what she was doing and abruptly pulled back. She looked at him with an expression of surprise, then shyly smiled.

"Oh, Quinn, how forward you must think I am," she said. "I shouldn't have done that. I'm sorry."

"No," Quinn said. "Please, don't apologize. If you apologize . . . it's like taking it back." He smiled. "On the other hand, if you want it back, allow me to just give it to you."

Putting his hand behind her head, he pulled her to him and kissed her a second time, marveling at how soft and sweet her lips were as they parted under his.

Finally, Kate pulled away from him. "I fear you

have made me breathless," she said. He reached for her again.

"No," she said. "Please, don't." She got up and began picking up the dishes and silverware and returning them to the picnic basket. "We must be getting back."

"I'm sorry if I offended you, if I tried to take it too far," Quinn said.

Kate looked at Quinn with eyes that were truly windows to her warming soul "Quinn, you didn't offend me. It's just that I know you are still suffering from the hurt Miss Parkinson caused you. That makes you particularly vulnerable to a woman's wiles, and I took advantage of that. But I find now that I am hoisted by my own petard, for both those kisses went straight to my heart. I don't want to be the woman you use to forget the one that you loved."

"I see what you mean," Quinn said. "And I wish I could tell you that I would never do such a thing. But honor requires me to say that there may be some truth in what you are saying."

When Quinn drove the rented carriage back into town, he saw a cavalry horse tied up at the hitching post in front of the Boots and Saddles Saloon. The piping on the saddle indicated that it was an officer's horse, and when he looked more closely, he recognized it as Tom Custer's.

Without making any mention of it, he drove Kate back to the hotel, then helped her down.

"I had a wonderful time, Quinn. Thank you so much for agreeing to escort me."

"I hope I wasn't out of line. Even though I am no longer an officer, I still consider myself a gentleman and—"

"Quinn, stop it," Kate scolded gently. "Nothing happened that I didn't want to happen." She looked toward the hotel. "Now, I really must see to Father. Will we see you for dinner?"

"Yes, I'm sure," Quinn replied.

Quinn escorted Kate to the front door of the hotel, then returned to the carriage, noticing that Tom Custer's horse was still in front of the saloon.

The horse was still there ten minutes later, after Quinn had turned in the carriage and team to the livery. Curious as to what Tom Custer was doing in town in the middle of a duty day, Quinn walked along the planked sidewalk until he reached the saloon. A burst of laughter spilled out onto the sidewalk, and he pushed through the bat-wing doors. He saw Tom Custer sitting at a table surrounded by several of the citizens of the town, and the expressions on their faces indicated that it was from here that the peals of laughter had come.

Quinn knew that there were many western forts in which an uneasy truce existed between the civilians and the soldiers. That was particularly true in

Kansas, where disagreements often resulted in a gunfight leaving civilians or soldiers, or both, dead in the street.

Here, however, the town of Bismarck existed only because of its proximity to Fort Lincoln. Many of the merchants depended upon the soldiers for their trade. And all depended upon the fort for their defense against the Indians, and for the protection of the railroad and river, which were their connections to the rest of the country.

"Sure it gets cold out here," Tom was telling the others. "But nothing like the winters back in Michigan. Why, I remember a winter back when I was just a boy, when it got so cold, that we needed only one candle for the entire winter."

"One candle? What do you mean?" someone asked. "What does being cold have to do with using only one candle?"

"Why, it was that cold that the flame pure froze on the wick," Tom explained. "It put out the clearest, bright light, and it was frozen solid, you see, so there was not a flicker. The problem was you couldn't blow it out."

Tom's story was met with more riotous laughter.

"Ye may not be Irish, Captain Custer," a big, red-faced man said. "But sure 'n' begorra if ye' don't have a bit o' the blarney in you."

Looking up from the table, Tom spotted Quinn and motioned to him. "Quinn, come join me." Getting up, he moved to another table. "You'll excuse me, gents, but I've some business to discuss with Mr. Pendarrow. Military business." He looked toward the bartender and held up two fingers. Nodding, the bartender drew two beers, and Tom picked them up as he moved toward a table in the back of the room.

"Have a beer," Tom invited, handing one of them to Quinn.

"Thanks. Tell me, Captain Custer, what brings you into town in the middle of the day?"

"Call me Tom. You aren't in my company anymore," Tom said.

"I guess not."

"But you are about to be in the regiment," Tom continued. "That is, if you are agreeable."

"What do you mean? Has something happened to my resignation?"

"No, nothing like that. But Autie wants to hire you. He wants you to come work for us."

Quinn shook his head. "I wouldn't make a very good scout, I'm afraid. Certainly, not as good as California Joe, or Isaiah Dorman, or any of the Indians."

"No scout is as good as California Joe, or Dorman, for that matter, even if he is a Negro," Tom said. "But scouting isn't what the general has in mind. He wants you to work with the wagons and mules. He wants you to make this expedition with us."

"I don't know," Quinn said. "I really would like

to work for the Seventh, and I would love to go into the field with you. But I don't know if I could work for Mug Turner. I have to tell you, Turner is the most unpleasant person I've ever met."

Tom laughed. "Why, you dummy, you won't be working for Turner. Autie fired Turner this very morning. You'll be taking his place."

"General Custer wants me to be the wagon master?"

"You got it," Tom said. "You'll have the equivalency of a captain in authority and pay. Why, when you think about it, it's like getting a promotion."

"Yes, I suppose in a way it is, isn't it?" Quinn replied.

"So, what do you say? Will you do it?"

"When would the general want me to start?"

"Is tomorrow morning too early?" Tom asked with a wide grin.

"I'll be there," Quinn replied smiling happily. "Bright-eyed and bushy-tailed."

Chapter Eight

Quinn's first impression of his new job was that he had made a terrible mistake. After looking things over, he realized that, as of now, he could count on no more than twenty out of one hundred assigned wagons. The remaining wagons suffered from such maladies as dry-rot of the hubs and bushings, split spokes and wheel rims, cracked axles, broken tongues and cross-trees, and rotted harness and traces.

The horses and mules were in nearly as bad shape, several needing reshoeing, and all needing currying. Less than half the pack saddles could be depended upon to carry its specified one-hundred-fifty-pound load.

But the worst thing was the condition of the stables, barns, and stalls. Whereas the stables for the cavalry mounts were kept spotlessly clean, here animals wallowed in their own filth. And the packers, a combination of soldiers and civilians, were as motley as the animals in their charge.

Quinn had barely finished his preliminary inspection when Custer's orderly showed up, bringing a message from the general, asking Quinn to pay him a visit. Shaking his head at the daunting task ahead, Quinn followed the orderly back to regimental headquarters.

"Well, you've had a chance to look the place over, Mr. Pendarrow. What do you think?" Custer asked.

Quinn shook his head. "General, the entire wagon and mule department is a disgrace."

"What is your recommendation for the remedy?"

"I recommend that we set a match to it and burn the whole thing down," Quinn said.

Custer sighed. "I had an idea it was pretty bad," he said. "I guess I just didn't know how bad. You know we'll be putting into the field in two days, don't you."

"Two days?" Quinn shook his head. "I didn't know it would be that soon."

"We'll be leaving the fort on the morning of the seventeenth. How many wagons do you think you can have ready?"

"If I cannibalize, take parts off one wagon to fix another, I might have as many as thirty ready for you. I know that's not enough but . . ."

Custer waved it aside. "That's more than enough," he said. "I'll only need wagons for the first part of the scout. As we get closer to the Indians, I intend to leave all wheeled vehicles behind and go with just the mules. The mules are all ready, aren't they?"

"They will be, General, if I have anything to do with it."

"Why, you'll have everything to do with it," Custer replied. "You are in charge of Trains company, and that includes wagons, horses, mules, and men."

"General, the men I have working for me all wear the same canvas clothing, civilian and soldier alike. And their bearing is so slovenly that it is impossible to tell one from the other."

"That shouldn't matter to you, Mr. Pendarrow. You have equal and absolute authority over all of them."

"The soldiers, too?"

"Yes." Custer cleared his throat. "I am not unaware that my commanders have been passing their disciplinary problems off to the Trains company. If there is a soldier in their company who can't stay sober long enough to make a formation, they make him a packer. As a result, you are left with the very dregs of the regiment. And I'm sure that the civilians aren't any better."

"General, would you give me the authority to promote or demote as I see fit?"

Custer drummed his fingers on his desk for a moment, then he shook his head. "Only *I* have that authority," he said. "But I tell you what I will do. I will honor your recommendations. If you want a man demoted, you may act on the spot, with full assurance that I shall make it so."

"Same with promotions?"

"You cannot create a new noncommissioned rating. But if you demote one man, you may promote another to his spot."

"Thank you, sir," Quinn said, and before he realized it, he started to raise his arm, catching himself in mid-salute, even as Custer was already returning it. Both men laughed.

"Old habits are hard to break, aren't they, Mr. Pendarrow."

"Yes, sir. I'm sorry, sir."

"Don't be sorry, my boy. As a soldier, you were an officer with very good habits. I'm sure those same habits will serve you well as wagon master."

At the Bismarck Hotel that morning, Kate stopped at the desk with a message to be delivered Quinn Pendarrow, asking if he would care to join her and her father for lunch. She was surprised, and not a little disappointed, when the hotel clerk informed her that Quinn Pendarrow was not available.

"He's checked out of the hotel?" she asked in surprise.

"Yes, ma'am. He left late yesterday afternoon."

Kate was puzzled that he would leave so quickly.

He had made no mention of his intention to do so during their picnic lunch.

"Did he say where he was going?"

"No, ma'am, he didn't say. If he returns, shall I tell him you are looking for him?"

"No, that's not necessary," Kate said quickly. "It's unimportant."

As she walked away from the desk, she wondered if she had done anything to cause Quinn to leave. Perhaps she had been too forward . . . or, perhaps when she pulled away from him, he had felt rejected. Having just been rejected by the woman he was to marry might cause him to be overly sensitive to a rebuff. The funny thing was, she realized, she had to force herself to rebuff him, for with all her heart and soul, she had wanted him to react to her just as he had.

As she crossed the lobby toward the stairs to the suite she was sharing with her father, P.G. came in through the front door of the hotel. He was grinning broadly and rubbing his hands together in glee.

"What is it, Father? You look like the cat who swallowed the canary."

"No, not here." P.G. put his finger to his lips in a shushing motion. "Come up to our room first, then I'll tell you."

P.G. was literally chortling as they climbed the stairs to their rooms.

"Now, what is it?" she asked.

P.G. looked up and down the hallway before he stepped into the room. He shut the door before he began to speak.

"I have the most wonderful news. I just spoke with Mr. Bell of the Bismarck livery barn. He has agreed to sell us a team of horses, a wagon, and all the supplies we will need to travel through the Indian territories."

"Father!" Kate said in surprise. "But you know we can't go. General Custer has forbidden it."

"And President Grant has authorized it," P.G. insisted.

"But isn't the army planning a major operation against the Indians? Yes, I'm sure they are, they were talking about it at dinner the other night."

"That's all the more reason why we should go while we have the opportunity. Kate, this may very well be the last year the Indians will follow their old ways. Don't you see? If we don't go now, the chance will be forever lost. Their culture will have disappeared."

"Do you not fear some danger?"

"Yes, there is some danger. I admit that. But, whatever else the Indians might be, my dear, they are human beings. I think they are savage only when they are protecting their homes, families, and lives. Surely an old man and a young woman, unarmed except for a few paintbrushes, will represent no danger to them. And if we aren't dangerous to them, I cannot but believe that they will be no danger to us."

"You are serious about this, aren't you? You intend to go, regardless of what Custer said."

"I'm very serious."

"Then I think we should at least hire Mr. Pendarrow to go with us," Kate suggested.

"No!" P.G. replied quickly. "His first inclination would be to attempt to talk us out of it. Failing that, he would insist that we be armed. And, as a former soldier, he could not expect to have anything but a hostile attitude toward the Indians. No, my dear, I think we would be safer without Mr. Pendarrow."

"But shouldn't we at least tell him of our plans?"

"No," P.G. said. "Not even that. For at best, he would attempt to stop us and, at worst, he might even tell General Custer. I have given this careful thought. I'm sure we will be all right if we only follow two rules. First, show no fear of the Indians, and second, give the Indians no reason to fear us."

Back at the fort Quinn had, by coercion, threat, intimidation, and persuasiveness, called together all the men under his command. Technically, as he was a civilian, they were not under his command because a civilian can exercise no military authority over a soldier. In this case, they were merely men who were assigned as packers to the Trains company.

With a barely concealed sense of disgust, Quinn looked over the men who were assembled before him, wearing loose-fitting, two-piece canvas coveralls. The uniforms were sodden with mud and dirt, bits of straw, and even manure. And as everyone was wearing the same garb, it was virtually impossible to tell soldier from civilian. Somewhere among this group of men was supposed to be the senior military person.

The noncommissioned officer in charge of the soldiers was Sergeant Buford Posey, who used to be in Captain Custer's troop, and Quinn remembered him. He remembered, too, that Posey had a serious drinking problem that caused him to be transferred to Trains company. None of the men were wearing stripes on their sleeves, so Quinn studied the faces of all the men, looking for Posey. Finally, he gave up.

"Sergeant Posey?" Quinn asked. "Is Sergeant Posey here?"

There was a general laughter at his question.

"This is Sergeant Posey's duty station, is it not?"

"Not so's you'd know it," someone replied. "Ole Posey just comes around from time to time as he sees fit."

There was another smattering of laughter.

"Where is he?" Quinn's tone of voice and expression were clear indications that he wasn't amused.

"Well now, Mr. Pendarrow, like as not, you'll find him in the tack room," one of the men replied.

"Yeah, sleepin' with his bottle," one of the others said. Again, everyone laughed.

"That's enough of that," Quinn shouted. This was going to be harder than he thought. "All right, as you probably know by now, I'm the new wagon master. I've just finished a thorough inspection of this entire company, and I have to tell you that I am very disappointed with what I have seen."

"Hang around long enough, sonny, and you'll get over it," someone called.

"You," Quinn said, pointing to the man had spoken. "Are you a soldier or a civilian?"

"I'm a civilian," the man replied, somewhat haughtily.

"You're fired," Quinn said. "You have five minutes to collect any personal belongings you might have, then I want you off this post."

"What? Now wait just a minute here," the man started. "You can't just up and fire me like that."

"I just did," Quinn said. Then he returned to the others. "The Seventh Cavalry will be going into the field soon. We'll be going with them, and I intend to provide General Custer with all the support he needs." He looked back at the man he had just fired. "And I have no patience with men like you."

"You can support the gen'rul all you want, Mr. Wagon Master. Long as you don't go tryin' to make a bunch of changes around here. Most of us is a'-likin' things just the way they are," one of the other men said.

Quinn glared at the man who spoke. "And you, my friend. Would you be army or civilian?"

"I'm army," the man replied.

"What's your name?"

"McMurtry. Corporal Logan McMurtry. Not that it's any of your business." McMurtry looked around at the others with a wide grin spread across his face. "Maybe you can fire the civilians, sonny, but there ain't nothin' you can do to me."

"As of now you are Private McMurtry," Quinn said resolutely.

"The hell you say! You got no authority for anything like that!" the soldier blustered. "You ain't nothin' but a civilian. You can't bust me back to private."

"You are right," Quinn conceded. "I have no personal authority to do that. But I do have General Custer's ear. And believe me, McMurtry, when I tell him I want you busted to private, he will do it." Quinn looked at the others. "That goes for all of you. Whether you men like it or not, from now on your fate is in my hands. If you are a civilian and I am displeased with you, I will fire you. If you are a soldier, I will reduce you in rank, fine you, or have you confined to the guardhouse—whatever it takes to get this sorry mess on its feet. Believe me, when I say I can, and will, do just that." He looked at the man he had just fired. "Why are you still here? Get out of my barn, get off of this post, or I'll have you thrown in the stockade."

Irate, but now aware that Quinn meant what he said, the civilian turned and left.

With the others more or less subdued, Quinn began assigning tasks. Within a few minutes the wagon and mule barn was a beehive of activity as the men began mucking stalls, washing stable walls, repairing wagons, and tending to the livestock.

Nearly an hour later, Sergeant Posey wandered onto the scene, still somewhat woozy from the previous night's drink. Bits of straw and manure in his hair were evidence that he had been asleep most of the morning. When he saw the men working, he rubbed his eyes in surprise and confusion. "What's all this? What the hell's goin' on here?" he finally asked.

"The new wagon master's got us workin', Sarge," one of the troopers said. Even as he spoke, he continued to work with the hoe, mucking out one of the stables.

"The hell you say. He's a Jim Dandy, is he? Well, don't worry. Like as not, he's tryin' to make an impression. He'll ease off in a couple of days. I'll take care of it."

"You tell 'im, Sarge," one of the soldiers said.

Putting down his rake, he started toward Posey. A second soldier joined him.

"You men, stop gathering around Sergeant Posey and get back to work," a clear, authoritative voice ordered.

Looking toward the man who gave the order, Posey saw a soldier, not in the stable fatigues, but in a field blue uniform. Corporal's stripes were on his arm and, from the looks of them, they were new.

"Who are you?" Posey asked. "Where'd you come from?"

"You know me, Sergeant Posey. I'm Corporal Adam Scott."

"*Corporal* Scott? You mean Trooper Scott. Yes, I know you," Posey said. "You're that has-been Reb colonel." Posey frowned, then pointed. "Here, what the hell are you doing in my platoon? And wearing corporal's stripes? Where's Corporal McMurtry?"

"It's Private McMurtry now, and you'll find him out behind the barn, shoveling manure," Scott said.

"*Private* McMurtry? Why wasn't I informed? Who broke him?"

"I did," Quinn said, arriving at that moment. By now, several other men had put their implements down as well, and were gathering around Posey, anxious to see what would happen when their NCO in charge butted heads with their new civilian commander.

Posey stared at Quinn for a long, contemptuous

moment, then he squirted a stream of tobacco juice between his teeth. The juice hit the ground very near Quinn's boots. "Well now, lookie what we have here," Posey said sarcastically. "A feather merchant with big ideas."

"I'm the new wagon master," Quinn said.

"You're a civilian, ain't you?"

"Yes."

Posey shoved another wad of tobacco in his mouth. "Yeah, I thought as much. I know all about you, Pendarrow." Posey purposely left out the respectful "Mister." "You give up your commission so's you could marry some gal back East, but she up 'n' found some other man to spread her legs for." Posey laughed. "So, you come crawlin' back to the army. Only the army won't take you back, so you have to be a civilian."

"That's enough, Posey," Corporal Scott said.

"I'll say when it's enough." Posey looked at Quinn. "Did I get anything wrong?"

"No, you didn't get anything wrong," Quinn said. "But you did leave something out."

"Oh? And just what is it I left out, Feather Merchant?"

The soldiers snickered, and even some of the nearby civilian mule skinners joined in.

"You left out that I'm going to make Trains the best company in the entire regiment," Pendarrow said.

"Now, how are you going to do that, Feather

Merchant?" Posey asked. "Bein' as how this here outfit belongs to me."

"Well, I would hope that you are going to help me with it."

Posey looked at Pendarrow for a long moment, then snorted. "I ain't doin' shit for you. Boys, you can work for this civilian if you want to. As for me, I got other things to do."

With a dismissive grunt, Posey turned to go back toward the back of the stables.

"Stop right there, Posey," Quinn called.

Without even turning around, Posey made a dismissive motion with his hand and continued to walk.

"Corporal Scott, as of now, you are acting sergeant and noncommissioned officer in charge, until such time as I get General Custer's approval to bust Posey and promote you in his place."

"What?" Posey spun around angrily and pointed a finger at Quinn. "Look here, Feather Merchant, you may have McMurtry fooled, but I ain't puttin' up with it. Troopers, take the rest of the day off," he barked.

The two soldiers who were nearest Sergeant Posey grinned broadly, then started to walk away.

"Sergeant Scott, detail two men as guards and escort Private Posey to the guardhouse. If he resists arrest, you are authorized to use whatever force is necessary. If need be, shoot the son of a bitch."

Those close enough to hear him gasped quietly. Posey blanched visibly.

"Yes, sir," Scott replied quickly. "You and you," he ordered, pointing to the two men who had already started to leave with Posey, "take charge of this prisoner."

One of the men held his hand out in supplication. "Hold on there, Corporal Scott. Posey's our friend. You don't expect us to put him in the guardhouse, do you?"

"It's Sergeant Scott," Scott said resolutely. "And you can either put him there, or you can join him. I don't care which."

With reluctant sighs and shrugs, the two men stepped up to Posey and grabbed him by each arm.

"Get the hell away from me!" Posey yelled, jerking his arms from their grip. He pointed his finger at Scott. "And you, you Rebel bastard, get them stripes off your sleeves before I—"

That was as far as Posey got before Scott brought the flat of a shovel down against his face. Posey went down like a sack of potatoes.

"Like I said"— Scott tossed the shovel to one side and rubbed his hands together—"you two take this man to the guardhouse."

Back in Bismarck at that very moment, Titus Bell was just closing a deal with P. G. McKenzie for the purchase of a wagon and a team of mules.

"Now, mind, if the soldiers catch you, you'll not be tellin' them I know'd where you was a'goin' when you bought this outfit," Bell said. "Why, Gen'l Custer'd boil me in oil iffen he know'd what I was doin'."

"You secret is safe with us," P.G. assured him. "You just be sure we have good animals and a sound wagon."

"You're gettin' the best I got 'n' that's the fact of it," Bell said. "Why, this rig could pull you all the way back to St. Louis if you was of a mind to go."

Bell took them behind the barn and turned over two fine-looking mules and a sturdy wagon, as promised.

"I got all the provisions you asked for, too," Bell said. "Flour, bacon, coffee, beans, a rifle, and bullets."

"I didn't ask for a gun," P.G. said.

"I know you didn't," Bell said. "But I figured as how you'd just forgot, so I throwed one in. There ain't no extry charge."

"I didn't forget," P.G. said. "I just don't want one. I'm going out there to paint the Indians, not shoot them."

Grumbling, Bell took the rifle out of the wagon. "It's your funeral," he said. "But you'd never catch me out there without a gun, that's for sure."

"It is likely, Mr. Bell, that we'll never catch you

out there at all," P.G. said laconically as he paid the money over to the liveryman for the rig.

"You're mighty right on that, sir," Bell said without embarrassment. "You're right as rain. I ain't in no hurry to get myself kilt, or my scalp lifted, and that's for sure and certain."

P.G. smiled broadly at his daughter and patted the wagon seat beside him. "Climb aboard, Kate, and we'll get under way."

Chapter Nine

"It's a miracle," Custer exclaimed. "Yes, sir, it is nothing short of an absolute miracle."

Custer was standing in front of the Trains company's wagon and mule barn. The walls and doors of the barn were scrubbed clean. Inside the barn all the stables were mucked and raked, and the ground was covered with clean, fresh-smelling straw. In front of the barn the civilians and solders of Trains company were drawn up in formation. The wagons that were fit for duty were cleaned and connected to their teams, with drivers sitting on the seats. The mules had been well curried, in harness, and outfitted with cargo packs. The packs were empty now, but they looked sturdy enough to easily carry the one hundred fifty pounds of cargo they were designed to carry.

All the men stood at attention, and all were in clean, inspection-ready clothing. The army was dressed in field blue uniforms. The civilians were wearing buckskin tunics and canvas trousers.

"Would you care to inspect the company, General?" Quinn invited.

"It would be my honor."

As Custer approached the soldiers, Sergeant Scott called them to attention. He saluted as Custer stopped in front of him.

"General, Trains company is ready for inspection, sir," Scott said.

Custer returned the salute, then began his inspection walk through the ranks. The first two men he encountered wore uniforms that sported the shadows of what had, at one time, been stripes on their sleeves.

"I know you, don't I, Trooper?" Custer asked one of the men, stopping in front of him.

"Yes, sir. The name is Posey . . . Seargent . . . that is, Trooper Buford Posey," Posey said, his eyes never wavering from their fixed position, staring straight ahead. He was locked rigidly at attention.

Posey was sporting two black eyes and a swollen purple bump on his forehead.

"Yes, you were the noncommissioned officer in charge of Trains company, weren't you?"

"Yes, sir."

"Do you have any questions as to why you were relieved from that duty?"

"No questions, sir."

"Well, keep your nose clean, work hard, and in four or five years, you may get your stripes back."

As if just noticing the wounds, Custer examined Posey more carefully. "Tell me, Trooper Posey, how did you come by your injuries?"

"I walked into the corner of a stable wall, General," Posey said, his eyes never wavering, his attention not slacking.

Custer chuckled. "Did you now?"

"Yes, sir, I did."

"You'll have to be more careful in the future," Custer said.

"Yes, sir. I suppose I will, sir."

Custer finished the inspection, then with Quinn walking one pace behind and to the left of him, exactly as would be his position if he were still in the army, they walked some distance away from the platoon.

"You have done an outstanding job here, Mr. Pendarrow," Custer said. "It is hard to believe what you have accomplished in less than forty-eight hours."

"Thank you, sir."

"In fact, Mr. Pendarrow, when you regain your commission, I intend to do all that is in my power to see to it that you are reinstated as a captain, and not a lieutenant."

"Thank you again, sir," Quinn said gratefully.

Custer walked back to address the men. "Troopers and packers, I am sure you are all aware that within a couple of days we will be going into the field on an expedition against the hostile Sioux. I want to tell you now that if the troopers of the line companies do their duty but one half as well as you have done yours this past forty-eight hours, we will have a great victory."

"Let's hear it for the general!" Sergeant Scott shouted. "Hip, hip . . ."

"Hooray!" the men all answered, soldiers and civilians alike.

"Hip, hip . . ."

"Hooray!"

"Hip, hip . . ."

"Hooray!"

Quinn dismissed the men.

"I can't tell you enough how proud I am of you," Custer said. He laughed. "And Boston and Autie Reed tell me that you haven't been afraid to work them, either."

Quinn grinned. "Well, General, if they want to get a taste of what life on the frontier is like, I'll accommodate them."

"It's good for them that you are working them as hard as you are. Also, it will give them an idea of what will be expected of them during the march. We leave tomorrow morning."

"Yes, sir."

"We're not going far tomorrow, no more than ten miles or so. I'm going to let Libbie and a few of the other officers' wives accompany us to our first night's encampment. We'll be just far enough away so that, when we pay the men, it'll be too far away from them to go into town and get drunk."

"Yes, sir, that's probably not a bad idea."

"What about you? Are you going into town tonight?"

Quinn smiled. "Aren't you afraid I'll get drunk?"

Custer laughed. "Not at all. I just thought you might want to say good-bye to Miss McKenzie."

"What makes you think I would want to do that?"

"I was watching her at the dinner table the other night. I'm somewhat a reader of people, Mr. Pendarrow. And my reading of Miss McKenzie is that she is very interested in you."

"You aren't trying to be a matchmaker, are you, General?"

"Well, why not? I find that the more married men we have out here, the more civilized we become. And, after all, you are free now, aren't you?"

"In a matter of speaking, I suppose I am."

"Then by all means, go into town, take Miss McKenzie and her father to dinner this evening. Farmers tell me that the earlier they prepare their field, the better the crop they have."

Quinn laughed out loud. "Ah, so now Miss McKenzie is a field of corn."

"Not a field of corn, a vineyard," Custer said. "Yes, a vineyard from which, I believe, will be produced a fine wine. And you, dear boy, if you play your cards right, are the vintner."

"What do you mean they aren't here?" Quinn asked the desk clerk at the hotel. "Of course they are here. Where else would they be?"

"I really don't know, sir," the clerk answered petulantly, offended by the fact that Quinn had questioned him. "All I can tell you is they checked out, bag and baggage. Where they were going in the wagon is anyone's guess."

"Wagon? Did someone pick them up in a wagon?"

"I believe Mr. McKenzie was driving the wagon himself, sir," the clerk said, smiling smugly that he had managed to withhold that important piece of information until the last minute.

When Quinn walked into the Bismarck livery barn, he saw Titus Bell hard at work, mending a double-tree.

"Bell, what do you mean you rented P. G. McKenzie a team and wagon?"

"I didn't rent them one," Bell answered.

"You didn't? But how can that be? The hotel clerk said he saw them leaving town in a fully loaded wagon. And you're saying they didn't get it from you?"

"Ain't sayin' that," Bell replied. He looked up

from his work. "I'm just sayin' I didn't rent it to 'em." He spit a stream of tobacco. "I sold it to 'em."

"Damn! How could you do that? You know the Indians are acting up right now."

"I know that," Bell replied. "That's why I tried to talk 'im out of it, but he wouldn't be talked to. Then I tried to get him to carry a gun, but he wouldn't do that either."

"So, they are out there alone, and unarmed?"

"I reckon so."

Quinn clenched his fist. "Have you no conscience, man? If anything happens to them I'll . . ." Quinn let the sentence die uncompleted.

"What was I supposed to do, Pendarrow?" Bell asked. "McKenzie's a grow'd man, and his daughter is a grow'd woman. I'm in the business of selling and renting wagons and animals. I can't say yes to some folks and no to others. What they do with 'em after they buy 'em from me is none of my concern, whether I want it to be or not. I told you I warned 'em against the Indians, now that's all I can do."

Quinn sighed. "I guess you're right."

Bell, who had been belligerently defensive, softened a bit. "Look here, the way I understand it, McKenzie an' his daughter ain't goin' to do nothin' but paint pictures of the Indians. Maybe they was right not carryin' a gun. If they ain't botherin' the Indians, maybe the Indians won't bother them."

Custer stood in the doorway of his quarters in a way that indicated that he had no intention of inviting Quinn in. Behind Custer, a lantern burned dimly in the parlor. Over Custer's shoulder toward the back of the house, a wedge of light spilled out into the dark hallway through the open door of the bedroom. Through that same open door, Quinn could see the mirror to the dresser. Fearing that he was intruding, he brought his attention back to Custer, as he explained how he learned that the McKenzies had bought a wagon and gone out in search of Indians to paint.

"I wish they hadn't done that," Custer said. "I specifically gave orders that they weren't to leave town and the protection of the fort."

"I know you did, sir. I was present when you told them," Quinn said. "But the point is, they did go. So, what do we do now?"

"There is nothing we can do now, Mr. Pendarrow, except hope for the best."

At that moment, in the mirror, Quinn caught a fleeting glimpse of Libbie. He was startled to see that she was naked. With his cheeks flaming in embarrassment, he looked away quickly.

"Is there anything wrong, Mr. Pendarrow?" Custer asked, puzzled by Quinn's strange reaction.

"No, sir, nothing is wrong," Quinn said quickly. He cleared his throat and continued. "General, maybe I could take a few men and go out looking for them."

Custer shook his head. "Absolutely not. Have you forgotten that we are getting under way tomorrow? No, Quinn, the best thing we can do for them now is push ahead, hard, driving the Indians before us until we are able to close in on them, and either return them to the reservations or destroy them. If we do our job properly, we'll have this area thoroughly swept clean of Indians. Mr. McKenzie and his daughter can wander around all they want. They won't see a thing."

Quinn sighed. "I hope you are right," he said.

Custer chuckled. "I'm George Armstrong Custer, Mr. Pendarrow. Have I ever been wrong?"

Although Custer laughed as he made the statement, Quinn knew that he wasn't entirely joking. He knew that Custer actually believed that about himself.

In the bedroom after Quinn left, Libbie lay on the bed, waiting for her husband to get undressed. She was already naked, her body subtly lighted by the golden glow of the lantern. She had a slender, athletic body, her legs smooth and tapered though remarkably muscled, her breasts small, firm, and well rounded. Right now the nipples were drawn tight from their exposure to the cool air. At the junction of her legs the tangle of hair curled invitingly.

Custer chuckled.

"What do you find so funny?" Libbie asked.

"The show you gave young Mr. Pendarrow."

"The show? Why, Mr. Custer, I have no idea what you are talking about," Libbie said innocently.

Custer looked at her. "Ah, yes, the picture of purity. Are you going to try and tell me that you didn't parade around in this room naked, while I was out front talking to him?"

"Well, perhaps I did, but I never approached the door."

Smiling, Custer nodded toward the mirror.

Libbie gasped. "Oh! Gracious!"

Laughing, Custer fell on the bed with her, then grabbed her. "Gracious indeed. You knew exactly what you were doing, old girl."

"Old girl, am I?" Libbie replied. "Well, it must've gotten some reaction from him, or you would never have realized I was doing it."

"Then you *admit* it! You *were* doing it on purpose!"

"If I was, it was just a little innocent play," Libbie insisted, putting her arms around Custer's naked shoulders and pulling him down over her.

The Indian territory was green with spring and running with streams swollen and sparkling with the melted snows. To the west, a ridge of purple mountains thrust into the sky.

Kate and her father watched as the first pink fingers of dawn spread over their camp. The last morning star made a bright pinpoint of light in the southern sky. The coals from the campfire of the night before were still glowing, so P.G. threw chunks of dried wood onto the fire, and soon tongues of flame were licking against the bottom of the coffeepot. A rustle of feathers caused P.G. and Kate to look up just in time to see a golden hawk diving on its prey. The hawk soared back into the air, carrying a tiny scrub mouse, which was kicking fearfully in the hawk's claws. A prairie dog scurried quickly from one hole to another, alert against the fate that had befallen the mouse.

P.G. poured them both a cup of steaming black coffee, and they had to blow on it before they could drink it. They watched the sun turn from gold to white, streaming its rays brightly down onto the plains.

Though P.G. and Kate didn't realize it, they had been watched since before dawn. An Indian, his face lined with age and experience, sat quietly behind a rock outcropping, studying them. Finally, he stood up and walked boldly into the camp. His sudden appearance startled Kate, and she gasped.

"I am White Wolf," the Indian said, speaking in English.

P.G. pointed to himself. "I am P. G. McKenzie. This is my daughter, Kate."

White Wolf studied both of them intently, for a long moment. "Do you have a gun?" he asked, finally breaking the silence.

"No."

"I will see," White Wolf said, starting toward the wagon.

"By all means, be my guest," P.G. offered.

White Wolf began poking through the wagon. He came across several drawings and held them out admiringly.

"You do this?" he asked.

"Yes," P.G. answered. "That is, I and my daughter do them."

"What you do with them?"

"Well, I finish them, then people buy them."

"I buy this one," White Wolf said, holding out a drawing.

P.G. looked at the drawing White Wolf had selected, then he smiled. He might have anticipated his choice. It was the preliminary sketch of a wolf, drawn while P.G. was on the train. In fact, he had a finished picture, painted in oil.

"You don't want that one, White Wolf," P.G. said easily. P.G. walked over to the wagon, then rifled through the same stack of pictures. A moment later he pulled out a beautiful depiction of a wolf, standing on a bluff, his head raised and silhouetted against a large, yellow moon.

"Ayiee!" White Wolf said, laying his picture down and reaching for the painting P.G. now showed him. "I buy this one!" he announced.

P.G. shook his head. "Sorry, my friend, that painting isn't for sale."

White Wolf looked crestfallen.

"Father," Kate said anxiously. "Let him buy it," she added through tightly clenched teeth.

P.G. held his hand out as if to indicate to his daughter that he knew exactly what he was doing.

"It isn't for sale," P.G. continued, "because I am making a gift of it. The painting is yours, White Wolf."

White Wolf thought for a moment, then he pulled out his knife and tried to give it to P.G.

"No," P.G. said, holding his hand in such away as to indicate that he didn't want the knife. "If you want to do something for me, you will let me paint your picture."

White Wolf held his hand in front of his face and made a circular motion with it.

"Yes," P.G. said. "I will paint a picture of you, and make a present of it to you as well."

Kate laughed. "If you give all the paintings you make to the Indians, won't you be defeating the purpose of our being out here?"

"Not at all, my dear. White Wolf will show his

painting to the others. That will do two things for us. It will assure the Indians that we represent no danger to them, and it will bring more of them to us," P.G. said with a wink.

If anyone had slept late on the morning of the 17th of May, they were, no doubt, awakened by the Seventh Cavalry band's rendition of "Garry Owen," the bouncy battle tune of the regiment. To the accompaniment of the music, columns of platoons, both mounted and dismounted, marched around the grounds of Fort Lincoln as the expedition performed its departure parade. Despite the grandiose show, there was a surprisingly small turnout of spectators to watch, though many tear-filled eyes did watch from the windows of the houses of the married officers and the Soapsuds Row quarters of the noncommissioned officers.

Never had Quinn been a member of such an impressive array of troops, and though he was glad he wasn't being left out, he wished with all his heart that he was still in the army, riding at the head of one of the line companies instead of back here with Trains.

Even so it was a magnificent sight, and was so recorded by Mark Kellogg, a reporter who, at Custer's personal invitation, would accompany the Seventh for the entire scout. The expedition consisted of the Seventh Cavalry, commanded by Lieutenant Colonel George A. Custer and consisting of 28 officers and 747 men; two companies of the 17th Infantry, and one company of the 6th Infantry, comprising eight officers and 135 men; one platoon of Gatling guns with two officers and 32 men; and 35 Indian scouts. Quinn was at the head of Trains company, which was made up of 37 wagons and 85 pack mules, as well as 25 soldiers and 65 civilians. General Custer's youngest brother, Boston, and his nephew, Autie Reed, were counted among the 65 civilians.

In addition to the Seventh Cavalry Trains, there were several wagons and pack animals from other supporting units, though as they maintained autonomy, Quinn didn't deal with them. When lined up in full order-of-march, the army of twelve hundred men and eighteen hundred animals stretched out for over two miles.

At that, they were but one-third of the army committed to the expedition against the Sioux. General Sheridan had developed a simple plan to crush the hostiles once and for all. It called for General George Crook to lead a column north from Wyoming, while Colonel Gibbon would bring a column east from Fort Ellis, in Montana. A third column, including the Seventh Cavalry and led by General Terry, would drive westward from Fort Abraham Lincoln into the Dakota Territory. The three columns would converge in southern Montana, the plan being to catch the Indians in the middle. Any one of the three columns, Sheridan believed, was strong enough to do the job on its own.

For the first few miles of march, Custer had authorized the wives and women of the post to accompany the men, and Libbie was riding alongside of her husband as if she were one of his staff officers. And indeed, in her blue-and-gold shell jacket complete with brass buttons, she looked as if she belonged.

Libbie was riding her horse Dandy, while Custer was riding his own, a stallion he had named Vic. They had already made arrangements so that when they separated, Libbie would switch to another horse, leaving Dandy with her husband. That way Custer would have two of the finest horses in the regiment.

It was early morning and, behind them, the sun was just peeping over the horizon as they headed west. In front of them a billowing cloud of morning mist appeared, and in an optical phenomenon, its water crystals coalesced into what seemed like a gigantic concave mirror that spread over the head of the marching column. As a result it not only reflected the soldiers, its concavity reversed the mirror image so that it was an exact reproduction of the army on the ground.

Quinn was alerted to the mirage by the gasps and exclamations of the men of the packers and skinners. Then the Indian scouts, believing it to be an omen, grew frightened and started to chant. To Quinn's surprise, even the most hardened soldiers were disturbed by it, and many swore they could pick out specific individuals, riding in the sky.

"That's ole Fred Wyllyams there, riding point. Damn me if it ain't," one of the soldiers said. "Me 'n ole Fred shared many a bottle of the creature. Onliest thing is, he was kilt near Pond Creek, back in '67."

"That there's Cap'n Hamilton, and just ahead of him is Major Elliot," another pointed out. "You'll recollect, we lost them two at Washita."

"My God," one of the soldiers said, almost reverently. "Boys, we're lookin' right into Fiddler's Green!"

"Mr. Pendarrow," Autie Reed asked, moving his horse over to ride alongside Quinn. "What is Fiddler's Green?"

Quinn chuckled. "You mean with two uncles in the cavalry, you've never heard of Fiddler's Green?"

"No, sir," Autie Reed admitted. "And if I asked them now, they'd just tease me."

"They probably would at that," Quinn agreed. "Fiddler's Green is where you go after you die."

"You mean, like heaven or hell?"

"Sort of like that, I suppose," Quinn said. "'Cept, it's just one place, and all cavalrymen go there, no matter what kind of life they lived here on earth.

Some say they've earned their way there, and Fiddler's Green is their eternal reward. Others insist that all cavalrymen are damned, and this is their eternal perdition."

"But what is it, exactly? I mean, if you go there, what will you find?"

"Legend says that it is a grassy glen where every man who has ever heard 'Boots and Saddles' goes after he dies. They stop there to water their horses, rest in the shade of the trees, and have a few drinks. The idea is that you'll wait there for all the troopers who will follow you and thus, will spend an eternity there, cheating the devil out of his due."

Autie Reed shook his head. "But that's not real, is it? I mean, it's just a silly old legend."

"Who is to say?"

"You don't believe it, do you?"

"If you believe in a hereafter, then heaven can be anything you want it to be. Who is to say that cavalrymen can't make it be Fiddler's Green if that's what they want?"

Autie Reed thought for a few moments, then shook his head. "You're right. I reckon it is real if people want it to be real.

In addition to Autie Reed, Boston Custer was also riding with Quinn and Trains company. For the moment, Autie Reed, Boston, Tom Custer, Jimmi Calhoun, who was married to the Custers' sister, and Margaret, along with General Custer and Libbie, meant that seven members of the Custer family were along on this one expedition.

"Hey, Autie Reed, let's ride forward!" Boston suggested, not even thinking to ask Quinn for permission. Like a pair of young colts, Autie Reed and Boston slapped their legs against the sides of their horses, urging them into a gallop and dashing ahead of the column, racing each other toward the mirage as they tried to catch up with it.

If it had been any other two men, Custer would have brought them back into line quickly, and sharply. But Custer, who was well known for the strict disciplinary standards he set for his officers and men, was remarkably lenient with members of his own family.

A galloper came up alongside the column to hail Quinn. "Mr. Pendarrow, Lieutenant Calhoun's compliments, sir, and he asks if he could please speak with you for a moment?"

"Sergeant Scott," Quinn called. "I'm going up the column for a few minutes."

"Very good, sir," Scott answered.

Quinn rode alongside the column, breaking into a gallop to gain ground on the others. He reined in when he saw Lieutenant Calhoun coming toward him. Calhoun's wife had been riding alongside, and she started to come as well, but Calhoun held up his hand to stop her. "I'll be right back, Maggie," he called back to her.

"What is it, Jimmi?" Quinn asked.

"Quinn, I don't know how to say this without it sounding somewhat foolish," Calhoun said. He cleared his throat nervously. "So I guess the best way is to just come right out and say it. But, if anything happens to me during this scout, I would like to think that you would help Maggie get resettled somewhere."

Quinn laughed it off. "What do you mean, if something happens to you?"

"If I don't come back," Calhoun said. "If I'm killed."

"Come on, Jimmi, don't tell me you are spooked by the mirage," Quinn said.

"The mirage? No," Calhoun answered quickly. "It isn't that. Actually, I've been feeling this way for a long time. I don't know how to explain it. It's . . . it's like a feeling of doom." Calhoun shivered.

Quinn remembered that Scott had expressed the same feelings to him a few days before.

"Well, I'm not going to make light of it," Quinn finally said. "I know that those feelings can be very unsettling. But I know, too, that they are just that—feelings—and I'm sure there's nothing to this one. It'll go away, and then you'll be just fine." He smiled reassuringly. "But in the meantime, if it will ease your mind, of course I'll help Maggie. Though I'm sure you know that the general will do everything that needs to be done. After all, she is his sister."

"No," Calhoun said, shaking his head. "That's just the point. I don't think the general, or Tom for that matter, will be coming back, either."

"Hey, it's gone!" someone said. "Look, everybody! The mirage is gone!"

The men broke into a cheer, and the mood changed quickly from gloom to cheer.

Calhoun smiled as well. "On the other hand, maybe it's nothing," he said. "But I did want to mention it. I guess I'd better get on back to Maggie. She'll be wondering what we're talking about, and I'm not very good at hiding things from her."

"Hide this if you can, Jimmi," Quinn advised. "There's no sense in making her worry for nothing."

Calhoun smiled, then slapped his hat against the side of his horse. "You're right," he called back over his shoulder. "Just forget I said anything, will you?"

Quinn waved, then returned to his own position.

The marching formation of the Seventh Cavalry was divided into two columns, designated right and left wings, commanded by Major Marcus Reno and Captain Frederick W. Benteen. Each wing was subdivided into battalions: One battalion was the advance guard, one was the rear guard, and one marched on each flank of the wagons and pack animals that moved at the center of the formation. The troops of the advance guard took care of pioneer or fatigue duty such as clearing the trail and finding creek crossings. The rear guard remained behind to take care of anything that happened along the way. If a wagon stalled in the mire, it helped push the wagon free.

The battalions on the flanks were to keep within 500 yards of the trail at all times, with instructions never to get more than a half-mile in advance or rear of the train. To avoid dismounting any more than necessary, one troop marched until it was about a half-mile in advance; it then dismounted, and the horses were unbridled and allowed to graze until the formation had passed and was about a half-mile in advance. At that time it took up the march again. Each of the other two troops would conduct their march in the same manner so that two battalions of troops would be alongside the train at all times.

In order to guard against surprise, half a dozen flankers were also thrown out to some distance on either side of the line of march.

The band was riding at the front of the column, and Custer had them play several numbers. Boston and young Autie continued to cavort around like schoolboys, and any mood of melancholia Quinn might have experienced from his conversation with Calhoun was quickly dispelled.

Chapter Ten

It couldn't be going better, Kate thought. For two days now she and her father had traveled unmolested through the Indian country. They visited a couple of small Indian settlements where the Indians turned out to pose for them and offered them food and shelter. The Indians were so cooperative and friendly that it didn't seem possible to Kate that there could any danger. She didn't understand how the army could possibly think these people hostile.

"You know, daughter," P.G. said, "a couple of weeks like this and I think we shall have everything we need."

"I know," Kate agreed. "It has been wonderful. The Indians have cooperated so well, and we have drawings of the villages and families in their tepees." She held up a couple of the sketches. "And I just love these drawings of the children. You were right, Father. By showing that we represent no

danger to the Indians, they have not been dangerous to us."

Kate propped the drawings up against the side of
the wagon that had served not only as their transportation, but as their living quarters and working
area as well.

"Here come some more," P.G. said, pointing to
four horsemen approaching the wagon. "No doubt,
they'll be wanting their pictures drawn."

Kate laughed. "You can't say we haven't been
getting cooperation from them, can you? In fact,
quite the opposite. They are so anxious to have their
pictures drawn that they keep coming to us and we
have a difficult time depicting them in their villages."

"Well, we can't turn them down," P.G. said. He
looked around. "Now, what happened to those
charcoal sticks?"

"Oh, I put them in the wagon," Kate said. "I'll get
them."

Kate climbed up onto the wagon, opened the canvas cover, and went inside. The canvas allowed only
a shaded light through, so that searching for the
charcoal was difficult. She began looking through
the blankets, papers, baskets, boxes, and other paraphernalia.

"I said I put them in here, and I know I did," she
called out to her father. "But I tell you, I can't find
them."

She felt the wagon tip as someone climbed on.

"You don't have to come up here, Father. I'll find them."

The curtain parted, and Kate looked around. There, grinning obscenely, was the painted face of a Sioux warrior.

Although she had become complacent and unafraid during their few days alone in Indian territory, Kate now felt a knife of fear stab into her heart, and she gasped. But she fought the urge to scream and finally managed to regain some measure of composure.

"Hello," she said. "Have you come to have your drawing made?"

"Come see," the Indian said, still grinning hideously. He jumped back down onto the ground, and Kate, puzzled by his strange behavior, followed him.

"What is it?" she asked. "What do you want me to see?"

The warrior made a broad, sweeping gesture with his hand. And then Kate saw the handiwork of which the warrior was so proud. Her father, with an arrow in his heart, lay sprawled on the ground, his eyes open but unseeing. His face wore a look of surprise and disbelief.

Kate felt the world spinning, then everything went black.

*　　*　　*

It was in the season the Sioux call the Moon of Making Fat, and the Hunkpapas were holding their annual Sun Dance. During the ceremony, the participant would have wooden skewers thrust into their shoulder blades, or into the muscles of their chest and back. The skewers were inserted as roughly as possible, to increase the pain. The Sun Dancer would bear the torture without a murmur, sometimes forcing himself to laugh at the pain. Leather thongs would then be tied to the ends of the skewers, then thrown over the crosstrees of the Sun Pole and the dancer would be hauled up into the air. There he would dangle, twisting in agony, but always keeping his face toward the sun, with his eyes wide open. The last act of this fierce ritual would be for the man to have others pull on him, helping him to exert all his force until his flesh was torn and he was free.

For three days Sitting Bull danced, then after going through the ordeal of the Sun Dance, sat in the sweat lodge until he finally fell into a trance. When he emerged from the lodge, he called everyone together to report on the vision that had come to him.

"Hear me," he said. "For voices came to me during my vision, and the words I speak to you are the words of truth."

The drums and the music stopped, and warriors and chiefs gathered around to listen. It wasn't only

Hunkpapas, but Oglala and Minneconjous, San Arcs, Blackfeet, and even Cheyenne. They all sat quietly to listen to the vision of Sitting Bull.

"A voice came to me and it cried: 'I give you this because they have no ears.' And when I looked into the sky I saw soldiers falling like grasshoppers, with their heads down and their hats falling off. They were falling right into the Indian camp. Because the white men had no ears and would not listen, Watkantanka, the Great Spirit, gave the solders to the Indians to be killed."

"Eeeeeeyyyaahhh," a warrior shouted in excitement, and others took up the cry so that the camp roared with their shouts of challenge. The drums began again, this time more ardently than before, and a hundred warriors took up the dance.

"Red Eagle," Sitting Bull said, patting the ground beside him. "Come, sit with me and we will talk."

Red Eagle sat beside Sitting Bull.

"I did not tell the whole of my vision."

Red Eagle remained quiet, realizing that a response was neither required, nor wanted.

"I did not tell the others all of my vision because it does not concern them." He looked at Red Eagle. "I think part of my vision was meant for your eyes. I don't know why the Great Spirit sent your vision to me. Perhaps because we once shared the sweat tent."

"Perhaps the Great Spirit sent the vision to you

because you are older and wiser and can interpret the meaning."

Sitting Bull nodded. "Yes, perhaps this is so." It wasn't vanity, it was a simple statement of fact.

They were silent for a moment, while Sitting Bull gathered his thoughts. Finally, he continued. "In my vision, I saw clearly that you will truly be a leader of our people."

"I am pleased that you saw this in the vision," Red Eagle said. "In the victory you have foretold I will prove myself worthy of your vision."

"I have told the others we will defeat the soldiers when they come, and this is true. What I have not told the others is that this victory will not bring us peace. More whites will come, and more still, until, like the blades of grass that cover the prairie, they will be everywhere."

"Perhaps your vision was a warning that we should fight more fiercely and kill more soldiers. I will do my part and kill many soldiers. This, I promise."

Sitting Bull shook his head. "No. This I saw too in the vision. Red Eagle, in the battle that is to come, you must not lift your hand against the soldiers."

"What? But surely this cannot be," Red Eagle said, baffled by Sitting Bull's strange request.

"The vision allowed me to see the future of our people for many winters yet to come. The time of the warrior leader is past. It is now time for the peacemaker. You are that peacemaker."

"But no," Red Eagle said, vehemently disagreeing with Sitting Bull's assessment. "I am a warrior."

"This is true." Sitting Bull nodded. "But it is also true that only a warrior can bring peace. For more courage will be required of the leader who would preserve peace than is required from him who would make war."

"If I remain in the village with the women and children in the battle to come, who will listen to me then, in time of peace?"

"You will not be in the village," Sitting Bull said. "This too came to me in the vision."

"Where will I be?"

"White Wolf has told of a white man and a white woman who are traveling through our land, making pictures with a drawing stick."

"Yes, Picture Man and Picture Woman. I have heard of them."

"They are not like the soldiers who kill our people. They are not like the miners who steal from our sacred Black Hills. They are not like the white hunters who kill buffalo for the sport and leave the meat to rot."

"If all white men were so, we could truly live in peace," Red Eagle said.

Sitting Bull put his hand on Red Eagle's arm.

"You must find them. You must find them and protect them from any harm."

"But if they are not with the soldiers, what harm can come to them?"

"You do not understand," Sitting Bull said. "In my vision I learned that I am in a sacred circle with them. Their fate is my fate. If something happens to them, then so shall it happen to me. If harm should come from a Sioux, then I shall be killed by a Sioux. If harm should come from a white man, then I will be killed by a white man."

Red Eagle stood and looked down at Sitting Bull. For his entire life he had prepared himself for and dreamed of the day when he could lead others in a great battle. Now the biggest battle in the history of his people was about to take place, and Sitting Bull had asked him not to take part. His blood ran hot, and he felt anger with this old man for asking such a thing of him.

And yet, beyond the anger and the frustration and the bitter disappointment, he saw the truth of what Sitting Bull was saying. And with that truth came a calm acceptance. He would not be the warrior he always thought he would be. He would follow the path the Great Spirit had chosen for him.

"I will find them," he said. "And I will protect them."

*   *   *

The regiment marched thirteen and a half miles on the first day, pitching camp at about two o'clock in the afternoon at the first crossing of Little Heart River. Libbie stayed that night with her husband. Living under canvas wasn't a new experience for her, for despite the fact that she now lived in the grand house of the regimental commander, there had been many times during their life together when quarters had been nothing more than a burlap tent. That the tent Custer used wasn't an army issue tent, but one presented to him by the Northern Pacific Railroad, did make it a bit easier. The NPRR tent was nearly twice as large as the Silbey tents provided by the army. It also had perpendicular walls, thus making every square foot of room more useful.

For breakfast the next morning, they sat at a field table that was laid with china and silver, as comfortable with this familiar setting as if they were in their own dining room.

"Would you like some more marmalade?" Libbie asked, holding a piece of buttered bread.

"Yes, thank you," Custer replied. He chuckled. "I hope all the men are enjoying their breakfast this morning. Eggs, bacon, butter, and marmalade. It won't be like this from now on. Nothing but hardtack and coffee, I'm afraid."

Libbie spread the marmalade on bread then passed it across to Custer.

"I'm still disappointed that you weren't more insistent with Captain Marsh. If he had allowed me passage on the riverboat *Far West*, I would have been able to follow you almost all the way."

Custer chuckled. "That's my Libbie," he said. "Following the colors as surely as any officer in the cavalry." He took a bite of his bread and jelly.

"I would have," Libbie said, "if Captain Marsh had not been so obdurate. Why didn't you speak to him?"

"I did speak to him, old girl. And he gave me a very good reason as to why he wouldn't let you and Maggie come with him."

"And that reason is?"

"He could not guarantee your safety against the Indians."

"Well, if that's all it takes, I would gladly release him from any responsibility for my safety," Libbie said.

Custer shook his head. "I won't."

"You won't? Why not?"

"Do you think I could go into battle worrying about the safety of my darling sunbeam?" Custer asked.

"But you will be keeping the Indians busy. What danger could there possibly be on a riverboat?"

"I do what I think is best," Custer said simply.

"Autie," Tom called from outside the tent. "The regiment is assembled for the march."

"Thank you, Tom," Custer said. Wiping his mouth with a napkin, he put on his hat, then leaned across the table to kiss Libbie. As he rose to leave the tent, Libbie heard him say to Tom, "If you are going to tell Libbie good-bye, you'd better do it now. She and the others will be going back to the fort with the paymaster."

Tom then stepped inside the tent and stood there for a moment, grinning at Libbie. Libbie got up from the table and walked toward him.

"So, you have come to tell me good-bye?"

"Yes."

Libbie hugged him. "Here all these years I have worried for you because you had no wife," she said. "At times like this I think you might have the right idea. It must be much easier going off to battle without having to say good-bye to someone you love."

"But I am saying good-bye to someone I love," Tom said.

Libbie chuckled. "You know what I mean."

"No, that's not the problem. The problem is, you don't know what I mean," Tom said.

Libbie looked puzzled. "Tom?"

"You are the only woman I could ever love, Libbie. And, as he has all his life, Autie has beaten me to the prize."

Libbie shook her head nervously, but Tom laughed easily.

"Oh, don't worry about it. I would never do anything to shame you or myself, or to harm my brother, for I love him as well. And I promise you that you will never again hear anything like this from my lips. But before we go on this scout—this scout above all others—I just wanted you to know."

"Why . . . this one above all others?" Libbie asked.

Tom was silent for a long moment, and Libbie tried to read his eyes. What is there? she wondered. Was it frustration that he was caught up in a situation he couldn't change? Was it fear of the upcoming mission? Or, was it a little of both? "No particular reason," Tom finally said.

"Tom, what can I say? You know—"

Tom put his finger on Libbie's lips and shook his head. "There is nothing to be said," he told her. "Come, the officers' wives are getting ready to leave. I'll escort you to the paymaster's wagon."

Maggie Calhoun, sister to the Custers and wife of Lieutenant James Calhoun, was already waiting at the paymaster's wagon. She kissed her brother Tom as he brought Libbie up.

"Do look after Jimmi for me, won't you, Tom?" she asked.

"He'll be with us until the end," Tom replied. For a moment, Maggie's eyes narrowed as if wondering exactly what he meant by "the end," then thinking that she might be putting more into his words than was necessary, she smiled. "I knew I could count on you."

"You two look after each other," Tom said. He left the two women, then swung into his own saddle as the regiment began marching out.

"Look at them, Maggie," Libbie said. "Isn't that a splendid sight?"

"Yes," Maggie agreed. "There is no sight more beautiful or inspiring than this."

"So magnificent," Libbie said. "How could any harm come to them?"

The words were strangely pensive, and were spoken almost as if Libbie had been talking to herself.

The column marched by as if on parade. Flags were snapping in the breeze, including Custer's personal colors. Though lieutenant colonels were not authorized their own flags, Custer kept the one Libbie had designed for him during the Civil War when Custer was a general. The flag was a swallow-tailed red-and-blue pennant, emblazoned with crossed white sabers. Also visible, when one looked more closely, was the embroidered name "Libbie."

As the column marched by, the officers paid their respects to the ladies by holding shining sabers up in a salute. The band was playing "The Girl I Left Behind Me."

Several times the paymaster started to call to his horses, but each time Libbie put out her hand to stop him. Finally realizing that she intended to watch the entire procession, he sat quietly until the last of the column had passed. Then they watched the long blue line recede into the distance, listening to the music fade away until just the drum and the high notes of the flutes could be heard.

Soon the only evidence that the army had passed them by was a cloud of dust hanging over the horizon. It was deathly quiet save for the whistling of the wind.

A paper blew across the prairie and plastered itself to the wheel of the paymaster's wagon. Libbie bent to retrieve it.

"What is it?" Maggie asked.

"It's a poem," Libbie answered.

"A poem? What sort of poem? Oh, do let me see."

"It was written by one of the soldiers, I suppose," Libbie said, a strange, faraway look on her face.

"Well, what is it? Is it a love poem?" Maggie asked.

"No," Libbie said. "Here, read it for yourself." She handed the poem over to her sister-in-law, who began to read it aloud.

> There goes first call blowing,
> Sergeant Flynn,
> And it sounds like taps blowing,
> Sergeant Flynn,
> Oh my lad, that's only a fancy

Take a brace there, Private Clancy,
You'll feel better when they strike up
"Garry Owen."

Ten thousand braves are riding,
Sergeant Flynn,
In the black hills they are hiding,
Sergeant Flynn,
Crazy Horse and Sitting Bull,
They will get their bellies full
of lead and steel from the men of
Garry Owen.

We'll dismount and fight the heathens,
Sergeant Flynn,
While there's still a trooper breathin',
Sergeant Flynn,
In the face of sure disaster
Keep those carbines firing faster,
Let the volleys ring for dear old
Garry Owen.

We are Irish, Scotch, and thrifty,
Sergeant Flynn,
We'll sell trooper one for fifty,
Sergeant Flynn,
For each Seventh scalp that's lifted,
Fifty heathen souls have drifted
To their happy hunting around for
Garry Owen.

Here they come like screaming Banshees,
Sergeant Flynn,
Sioux and Blackfeet and Comanches,
Sergeant Flynn,
Let your blades run red and gory
In their blood we'll write our story
We will die today for dear old
Garry Owen

We are ambushed and surrounded
Sergeant Flynn
But Recall has not sounded
Sergeant Flynn
Our story will echo from the grave
How we fought, oh so Brave
But there are better days to be in
Garry Owen

Maggie laid the paper in her lap and looked at Libbie. "Oh, my," she said. "Libbie, you don't think . . ."

"What?" Libbie asked.

Maggie looked at the cloud of dust, which was now little more than a small puff on the horizon. "You don't think anything will happen to them, do you?"

"No, of course not," Libbie replied "Why, one company of the Seventh could handle the entire Sioux Nation. I've heard Autie say that, I don't know how many times."

"I know," Maggie said. "Still . . ."

"Maggie, you were right here as I was when the army marched by. You saw how magnificent they were. Do you really think they are in any danger from savages?"

"No," Maggie said. "No, I suppose not."

"Good. I thought you would see it that way. Now, driver, let us hurry back to Fort Lincoln."

"Yes, ma'am, Mrs. Custer," the driver said, and he clucked to the horses.

Chapter Eleven

There were four Indians in the party that captured Kate. She had been their prisoner for two days now, and to her surprise, and relief, they had not harmed her in any way. The only complaint she had was that they rode, while she was forced to walk along behind them. She was thankful that they did, at least, ride slowly.

As a result of three days of walking, she was very tired. She was also hungry, because though they hadn't harmed her, they weren't particularly generous with food. Her meals came from the scraps they tossed her way, much as one would feed a dog.

At the end of the third day of her captivity, they stopped for camp. One of the Indians killed a rabbit and skewered it over a fire. As usual, Kate sat quietly, waiting for what was left. As she sat by the fire, dirtier than she had ever been in her life, her hair hanging in matted strands, her dress tattered and torn, her fingernails broken, as wild-looking as any creature who ever wandered the plains, she thought about her life back in New York. She saw in her mind the elegant gowns and handsome clothes of the men, and the beautiful carpets and appointments of the art gallery. She remembered the fine restaurants where refined waiters served a variety of foods drawn from all over the world.

For some strange, inexplicable reason, the contrast between her life then and her current existence struck her as funny, and she began to laugh.

The Indians looked up in shock.

"Why do you laugh?" one of them asked.

That any of them spoke at all surprised her. For three days she had been speaking to them, trying to get one of them to say something—anything—to her. Until now they had been completely silent.

"Why you laugh?" the Indian asked again.

Kate thought of all she had been put through for the last three days, not the least of which was the refusal by any of them to even speak to her. Now that they were curious, they were willing to speak to her. She knew she couldn't explain the humor of the situation to them, even if they spoke perfect English. So she made no effort to try. Let them see how it felt, she thought.

Kate found the sight of confused disbelief on the faces of the Indians to be even funnier, so she began laughing again, so hard this time that tears streamed down her face. She had no idea why she was laughing, she knew that only she could appreciate the irony of her situation, and its tragedy was greater than any humor. But she couldn't help it. Her mirth was wild and uncontrollable.

"You stop laughing," the one she believed to be the leader ordered.

"I can't," Kate gasped.

The Indian stood up and, drawing his hand back to hit her, started toward her. Even under imminent threat, Kate couldn't control her laughter, and the Indian began cursing her in his own language.

Suddenly, a shot rang out of the night, and the Indian grabbed his chest. He looked down to see bright red blood spilling through his fingers.

The other three Indians shouted and jumped up, reaching frantically for their rifles. Three more shots cracked through the night and they, too, went down.

Kate screamed at the sound of the shots, then stared into the dark to see if she could determine where they came from. Two men stepped out of the dark then, into the golden circle of light thrown by the campfire. They were both white men, one tall and thin with a prominent Adam's apple and large eyes. He looked to be in his mid- to late twenties. The other was shorter, stocky, with a head full of bushy hair and a great gray beard. He could have been as old as fifty.

"Well, now, Harley, lookie here, would you?" the

young one said. "What think ye o' this now? These here heathens had 'em a white woman."

"Can't be too much of a woman, Luke, 'cause she ain't dead. Any white woman that was decent would'a already kilt herself."

Luke laughed. "Well now, ain't it just our luck that we'uns found us a woman out here who ain't decent." He rubbed himself gleefully.

With a sinking heart, Kate realized what the man meant. She had been with the Indians for three days, without being hurt. Was her situation worse, now that she was with her own people? she wondered.

It was the next day before Red Eagle found the camp. Two days earlier he had discovered Picture Man's body lying along his wagon. The signs told him that Picture Woman had not been harmed, but was taken prisoner by the Indians who captured her. He followed their trail, not sure as to how he would deal with them when he caught up with them, but determined to rescue Picture Woman, whatever it took. Now he was at the place where they had stopped for the night.

Red Eagle dismounted and crawled up to the top of the ridge on his hands and knees, then crept on his stomach for the last few yards. Finally, he reached the summit and peered down toward the encampment.

It was strangely quiet. Those who captured the white woman should have been making preparations to move. And there should have been a smell of cooked food in the air, for surely they would have had their breakfast by now. Also, where were the horses?

Red Eagle studied the campsite for a few minutes longer, then looking all around to make certain that no one was watching him, he rolled over the top of the ridgeline. Keeping low, he darted quickly and silently down into the camp.

Just as he reached the campsite, he saw the bodies of the four Indians. Cautiously, he walked the rest of the way into the campsite, ever alert for any sign of danger.

Picture Woman wasn't here, but Red Eagle didn't really expect her to be. He sighed, then looked back toward the dead Indians, wondering who had killed them.

Red Eagle dropped to one knee to examine the site more closely. Reading the sign, he saw that the four had been killed by white men. He knew that because of their horses' tracks. They had arrived with two shod horses, and left camp with an additional unshod pony. That pony wasn't carrying as much weight as the two shod horses, so Red Eagle knew that they had taken Picture Woman with them.

For a moment, Red Eagle wondered if he should

continue his search for her. After all, she had been rescued by her own people. If he followed them, they might think he was trying to get her back. Standing, he returned to his horse. He had not been able to save both the father and daughter who had come onto their land to make pictures. But now, at least, Picture Woman was safe.

He wondered about Sitting Bull's vision that he would be killed by one of his own people if an Indian harmed the picture-makers. Picture Man was harmed by an Indian, but Picture Woman was free. Would Sitting Bull's prophecy be carried out? Red Eagle wondered. Or would he be spared, as Picture Woman was spared?

Chapter Twelve

On the third day of the march, the regiment was up by three in the morning and on the move by five. It began raining just before noon. The rain turned into a thunderstorm, including large balls of hail, by early afternoon. The ice pellets stung and bruised man and beast alike, but there was little the men could do about it besides hunker down in their ponchos and ride it out. The rain was hard on the soldiers, for despite the ponchos they wore, it managed to get through to soak their wool uniforms. As a result, even when the rain stopped in the late afternoon, the men were still miserable in their water-soaked, heavy, chafing wool uniforms

If the weather was hard on the line soldiers, it was twice as hard on Trains company. They had the same uncomfortable conditions with regard to their persons, plus they had to contend with the wagons. The wheeled vehicles became mired in the mud, often hub deep, and the teams would have to be doubled, sometimes trebled, in order to get the wagons free.

Gradually, the wagons began falling behind despite the best efforts of the drivers and skinners to keep up with the march. Once Custer himself rode back to check on their progress.

"Mr. Pendarrow, I can't run off and leave my supplies. On the other hand, I can't afford the time it takes to wait for you. You are going to have to keep up with the regiment," Custer said.

"Yes, sir," Quinn replied. Unasked was the logical question . . . how could they go any faster than they were going?

"Is there any wonder why I don't want wagons to accompany me beyond the rendevous with the *Far West?*" Custer asked. Frustrated, he wheeled Dandy around and urged the animal into a gallop to return him to the front of the formation. In the mud the horse's hooves lost purchase, and for just a moment it went down on one knee. Only Custer's skill as a rider and the horse's reflexes avoided a spill.

Quinn turned his attention back to the task at hand—that of getting the wagons free.

"Mr. Pendarrow, I have a suggestion, sir, if you don't mind my making it," Scott said.

"Mind? No, of course I don't mind," Quinn said. "I welcome anything that will help."

"These last three wagons are the heaviest loaded, and they are the ones giving the most trouble. Why don't we just leave them here?" Scott suggested.

"You mean just abandon the wagons and the supplies?"

"No, sir, not the supplies. And not even all the wagons. Just these three. We'll rig up some carrying frames and use the team animals as pack mules and horses."

"At one hundred fifty pounds per animal, they won't be able to carry all that's in the wagons," Quinn said.

"I know the army regulations say one hundred fifty pounds, but we both know they can carry double that weight. I figure if we spread the loads out, put no more than, say, two hundred pounds on each of the pack animals, we'll make it just fine."

Quinn thought about Scott's suggestion for a moment as he looked at a double-teamed effort to pull one of the wagons free. Finally, he nodded his head. "Do it."

Though the regiment made camp by five that afternoon, it was well after dark by the time the last wagon came up. Quinn stayed with the lagging wagon until it finally reached camp.

"You men get something to eat," Quinn said. "Then you'd better get some rest. I figure today was just a sample of what it's going to be like."

"You want me to get something for you to eat?" Scott asked as Quinn dismounted.

Quinn shook his head. "No, thanks. Custer wants all the element leaders to meet with him at the end of each day. I'm sure I missed it, but I had better get on up there and let him know that I am here, nevertheless."

As Quinn started toward Custer's location, he saw Boston and Autie Reed leaning against a tree. The young men looked totally exhausted.

"I'm going up to see the general. You two want to ride up with me?"

They looked at him, then Boston dismissed his invitation with a wave of his hand. "Give Autie our regards," he said. "But I think we'll stay here."

Quinn chuckled to himself as he rode away. He had to give the two young boys their due—they were working as hard as any of the other men in the company. But the extraordinary display of energy they had exhibited when the march began had since been greatly reduced.

"Quinn, you made it, I see," Tom Custer said when he saw Quinn approaching.

"Yes."

"And without leaving any wagonloads out on the trail?" Custer asked. He asked it in a joking manner, but Quinn thought bitterly of the three wagons he had to abandon.

"Every ounce of cargo is present and accounted for, General," Quinn said.

"Good for you," Custer said. He pointed to the fire, over which a large joint of meat was spitted. "One of our scouts, Charley Reynolds, shot an elk today. It's quite tasty—you'd better have some. Anytime you are in the field and can eat something more than hardtack, beans, and jerky, you need to take advantage of the opportunity."

"Thank you, General." Quinn then walked over to the spitted carcass and, using his knife, carved off a piece.

Custer cleared his throat. "Quinn, I'm afraid we received some bad news today."

Quinn looked at Custer, but didn't say anything.

"Two of our scouts came in with a report that they found the McKenzie wagon."

"And the McKenzies?" Quinn asked.

"They found the father, lying beside the wagon, scalped. No sign of the girl."

"Damn," Quinn said quietly. He sighed. "I should've gone after them the moment I learned that they had left."

"How do you know that would've been in time?" Custer asked. "It could very well be that they were attacked their very first day out. There's nothing any of us could've done about it, short of putting them in jail to make certain they didn't leave. We certainly couldn't have done that."

Quinn shook his head in agreement. "No," he said. "We couldn't have."

"In the final analysis, Quinn, the McKenzies have no one to blame but themselves. They were warned about the Indian situation. In fact, they were ordered not to go. They didn't heed the warning, and they disobeyed the order. As a result, they have paid for that bit of foolhardy bravado with their lives."

"I thought you said they haven't found the girl."

"No, they haven't," Custer said. "But if there is a merciful God, Miss McKenzie is dead."

Kate had not been rescued. She had been captured, and was as much a prisoner of the two white men as she had been of the Indians. She was riding instead of walking, but her condition was just as difficult and, she believed, just as precarious. At least the Indians had ridden at a slow enough pace to allow her to keep up. And they had made no overt move toward her person.

Harley and Luke were riding fast and hard, and, unlike the Indians, they kept Kate tied up. Her hands were secured behind her back with a strip of rawhide, and her feet were tied with a rope that passed under the pony's stomach. She had to hold on with her knees lest she fall and be dragged by the animal, and the constant pressure of her knees turned into agony. Just as difficult was the mental anguish she was experiencing. Whatever they had in mind for her couldn't be good.

When the storm broke, it was worse. Her captors made no effort to get out of the rain, but they did put on their own ponchos. Kate had no protection from the rain and no way to ward off the stinging effect of the hailstones.

She thought that when the rain stopped she would get some relief, but that was when an even more serious situation began to develop. As the sun dried the wet rawhide, it began to shrink. And as it shrunk, it grew tighter and tighter around her wrists, and the pain became more and more acute. Finally, she called out, "My hands! Please, these ties are so tight! Loosen my hands!"

Harley looked around in surprise. "Damn, Luke, we forgot about the rawhide shrinkin' when it got wet. We don't loosen them binds, she's goin' go all gangrenous on us." Harley rode back and cut the cords. If she had felt pain before, it was nothing like the excruciating pain she felt when the blood started rushing back into her hands and fingers.

The longer they rode, the more her discomfort increased until she felt as if she would be unable to take it any longer. Finally, as the sky in the east began to lighten, Harley called for a halt.

"We may as well stop here and sleep awhile. Like

as not any Injuns that might have come up on them four we kilt is far away by now."

"Yeah, that's what I'm thinkin'," Luke said.

Harley stretched and yawned, then scratched himself. "Besides, which, I'm plum tired."

Though Kate no longer had her hands tied, her feet were still tied under the belly of the pony, and Harely walked over to untie her. Gratefully, she climbed down.

"Well, you ain't too tired, are you?" Luke asked.

"Too tired for what?"

Luke laughed. "Maybe I should ask if you're too old," he said. "Too tired for . . . you know." He looked pointedly at Kate.

"Go on over there 'n' lie down in the grass under that tree," Harley said to Kate, nodding toward a nearby tree. "You'll be comfortable over there."

"Yeah, 'ceptin' don't you go gettin' yourself too comfortable now," Luke warned, giggling and rubbing himself. " 'Cause me 'n' ole Harley here, we got plans for you. Ain't we, Harley?"

Harley was quiet for a moment.

"Harley? I said, me 'n' you got plans, right?"

"I don't know that we do," Harley finally answered.

Luke opened his eyes wide in surprise. "You don't know? What do you mean, you don't know? Didn't you tell me no more'n a hour ago that you thought this here girl was prettier'n any whore you'd ever had?"

"Yes. "

"Well, there you go. How many times you ever had somethin' like this just dropped into your lap? Prettier'n any whore, and it ain't goin' to cost us a thing."

"You're wrong," Harley said. "It would cost more than I'm willin' to pay."

"What are you talkin' about?"

"Look here, Luke, iffen this was some Injun gal, why, I wouldn't think nary a thing about it. But she ain't a Indian. She's a white girl."

"She was with Injuns when we found her," Luke insisted. "That's the same thing as her bein' an Injun girl. Hell, you said yourself that any decent white woman would'a done kilt herself by now."

"I know that's what I said, but when you get right down to it, I don't know that a body can kill themselves all that easy, be they man or woman."

"Harley, you're not goin' soft, are you?"

"Maybe. All I know is I don't feel none too good 'bout doin' anythin' to this girl. I think it might be best if we just left her alone."

Luke snorted in frustration, then he ran his hand through his hair. "Look, old man, you don't want to do nothin' to this girl, why, then don't you do nothin'. But me, I'm goin' to have myself some fun." He started toward Kate, loosening his belt as he did so.

"No, you ain't," Harley said. His voice was quiet, but it was cold and ominous.

Kate had been following the conversation, praying that Harley would prevail. Now she was shocked to see that he had actually drawn his pistol, and he was pointing it at Luke.

"What the hell are you doin', Harley?" Luke growled.

"I told you, Luke, we ain't goin' to do nothin' to this here girl."

"The hell I ain't. You just watch me." Luke once again turned toward Kate.

Harley pulled the hammer back on the pistol, and the deadly sound of a double metallic click as the sear engaged the cylinder stopped Luke in his tracks.

"You try it, Luke, and I'll put a bullet in you," Harley said.

"Dammit, Harley, have you lost your mind?" Luke shouted in frustrated rage.

"No. But I reckon I've found some conscience. Girl, get on that pony and go," Harley said.

Kate was totally exhausted, and whereas one minute earlier she didn't believe she could take one more step, she was now galvanized into action. She was being offered the chance to escape, and her tiredness fell away.

"You don't think you're doin' this girl any favors sendin' her out like that, do you?" Luke asked. "Hell, if she stays with us, all we'll do is have a little fun with her, then we'll turn her loose first white settlement we come to. But if she goes out there, she's goin' to die for sure. If the Indians, or a bear, or a snake don't get her, she's goin' to die of hunger. You know that as well as I do."

Harley looked over at Kate. "He's right," he said. "It ain't likely to be easy out there. So I'm goin' to leave it up to you, girl. Which do you want? You want to stay with us? Or take your chances?"

"Yeah, girly, let me hear what you got to say now," Luke said.

Kate climbed onto the back of the pony without answering. Then she looked at Luke with an expression of anger and hate. "That question doesn't even deserve an answer." She jerked the horse around, then, slapping her knees against the animal's side, caused him to bolt away quickly.

It was May 22, six days into the expedition. The march was encountering a rough section of the trail, one that necessitated doubling up the teams. In this case the teams were being doubled not to pull the wagons, but rather to help stabilize them. The trail angled off down a sharp incline, and they had to use ropes on the top side of the wagons to hold them upright.

"Now!" Sergeant Scott shouted. "Bring it down now!"

The wagon driver started forward a few feet.

"Wait! Hold it! Whoa!" he shouted, hauling back on the reins. The team stopped.

"What is it?" Scott asked. "What'd you stop for?"

"I ain't goin' down this here incline," the driver said.

"Well, what do you plan to do, just sit here and wait till we come back?" Scott asked.

The driver climbed down from the wagon. "Look, I'll do my work same as anyone else, and I'll work as hard as anyone else. But I ain't a soldier and I ain't a fool, and by God, there's no way you or Pendarrow either one can make me take this wagon down that hill."

"I'll do it," McMurtry said, climbing up the left front wheel to get to the driver's seat.

"Mac, wait," Scott called to him. McMurtry was the soldier Quinn had busted from corporal on the first day he took over Trains. Ironically, he was now one of the best soldiers in the platoon, showing the stuff that had gotten him promoted to corporal in the first place.

"We ain't got time to wait, Corporal, you know that," McMurtry said. "Custer is takin' this regiment on with or without us. We wait around, we get left behind."

"I know," Scott agreed. "But maybe Sterns has a

point. Let's take another look at the rigging before we try it."

"Hell, Sterns is just scared," McMurtry said. "Let's just do it, and be done with it. Hyar, giddap!" he shouted.

"Mac, wait! We don't have anyone on the hold lines!" Scott shouted, noticing that the men had dropped the lines when Sterns stopped. Scott's warning was too late. The wagon started down the incline, then rolled hard to the right, upsetting with a loud crash. McMurtry was thrown from the wagon seat, then the entire weight of the wagon rolled over him.

"Mr. Pendarrow!" Scott shouted, running to the injured man.

Quinn didn't have to be summoned. He was back by the next wagon in line, and when he heard the sound of the crash, he looked around just in time to see the wagon rolling over. He ran toward it, then scrambled down the hill where Scott and several others were already gathered around McMurtry.

"How bad is it?" he asked.

Scott looked up at Quinn, but didn't say a word. He didn't need to. Quinn could tell by the way McMurtry was lying that he was dead from a broken neck.

Kate was exhausted and weak from hunger. There had been very little to eat while a captive of the Indians, and only a single piece of jerky during the day she spent with the two white men who found her, then nothing since. She had wandered around during the last three days, trying to find something that looked familiar, something she had seen before in hopes it would at least give her the right direction. She had been unsuccessful, and was now hopelessly lost.

When Kate lay down late in the afternoon of the third day, she made no effort to tether the horse. It didn't matter to her whether the horse wandered off or not. She wouldn't need him. She wasn't planning on moving from this spot.

Kate had no idea how long she had been sleeping. She was awakened by the smell of cooking meat and, at first, thought she must be dreaming. But when she woke up, she could still smell the meat. It was dark, but when she opened her eyes, she could see an Indian, front-lighted by the golden bubble of light that emanated from a small fire. The Indian was holding a stick over the fire, and skewered on the end of the stick was a bird. She had no idea what kind of bird it was, but the smell of it roasting actually made her salivate.

Kate's first thought was to run, but she was too weak to move. Besides, she reasoned, if he had wanted to kill her, he would have already done so.

"Hello," she said.

The Indian looked around, then he held up the stick. "I make food for you."

"It smells delicious."

"You are Picture Woman?"

"Picture Woman?" Kate thought for a moment, then realized that that may be what the Indians called her. "Yes," she said. "I am Picture Woman."

The Indian pointed to himself. "I am called Red Eagle."

"Red Eagle. My, that is a . . . a fierce name," Kate said. She didn't know what else to say.

Red Eagle pulled the bird away from the fire, looked at it, smelled it, then nodded. He put it on a flat slab of bark, then cut the meat into smaller pieces with his knife. He brought the entire thing over and handed it to her. "Eat," he said.

"Thank you." Kate grabbed a large piece. It burned her fingers, and she had to pass it from hand to hand to hold it, but she didn't put it back down. She blew on it to cool it, then took a bite. Even without salt, she believed it was the best thing she had ever tasted. "It's delicious," she said.

Red Eagle said nothing.

Kate ate all of the first piece and started to reach for another, then pulled back. "Where are my manners?" she said. She indicated that he should take a piece.

"No. You eat. You need food."

"I won't argue with you," Kate said, selecting another piece.

She had no idea what this Indian had in mind for her, but for now she didn't care. He had saved her life. That was enough.

Chapter Thirteen

May 26 was an easy day, the easiest day of the entire march. The trail was wide, flat, and free of any obstacles, and that enabled Trains company to keep up with the march quite easily. The weather was hot and dry, but there was plenty of forage for the animals, and they were near water. They made twelve easy miles, then stopped for camp at two o'clock that afternoon. By three o'clock, a courier had arrived from Fort Lincoln, bringing up the mail.

There was a great deal of excitement as the men gathered around for mail call. Quinn watched from just outside the circle. A man's name would be called, he would answer, then the letter would be passed back to him. After that, the man would wander off, clutching the letter tightly. Finding some place all his own, he would open the letter and for the few minutes it took him to read it would be transported away from the rigors of the trail back to home and hearth.

Quinn remembered those times at the fort when

he would wait anxiously for mail from Suzie Parkinson. He was over the heartbreak of seeing Suzie marry someone else . . . but he still missed the magic that receiving a letter could bring.

Sitting near a tree and sucking on the root of a stem of grass, he had to be content with watching the others read their letters. Tom Custer was nearby, and when he finished his letter he looked over at Quinn.

"No mail?" he asked.

Quinn shook his head. "I don't get mail anymore." The comment sounded like self-pity, and he immediately wished that he hadn't said it. "I mean, I don't need it. I don't have anyone anywhere."

"Well, a man shouldn't go into the field without a letter to read," Tom said. He held up the letter he had just finished. "Here, you can read this one."

"I can't read your mail, Tom."

"Hell, don't let that bother you. It isn't my letter, anyway. It's Autie's. It's from Libbie."

"The general's personal mail? All the more reason I can't read it."

Tom laughed. "Believe me, there's nothing really personal about it. You don't know my sister-in-law all that well, do you? She doesn't write to Autie . . . she writes to posterity. She has a sense of history about her, and I think she fully intends for the world to read all her letters someday. In fact, she often questions me about them when we come back, wanting to know what I thought about something she wrote."

"Still . . ."

"Read it," another voice said. It wasn't until that moment that Quinn realized General Custer was lying down nearby. He made the comment without even opening his eyes. "Libbie's a bit vain. She enjoys having others read what she writes."

"All right, if you're sure," Quinn said, reaching for the letter Tom held toward him.

My dearest Bo,

The servants are doing very well. We are raising chickens. We have forty-three. So many cats about the garrison keep the rats away. The weather is very hot, but the nights are cool. The lights about the hills and valleys are exquisite. The river now is too high for sandbars to be seen.

About a hundred men with John Stevenson in command have gone to the Black Hills. Nearly twenty-five teams have passed by.

I still feel that I could have come upriver on the Far West and, while some distance from any danger, would be that much closer to you . . . indeed, would have been with you much longer. I feel an emptiness during this expedition that transcends anything I have ever felt before. I cannot but feel the greatest apprehensions for you on this dangerous scout. Oh, Autie, if you return without bad news, the worst of the summer will be over.

Carter has returned and is chief trumpeter. He really sounds the calls beautifully. But his long-drawn notes make me heartsick. I do not wish to be reminded of the cavalry just now, for it only increases my feeling of nervousness.

The papers told last night of a small skirmish between General Crook's cavalry and the Indians. They called it a fight. The Indians were very bold. They don't seem afraid of anything. Please, do be careful, Autie.

The wildflowers are a revelation, almost the first sweet-scented I have ever known. The house is full of bouquets.

With your bright future and the knowledge that you are of positive use to your day and generation, do you not see that your life is precious on that account, and not only because an idolizing wife could not live without you?

I shall go to bed and dream of my dear Bo.

Libbie

"My wife writes well, doesn't she?" Custer asked, getting up and walking over to a simmering pot of stew.

"Yes, she does," Quinn answered, still feeling a little self-conscious about reading such a private missive.

"It's no wonder people make the accusation that she writes all my articles for *Galaxy*." Custer tasted the stew, then smacked his lips appreciatively, mostly for the benefit of young Autie Reed, who was enjoying his uncle's antics. "Libbie can write, but I tell you, nothing she cooks is as tasty as this trail stew."

"You'd better not let Aunt Libbie hear you say

that, Uncle," Autie Reed teased. "She would grab you by the hair."

Tom laughed. "She wouldn't have much hair to grab. The General shaved most of it off. Did you hope to cheat the Indians of their prize, Autie?" he asked.

Custer joined in the laughter and, removing his hat, ran his hand across his newly shorn hair. "I needed a change," he said. "And besides, there's no sense in making it easy for them."

"Tell me, Mr. Kellogg, what does the newspaper think about the general's new look?" Tom asked the newspaper reporter.

Kellogg, who was reading the newspaper he had received with the mail, looked up and chuckled. "I don't think the readers will find him quite as dashing," he said. He ran his hand over his own hair. "But if I thought it would keep the Indians from being interested in me, I'd shave myself bald."

"Don't you worry, Mr. Kellogg," Autie Reed said. "If the going gets rough, I'll protect you."

"I'm certain Mr. Kellogg will sleep much easier for that," General Custer said.

Boston called to Autie Reed and Tom, anxious to show them something interesting he had found, and they walked off to see what it was. That left only Quinn, General Custer, and the newspaper reporter. Kellogg read in silence for a few moments longer, then Custer called over to him.

"Tell me, Mr. Kellogg, what do you find so interesting in the paper?"

"There is a story of three men killed in the Black Hills," Kellogg said. "Tomahawked and scalped by Indians."

"No report of P. G. McKenzie yet?"

"No."

Custer held up his finger. "You wait until news gets out that McKenzie and his daughter were killed. Maybe there is not that much of a public outcry over innocent and unknown prospectors. But a man of McKenzie's prominence will cause a roar against the Indians, and this campaign will be looked upon as a crusade as meaningful and necessary as any during the great rebellion."

"I'm sure it will, General," Kellogg said. "And I certainly intend to do all I can to make certain that happens."

"And what news is there of politics?" Custer asked.

"It appears that Governor Tilden has announced that he is withdrawing his intention to place a name into nomination in order that his own name may be entered."

"What?" Custer asked in a small voice. "What did you say?"

"Oh, it's all political strategy and hokum anyway," Kellogg said. "You see, Tilden's biggest opponent for the nomination is clearly General Winfield

Scott Hancock of Pennsylvania. So Tilden spread the rumor that he was going to place another prominent military man's name into nomination for president, in order to dilute the support for General Hancock. Of course nobody knows who the military man was who would be so base as to allow his name to be used for such a purpose. Certainly it could be no one with political ambitions of his own, for such a thing would be the death knell to any future political aspirations."

"I see," Custer said quietly. "Did they find who this military fellow was?"

"No," Kellogg said, looking through the paper. "No, I don't think so. It may be, though, that the fellow whose name Tilden was going to propose had no idea of the real reason for the nomination, and, when he realized it, he ordered Tilden to withdraw him."

Custer turned red in the face, then turned and walked away.

"General!" Kellogg called. "General, are you all right?"

Because Tom and Autie Reed had been called away, Quinn was the only other person near enough to overhear the conversation. He remembered the dinner at the Custer house the night before his resignation took place. During that meal, Custer had brought up the possibility of becoming president and mentioned, also, that Governor Tilden would be submitting his name for nomination.

No doubt Custer was the military officer Kellogg was talking about. Blaine was going to make the nomination, but he had no intention of backing him. He was just using him . . . and it was obvious that until this moment Custer didn't know that.

Glancing over toward Kellogg, Quinn saw that the reporter was once again engrossed in his newspaper. Quinn decided to go after Custer, to offer . . . what, he wondered. His support? Sympathy? He was sure Custer wouldn't want that. And yet he felt compelled to do something.

He found Custer standing by the front wheel of a wagon, his hands around the spoke, pulling on the wheel. "General, are you all right?"

Custer pulled on the wheel so hard that the hub and axle squeaked.

"You'd better get on your men, Pendarrow," Custer said. "If they don't keep these wheels lubricated, we could be having a great deal of trouble before the expedition is over."

"Yes, sir, I will see to it personally," Quinn said.

"And not just the hubs," Custer said. "The tie-joints as well."

"Yes, sir."

Custer walked around to the other side of the wagon and pulled at the wheel on that side as well.

"I was a fool," he finally said, speaking so quietly that Quinn could barely hear him.

"No you weren't, General."

Custer laughed, a quiet, self-deprecating laugh. "Oh, yes, I was. I sat there in that hotel suite in New York with Tilden, and I let him convince me that he would be submitting my name for nomination for president because he really believed I would be the best man for the job. Who was I fooling? How could I have been so naive as to think I could be president?"

"You would make a fine president, General," Quinn assured him. "And you weren't being naive, you were being confident. Your problem is you are too honest a man. Your word is your bond, and you aren't prepared to deal with duplicity. You had no idea Tilden intended to use you for his own purposes."

"I can tell you this, Quinn. Never again will I be such a fool."

"General, I hope you aren't considering withdrawing from all political considerations."

Custer looked at Quinn and smiled. "Quite the contrary. I shall be even more forceful in my political pursuits from now on. But I shall do it all myself and never again will I depend on someone else."

Although they had encountered some very hot days during the march, it turned colder on May 31.

At midnight it began to snow, and when everyone awoke on the morning of June 1, they discovered a three-inch covering blanket of snow.

It was still snowing, and continued to snow until midmorning. Custer decided to remain in camp that day. For most of the men, the respite was welcome. For the men of Trains, however, it was just an opportunity for work. Quinn had all the wagons inspected, then his men made such repairs as was required.

It snowed again the next day and turned even colder. The chief medical officer, Dr. Williams, advised Custer to remain in camp, warning that to march the men in such conditions could bring on a lot of illness such as diarrhea and flu. Custer agreed, so the Seventh stood down for yet another day.

There was no rest for Trains, however. Just across the river was a high hill to be crossed, and Quinn decided that if they were going to be able to keep up with the regiment once the march was resumed, they would be better served by tackling that hill today.

Under the best of conditions the hill would have been hard to negotiate. Covered as it was with several inches of snow, it was exceptionally difficult as the teams had a hard time with their footing, and the wagons slipped and slid in the snow. Quinn started his wagons up the hill at nine o'clock in the morning. Trains worked throughout the long day without a break, finally getting the last wagon over by six o'clock.

Supper that evening was hardtack cooked in bacon grease and coffee. Quinn was just finishing when Tom Custer rode up.

"Everyone all right up here?" Tom asked as he dismounted.

"Fine. Tired, but in good spirits," Quinn answered.

Tom looked around at the wagons, all in place ready to start the march the next morning. The men were in groups eating their supper, talking and laughing together, soldier and civilian alike.

"I have to hand it to you, Quinn. You have done one magnificent job with these people."

"Thanks," Quinn replied. "But these men are the ones who have performed. Basically, I believe they are as good a group as I've ever worked with."

"The general is very pleased with you," Tom said. "He has commented on it several times."

"What did you come up here for, Uncle?" Autie Reed asked from a group of men. "Did you come for some of our fine supper?" he teased, holding up his hardtack.

"Now, why would I want that when we had beef with roasted potatoes, corn on the cob, and cherry pie. Oh, the cherry pie was simply delicious," Tom said, rubbing his belly appreciatively.

"You had beef . . . and . . . cherry pie?" Autie Reed complained.

Boston chuckled. "Can't you tell when he is teasing you, Autie Reed? You are such a greenhorn sometimes."

"Oh, like he and Uncle Autie have never teased you? What about that sponge rock?"

Autie Reed was talking about a strange-looking rock filled with holes that they found the first day out. Custer told Boston that it was a sponge rock, unique to Montana. When Boston questioned him on it, Custer told him that he had seen many just like it when he made his grand expedition two years earlier.

"All you have to do is soak it in water and it becomes soft, and makes the most wonderful sponge," Custer had insisted. "Not only that, it has its own unending supply of soap, so you could use it over and over again, though I don't know what good it is, other than as an oddity."

Boston got very excited over the possibility of marketing the sponge rock, insisting that they could get rich from it. He carried the rock in a bucket of water for several days, waiting for it to get soft and produce soap. Not until he heard his brothers laughing about it did he know he had been taken.

"That's different," Boston said in response to Autie Reed's reminder. "It could have been true. There are rocks like that, I'm sure. Tom, do you have any idea how many Indians we might see?" he asked in an attempt to change the subject.

"You know, boys, I've been thinking," Tom replied. "You've had your adventure now, it might not be a bad idea for you two to return with the dispatches tomorrow."

"What? Whatever makes you say such a thing?"

"I just don't think what's coming up will be good for civilians, that's all."

"We aren't just civilians, Tom," Boston insisted. "We're family. Mr. Pendarrow is going, and he is a civilian."

"Mr. Pendarrow is our wagon master. It's his job to go. Also, he is an ex-cavalry officer and he knows exactly what he is getting into. Besides, being family has nothing to do with it, except maybe that it makes me more anxious for your safety."

"Tom, are you afraid?" Boston asked, awed by the possibility. "I've never known you to be scared of anything."

"There are only two kinds of people who are never afraid," Tom said. "Fools and those who want to die."

"Ready to spar, Cap'n," the bo'sun called up to the wheelhouse of the riverboat *Far West*.

"Who you got on the poles?" Captain Grant Marsh called back down.

"Willie and Pete are on the poles, Hank is working the steam capstan," the bo'sun answered.

Under Captain Marsh's careful manipulation of the wheel, the boat moved slowly up to the sandbar. Then he gently pegged the nose to the bar.

This was all part of the plan, for the only way the boat could move all the way up the Yellowstone was to negotiate the frequent sandbars by working over them through a procedure known as sparring.

"We're aground," March called down from the wheelhouse.

"All right, laddies, here we go now!" the bo'sun shouted.

Willie and Pete put their poles into the water, then the bo'sun signaled Hank, who opened the throttle on the engine that operated the capstan. The capstan began winding up, pulling on the cable, and the cable put tension on the spars. That caused the front of the boat to lift slightly, which was just what they were after. At the stern of the boat, the paddlewheel churned mightily, whipping up a muddy froth. Gradually, the boat began to slide forward until finally enough of it was over the bar that it could move under its own power. After only a hundred feet or so, they had to spar again.

They had just completed their third spar when Captain Marsh saw her. At first, he was almost ready to believe that he was hallucinating, and he grabbed his field glasses for a closer look.

It was real! A woman was standing on the bank, waving at them. And, most bewildering of all, it was a white woman.

Captain Marsh pulled the whistle chain, and the heavy bleat of the whistle rolled across the flat water, then back from the trees along either bank. He reversed engines, and the paddle began spinning in reverse, causing such a froth that water splashed all the way up onto the texas deck.

"Bo'sun, put a boat over!" Captain Marsh shouted. "Pick up that woman!"

Chapter Fourteen

When word drifted back along the line of march that the regiment had come across an Indian burial ground, both Boston and Autie Reed begged to be allowed to ride ahead. Quinn granted permission, and when he and the wagons reached the burial site half an hour later, he got his first glance of the site.

Highly decorated corpses were laid out on elevated scaffolds, or stuffed in the forks of trees.

"Look at that one," Boston said, pointing to a scaffold that seemed more elaborately decorated than any of the others. The support poles were painted red and black.

"Him very brave warrior," the Indian scout named Bloody Knife said.

"How do you know he was brave, Bloody Knife?" Boston asked. "Did you know him?"

"These colors mean very brave," Bloody Knife said, putting his finger on the red and black rings.

"Yeah?" Custer said. "Well, if he was brave, that means he probably killed some white men. Pull it down," he ordered.

"No!" Bloody Knife said. "It will be bad medicine to pull down the grave."

"Come on, Bloody Knife, those heathen bastards have certainly desecrated our dead. What's good for the goose is good for the gander."

With Boston and Autie Reed's enthusiastic help, a couple of the soldiers pulled on the scaffold until they brought it down. Lieutenant Maguire removed the blankets wrapping the body, then examined the remains.

The body, not yet decomposed, was that of a fairly young warrior in his late twenties to early thirties. A terrible gaping wound just below the right shoulder was the probable cause of death.

"They sure buried him with all his treasures," Autie Reed said.

"You want some souvenirs? Take what you want," Custer suggested.

Autie Reed got a bow with six arrows and a pair of moccasins. Several others stepped forward then to help themselves, not only from the body of the recently slain warrior, but from the other graves as well. After half an hour of looting, officers and men were proudly displaying beaded moccasins, rawhide bags, horn spoons, and in some cases, even skulls or other bones from those bodies that had already turned into skeletons.

Back on the Yellowstone, Red Eagle had hidden in the trees, watching as the big boat stopped, and a little boat came to pick up Picture Woman. Not until he saw that she was safely on board did he leave. He had done what Sitting Bull asked of him . . . he had been a peacemaker. Now he would return to his people and be there to fight in the great battle that was soon to come.

Three days later as he approached the Rosebud, he saw a great column of dust rising ahead of him and, thinking it was the village on the move, he hurried forward. As he drew closer, though, he could tell by the sound that he had happened across a large body of soldiers. The Plains Indians always laughed among themselves at the way the army moved. Some of the Indians had attended the agency schools, and they had read a story in the schoolbooks about "belling the cat." They made jokes about belling the cat, saying that there was no need to pin a bell on the soldiers, for all of them carried bells. The bells were the metal bridle bits and harness accouterments, canteens, mess kits, sabers, belt buckles, wagon chains, and half a dozen other noisemakers. That was exactly what Red Eagle heard now, and as he sneaked forward, he saw a large column of soldiers moving down the Rose-bud.

He walked his horse for some distance before he mounted, not wanting the soldiers to hear the sound of his horse's hooves.

"Yes," Sitting Bull said when Red Eagle told of the presence of the army on the Rosebud. "Others have told us they are there. They are the soldiers of General Crook."

"If they continue as they are going, they will find our encampment," Red Eagle warned.

"Many warriors are preparing to go meet them now. I believe they will stop the soldiers from coming to our camp."

"Is this the great battle you have foreseen in your vision?"

Sitting Bull shook his head. "I am puzzled. In my vision there were women and children moving among the dead. I think this cannot be them, for if our warriors go to the Rosebud to fight the soldiers, there will be no women or children with them."

"How do you explain this?"

"I believe there are two armies—one at the Rose-bud, and one that will deliver themselves to us at the village, so that we may kill them."

"Then there are two battles to be fought?"

"Yes."

"To fight two battles, we will need every warrior.

Sitting Bull, I have done as you asked. I found Picture Woman, and I took her to a place where she would be safe. Now I ask you to free me from the role of peacemaker, and let me be a warrior once more."

"I have thought on this," Sitting Bull said. "And an answer has come. You will lead the warriors when they attack General Crook. I believe you will have a great victory."

"Hiyee heyii, huka hey!" Red Eagle yelled in excitement.

General Crook's men had just paused for a midafternoon break and were boiling water for coffee over dozens of small fires when Red Eagle attacked. Five hundred painted, screaming warriors came streaking down from the hills, firing rifles and loosing arrows with devastating effect. It was a bold move, for General Crook had as many men as Red Eagle had warriors, and an attack against an army unit of equal or greater strength was not a tactic the Indians ever used. The very unexpected nature of the attack stunned the soldiers into disorder, delaying for several critical moments any organized response. The soldiers suffered dozens of casualties as bullets tore through their ranks and clouds of arrows rained down on them.

"Hoka hey! Kill them!" Red Eagle shouted, firing and loading and firing again as fast as he could. He saw a soldier drop, then another, then another, as

the soldiers threw down their coffepots and began to run about their camp as if unsure of what to do.

These were, however, experienced cavalrymen and after the initial shock, they recovered from their fear and began firing volley after volley back at the Indians. Red Eagle was kept busy dodging the bullets that whizzed by his head like angry bees. With gun smoke hanging thick in the still air and no letup in the firing, the soldiers began moving back until they finally managed to organize a line of defense that was strong enough to hold the Indians off.

The defensive line was established some one hundred yards distant from where the first attack had come. As the soldiers gave up the field, they took their wounded with them, but left their dead behind. They also left a field that was strewn with rifles, carbines, and pistols.

Red Eagle realized that in the army's current defensive position he would not be able to dislodge them, but he launched one more attack anyway. He did this for the sole purpose of providing cover for those warriors who swept across the original battlefield, gathering the discarded weapons, ammunition, and even stripping the dead of their uniforms. With their supply of arms greatly increased, and the soldiers badly mauled by the attack, Red Eagle regrouped his warriors at top of the ridge.

So shaken was General Crook by the audacity of the attack, and so pummeled was his army, that he began to retreat, heading back to his base camp at Goose Creek.

From the top of the ridge, several of the warriors saw the army leaving. *"Hoka hey!* They are going!"

It was true. Red Eagle saw the soldiers falling back and for a brief moment he thought of attacking them one more time. When he looked around at his warriors, though, he saw that more than half of them, including the ones who had picked up some of the battlefield bounty, were heading back toward the encampment. That left his strength now at less than half of what it had been when he made the initial attack. And with the soldiers warned and organized for a more powerful defense, Red Eagle knew that the opportunity for a complete rout had passed him by.

He turned and started back toward the camp. With shouts of victory and exhilaration, the remaining warriors went with him. His leadership during the battle had been accepted without question, and already as they rode home some of the warriors were composing songs in his honor.

It was the largest encampment Red Eagle had ever seen. A large circle of Cheyenne anchored one end of the valley, the Hunkpapa the other end. In between were Ogalala, Sansarc, Minneconjous, and Blackfeet. A smaller circle of Brule also encamped within the valley. To any white man who might see it, the encampment would look like one huge Indian village. In fact, it wasn't a single village, nor even a single tribe. It was actually a series of individual neighborhoods and tribes. But the Indians did move freely from neighborhood to neighborhood, and they were keeping their pony herds together. In all, it was a settlement of from eight to ten thousand Indians.

The Indians were well aware of the army's putative expedition, so they had come together from several smaller villages and tribes, even the agency Indians, for mutual protection. However, such a large settlement put a tremendous strain on the wood, forage, and food supply, so Red Eagle knew they wouldn't be able to sustain the gathering for very long.

On the night of their victory over General Crook's men, the Indians celebrated with food, dancing, music, and stories of the battle. Those who had acquired guns from the battle showed them off. Others wore the soldier coats or soldier hats, and some of them made a game of frightening the young ones, pretending to be evil white soldiers.

In the Hunkpapa circle, Red Eagle sat on the ground with Sitting Bull. The camp resonated with the sound of drums, nose-flutes, and singing. They were eating a tasty highly spiced stew that Sitting Bull's wife, Walks Alongside, had prepared for them.

"There is much celebration tonight," Sitting Bull's wife said.

"Yes, the warriors fought well. They have reason to celebrate," Red Eagle said.

"They sing songs of your bravery and success," Sitting Bull said.

"I am pleased that they do so."

"Now," Sitting Bull said, "when the battle comes, you can stay in the village and no one will think you are a coward."

"You ask much of me."

"Yes," Sitting Bull agreed. "I could not ask this of a lesser man."

"To stay in the village when my brothers fight would be a hard thing to do."

"You must do this, for only if our people have a peacemaker such as you can we survive the long winter that is coming. You will do this?"

For a long moment Red Eagle ate his stew in silence. Then he put the bowl down and looked up at Sitting Bull. The old chief's eyes had not drifted away from him for the entire time. "I have listened to your council, and I will do this thing," Red Eagle replied.

Sitting Bull nodded, then went back to his stew without saying another word.

Had Red Eagle not proven himself in battle against General Crook, he would not have been able to follow the path Sitting Bull said had been chosen for him. Now he could do so. Sitting Bull was a very wise man, Red Eagle mused, taking another mouthful of stew.

Quinn and his wagons had come twelve miles since leaving camp early that morning. There was a broken axle to deal with just before noon, and one hill that required a double-team to climb, but other than that, the wagons had maintained a comfortable pace.

They were now less than a mile from the head of the Powder River where they were to meet the steamer *Far West*. It had been their belief that they might have to wait a few days for the *Far West* to arrive, but a rope of smoke curling up from beyond a low-lying hill indicated that the boat was already there, waiting for them. Shortly after the lead element of the march reached the river, the captain blew his whistle, resulting in a deep-throated, two-tone bleat that was audible for several miles. If there had been any doubt in anyone's mind what the smoke was, it was resolved now.

Just before they crossed the final hill that would take them down to the water's edge, Quinn saw Tom Custer riding toward him at a gallop. Quinn moved forward to meet him. "Tom, what is it? Is something wrong?"

Tom grinned broadly, and shook his head. "No, nothing is wrong. But something is right."

"What do you mean?"

"You'll see," Tom said. "Come with me."

Quinn looked back toward the slow-moving line of wagons. "I should stay with the wagons until they get in."

"You can leave them now—they're almost there. Sergeant Scott can handle it from here. Come on, there's something you should see."

Curious about Tom's strange behavior, Quinn signaled to Sergeant Scott to bring the wagons on in, then he rode back toward the river with his former commander.

The *Far West* was an impressive sight, an unbelievably large craft to be that far up river. It was secured against the riverbank by lines tied around trees, fore and aft. The riverbank was piled high with crates and bundles, representing the supplies the *Far West* had brought up.

About twenty yards north of the last pile of bundles, something seemed to be especially attractive to the men, for scores of soldiers were gathered around.

"What's that?" Quinn pointed to the gathering of soldiers. "What are they doing over there?"

"That's a saloon," Tom said.

"A saloon?"

"Well, a makeshift saloon, anyway. Some planks laid across a couple of barrels. The sutler, John Smith, came up with the boat."

Quinn chuckled. "I'll bet the general likes that.

"He's a teetotaler. He doesn't even like it that Smith sells liquor back at the fort," Tom said. "I, on the other hand, think it's grand. I think it will give the men an opportunity to let off a little steam."

"I suppose, if it doesn't lead to trouble," Quinn said. He laughed. "But what trouble could it possibly lead to? Most liquor fights start over a woman, and since we don't have any, I guess we are safe there."

"What makes you think we don't have any women?" Tom asked.

"Surely, we don't. Good heavens, Tom, the boat didn't bring up a bunch of whores, did it?"

"Ohh! " Tom said, smiling as he winced. "I don't want to be around when she hears you called her that."

"When I called who what? Tom, what are you talking about? You are being very circumspect."

Tom pointed toward the stern of the boat. "Look there, on the boiler deck."

Looking in the direction Tom pointed, Quinn saw someone in denim trousers and a blue plaid shirt, standing by the steam escape pipe with one hand resting on the rail. "Are you talking about that fellow by the steam pipe?"

"Fellow?"

Quinn looked closer, then gasped in surprise. The

"fellow" was Kate, in men's clothes. "That's Kate! But it can't be!"

"Maybe it can't be, but it is, my friend," Tom said. "Captain Marsh picked her up alongside the Yellowstone four days ago."

Quinn urged his horse into a gallop, covering the remaining distance in a matter of seconds. Then leaping down from the saddle, he took the gangplank in only two large steps and started toward the stern. Seeing him coming toward her, Kate met him halfway. Without a second thought as to where they were, or who might be watching, they embraced and kissed.

Their performance was greeted with good-natured whistles and catcalls from several of the men.

"I almost didn't recognize you, dressed like this," Quinn said. "Is this the latest fashion?" he teased.

"Oh, I must look awful. My dress was beyond repair," Kate said. "I had no choice but to wear this."

"You look beautiful no matter what you're wearing," Quinn said. "But tell me, what are you doing here? I thought you were dead and—"

"It's a long story, but as you can see, I am not dead."

"What about your father? Is he here with you?"

The smile left Kate's face and her eyes welled with tears. She said nothing, shaking her head.

"I'm sorry," Quinn said.

Kate took a deep breath. "We should have listened to you and General Custer. But Father was such an independent, proud, and stubborn man. He was convinced that if we showed no hostility toward the Indians, they wouldn't be hostile to us. And for several days, it worked."

Kate told the story of her captivity, including the part where she thought she was being rescued by white men, only to find out that she was going from the frying pan to the fire.

"One of them eventually had an attack of conscience," she said. "And he forced the other one to let me go."

"Yes, well, even at that, I don't know how good he was being to you, turning you out on your own. You were very lucky to stumble across the river at just the right time to see Captain Marsh."

"Oh, but that is the most amazing part of all. My being on the side of the river, waiting to meet Captain Marsh, wasn't luck," Kate said. She continued her story, telling about her time with Red Eagle.

"Red Eagle found you and led you to safety?" Quinn asked incredulously.

"Yes."

"That is truly amazing," Quinn said. "Red Eagle is said to be one of the worst of them."

"Maybe not."

"Well, sure, you would think that. I mean he decided to spare you. But, believe me, with him it is all a matter of caprice."

"He said leading me to safety would be a sign for the white people that the Indians mean no harm. They want to be allowed to live in peace, and he wants to be the peacemaker who brings it about."

"You talked to him?"

"Yes. He is a very unusual man, Quinn. There is a sense of quiet dignity about him, a dignity that is the equal of any congressman, senator, or governor I've ever met."

Quinn thought of the time he had tried to shoot Red Eagle but missed because the distance was too great. He remembered how his bullet clipped the feathers in Red Eagle's headdress, yet the Indian had stood there as stoically as if Quinn had done no more than wave to him.

"I can understand how you might come to that conclusion," Quinn said. "And I will admit that he is a most impressive man."

"What are you doing here with General Custer and the others?" Kate asked. "I thought you were out of the army."

"I am out of the army," Quinn replied. At that exact moment, Trains company started down the last long slope as they approached the riverside campsite. Quinn pointed to them. "I'm the civilian wagon master," he said. "I brought up Trains company."

"Trains? That's a funny name." She made a motion with her hand as if she were pulling on a whistle rope.

"Not exactly," Quinn said. "But you aren't too far off, either. It means wagon train, mule train, pack horse train. The general can't fight without us. We are carrying all of his supplies, including the ammunition."

"Why, it's almost as if you had never left the army at all, isn't it?"

"In a manner of speaking, I suppose it is," Quinn agreed.

"And this job pleases you?"

"I would rather be back in the army," Quinn said. "I am . . . that is, I *was* Tom Custer's executive officer. When the fight with the Indians comes, Tom will be forward at the point of attack. I could—and should—be there as well. And I would be there if I were still in active service. As it is though, when the fighting starts, I will be far from the sound of battle. I will be safe with my pack mules, while he and the men I trained will be facing mortal danger."

"You say that almost as if there was something disgraceful about staying safe," Kate said.

"For a career soldier there can be no greater disgrace than to be in the rear when his comrades are in harm's way."

Suddenly, a loud shout rang out, then a splash, followed by the sound of laughter. Immediately afterward, there were several more splashes. When

Quinn looked toward the source of the sound, he saw that several of the men who had been availing themselves of the sutler's liquor were now jumping into the river for an impromptu swim.

"Sounds like they are having fun." Kate leaned over the rail to look at them. "Oh, my!" she gasped, turning around quickly.

At first Quinn was confused, but when he looked as well, he saw that many of the men were skinny-dipping. Stripping naked on the riverbank in clear view of everyone, including Kate, they ran screaming and laughing at the top of their lungs and jumped into the water.

"I'll go tell them to—"

Kate put her hand on his arm, interrupting him. "No! Let them have their fun," she said. "I'll stay in my cabin until it's safe to come out again."

Quinn watched Kate as she returned to her cabin. He was concerned that she might be terribly embarrassed, but was surprised to see that she was barely able to contain her laughter as she slipped out of sight. Quinn wasn't sure he would ever understand women.

Chapter Fifteen

The steamer *Far West* was specially equipped to support the expedition against the Sioux. Its wheelhouse was reinforced with two-inch boilerplate, and its lower deck was protected by oak planking backed by bales of hay. The riverboat, under the command of Captain Grant Marsh, had pushed farther up the Yellowstone than any boat had ever gone before.

General Terry was actually in command of the operation, though Custer had operated with near total autonomy for the entire expedition. This wasn't entirely without Terry's approval, since he rightly believed Custer to be a far more experienced Indian fighter than he.

On the night of June 21, General Terry held a strategy conference in the great cabin of the boat. Although the great cabin was large as boat cabins go, stretching all the way across the width of the boat, there were too many officers for all to sit. As a result, many stood, Custer among them, even though his rank would have allowed him to sit had he wanted. It wasn't a lack of room, as much as his restless energy that kept him on his feet.

"Now, Custer, look at this map," Terry said. "I have marked your route with pins." Terry adjusted his glasses to stare at the map. He leaned closer, then sighed in frustration. "I can't see those damned pins. Does anyone have a pencil?"

"I do, General," Lieutenant W. W. Cooke said. Cooke, who wore his beard in two long forked tails, had been Custer's adjutant for the last twelve years.

"Trace along these pins with your pencil, would you, Lieutenant?"

Cooke did so, and for a moment there was no sound save the voices rising up to the cabin from the soldiers resting on the riverbank and the quiet whisper of the current as it slapped against the hull.

"There," Terry said when Cook finished. "Now, General Custer, what I want you to do is take your troops up the Rosebud and . . . well, perhaps it would be best if I had your orders read aloud. That way there will be no misunderstanding. Ed?"

General Terry's adjutant, Captain E. W. Smith, opened a folder, then began reading:

Lieutenant Colonel Custer, Seventh U.S. Cavalry. Colonel: The brigadier general commanding directs that as soon as your regiment can be made ready for the march, you will proceed up the Rosebud in pursuit of the Indians whose trail was discovered a few days before. It is, of course, impossible to give you any definite instructions in regard to this movement, and even if it were, the department commander places too much confidence in your zeal, energy, and ability to impose upon you precise orders, which he feels might hamper your success. He will, however, indicate to you his own views of what your action should be and desires that you should conform to them unless there is sufficient reason for deviating from them.

Captain Smith paused in his reading and looked up at Custer, as if charging Custer with the specific instruction that he was to conform to Terry's orders.

"Yes, yes, I'm quite prepared to do that," Custer said impatiently. "Go on, Captain."

Captain Smith resumed reading.

He instructs you to proceed up the Rosebud until you ascertain definitely the direction in which the aforementioned trail leads. Should it be found, as it appears almost certain that it will be, you should continue southward, perhaps as far as the headwaters of the Tongue, and then turn toward the Little Bighorn, feeling constantly to your left so as to preclude the possibility of the escape of the Indians to the south or southeast by passing around our left flank. Colonel Gibbon's column will head for the mouth of the Bighorn. As soon as it reaches that point, it will cross the Yellowstone and move up at least as far as the forks of the Bighorn and Little Bighorn. Of course, its movements will be controlled by circumstances as they arise, but it is hoped that the Indians, if upon the Little Bighorn, will be outflanked by two columns so that their escape will be impossible.

The department commander desires that, on your way up the Rosebud, you should thoroughly examine the upper part of Tulloch's Creek, and that you should send a scout through to Colonel Gibbon's column with the results of your examination. The lower part of this creek will be examined by a detachment from Colonel Gibbon's command. The supply steamer will be pushed up the Bighorn as far as the forks of the river are navigable, and the department commander, who will accompany Colonel Gibbon's column, desires that you report to him there no later than the expiration of the time for which your troops are rationed, unless in the meantime you receive further orders.

Captain Smith cleared his throat, then handed a copy of the orders he had just read to Custer.

"By my reckoning," Terry said, "we should make contact with the Indians on the twenty-sixth. With our two columns converging, there will be no way for them to escape. Do you have any questions?"

"No questions, General," Custer replied. "And I thank you for your confidence in me."

"I'm certain that my confidence is well placed, Custer. But remember, the most important part of the entire plan is for us to reach the Indians in concert by the twenty-sixth. I have to inform you that the scouts tell me the signs are for the largest encampment they have ever seen. We may very well be going up against a thousand or more armed warriors."

"Even so, General, I don't think we are likely to encounter any more than the Seventh could handle," Custer said.

Colonel Gibbon looked up in surprise. "Any more than the *Seventh* can handle?" he asked. "I hope that with that attitude, you aren't planning on handling them alone, General."

"I will be following my orders, Colonel," Custer replied.

"Very good," Terry said, straightening up from the map. "Any more questions, gentlemen?"

"Just one," Custer said. "It is not a question as much as it is a request. I plan to leave the Gatling guns behind."

Although Custer had said it was a request, it sounded far more like a peremptory statement.

"Leave them behind? Why would you want to do that, Custer? Why, just four of those guns can put out as much firepower as an entire company."

"Yes, sir, if we are in a static position," Custer replied. "But they must be pulled by horses . . . and I remind you that the horses we have pulling these guns are marked IC: inspected and condemned."

"That just means they are condemned for riding.

211

They are quite capable of pulling the gun caissons," Gibbon said.

"Maybe so, but the terrain we'll be going through is not suited for wheeled vehicles. I'm leaving my wagons behind as well. Already we have had quite a few upsets."

"Perhaps if you had men working the wagons who knew what they were doing," Gibbon suggested.

Quinn, who had been listening quietly to the conversation, now perked up.

"I beg your pardon, Colonel Gibbon, but these men have worked long and hard in extreme conditions to get these wagons here," Quinn said.

"Colonel Gibbon, I will not have my men criticized by you," Custer shot out. "My decision not to take wagons beyond this point has nothing to do with the quality of the men handing the wagons, nor do I find fault with Mr. Pendarrow's leadership. I am exceptionally well pleased with their efforts. It is the nature of the terrain and the vehicles I am concerned about."

"Without wagons, how will you be able to take enough supplies forward to support your march?" Terry asked.

"We'll use pack animals."

"You don't have that many mules."

"We have been working with our team animals, General," Quinn said. "I believe I will be able to convert enough of them into pack animals to make up for the loss of the wagons."

"I've seen that tried before, Mr. Pendarrow. It rarely works," Gibbon said.

"It is difficult, I'll admit. But it isn't impossible."

"Well, good luck to you," Gibbon said.

As the others began poring over the map and discussing the particular details of the upcoming operation, Quinn excused himself and left the boat to give instructions to Scott to begin breaking the wagon loads down into packs for transport on mules and horses.

That evening Captain Marsh sent a note to Quinn, inviting him to have dinner on board the *Far West.* The other dinner guests would be General Terry, Colonel Gibbon, Colonel Custer, Major Brisbin, Major Reno, Captain Benteen, and Kate McKenzie.

"Well, now, you truly are in august company," Scott said.

"Yes, but what will I wear?" Quinn laughed. "I have but one civilian suit, and I didn't bring it along."

"Don't worry about that. I'll come up with something for you," Sergeant Scott said.

Later, as Quinn was standing behind one of the wagons, shaving, Scott came up to him carrying a bundle. He held it toward Quinn.

"So you did come up with something for me.

Thanks." Opening the bundle, Quinn saw a gold-trimmed gray tunic and gray pants with a gold stripe down the side of the legs. "What is this?" he asked.

"It was the uniform of a colonel in the Confederate cavalry," Scott said. "But with all the insignia removed, it is just a gray suit."

"Sergeant Scott, I can't wear this," Quinn said. "If you've kept it all these years, it must be very meaningful to you."

"It would be very meaningful to me if you would wear it, Mr. Pendarrow," Scott said. "Unless, of course, you would rather not. It being a Confederate uniform, I would understand."

Quinn took the bundle. "I would be honored to wear it," he said.

When Quinn put the uniform on later, he examined himself as best he could in the small shaving mirror. With all rank and accouterments removed, it became a good-looking gray suit, cut in a military style. In fact, many of his men who saw him just before he went on board the *Far West* for dinner, commented on his "classy duds," not even realizing the significance of the uniform.

Even Custer was fooled, for when he saw Quinn he looked at the suit in admiration. "I see you have designed a uniform for the position of wagon master," he said. "And a handsome one, too."

"Thank you, General," Quinn said without further explanation.

Custer laughed. "During the war, when I was promoted to general, I designed my own uniform. Generals can do that, you know. It was quite an attractive outfit, too. It consisted of a black velvet tunic with gold braid from my cuffs to my elbow. Under the tunic I wore a sailor-suit collar with a general's star in each corner, and a scarlet cravat. It was a fine-looking uniform. Of course, as I am only a lieutenant colonel, I can't do anything like that now."

"No, sir, I suppose not." Quinn didn't mention that the white buckskin uniform Custer sometimes wore wasn't exactly regulation, nor was the brown, fringed buckskin jacket he was wearing during this scout.

Quinn wasn't the only one who had gone out of his way to wear something special for the dinner. Kate had changed from the blue denim trousers and blue plaid shirt she was wearing earlier in the day to a dress.

"I must again apologize for my appearance," Kate said. "This is the dress I was wearing when I was captured. I've cleaned it and made as many repairs as I could, but it still leaves much to be desired."

"Mademoiselle, it looks as if you just bought it

from the finest dress shop in New York," Custer said gallantly.

"I agree," Quinn added, a bit chagrined that Custer was quicker and more glib of tongue than he was.

Dinner was excellent, consisting of boiled ham, canned corn, and potatoes. For dessert there was a pie made with dried peaches.

"General Terry, I've been thinking about your plan," Colonel Gibbon said as he carved a piece of ham.

"Do you find fault with it?" Terry asked.

"With the basic plan? No, sir, I think your idea of creating a pincer maneuver is excellent. But, as I understand it, one pincer will be a strong, swift-moving strike force that will search out the Indians and then drive them against a blocking force. Is that correct?"

"That's the plan," Terry agreed.

"Custer and the Seventh are to be the mobile force, and I will be the blocking force?"

"That is correct."

"General, would it not be better if Custer and I moved toward each other? It would still trap the Indians between us, while giving each of the regiments an equal responsibility in the attack. As it is now, that honor is reserved for the Seventh alone."

"Colonel Gibbon, I haven't conceived this plan as a means of bringing honor or glory to any one regiment. I have conceived it as the best way to accomplish our goal of finding and defeating the renegade Indians. I have the utmost confidence in you and your regiment, but General Custer and his men are the most experienced Indian fighters in the field today. It would be foolish of me not to go with the strongest possible plan, and that is for you and your regiment to be the anvil against which the Indians will be driven and smashed. It is no small responsibility, and I must know if I can depend on you."

"Yes, sir, of course you can depend on me," Colonel Gibbons replied.

"Good. Then let us have no more talk about the efficacy of the plan. Rather, let us concern ourselves only with its implementation. I'll tell you what I will do. If you wish, I will send your second battalion, under Major Brisbin, with Custer. That way, the honor will be shared between your regiment and Custer's."

"General Terry, may I speak frankly?" Major Brisbin cut in, speaking up quickly before Custer could respond to General Terry's offer.

"Yes, of course. It gives me no offense to have my officers be frank with me."

"If you attach my battalion to the Seventh, then it would become a combined command. Therefore I would want you, and not Custer, to be in command. If this is not to be, then I would prefer that you not send my battalion."

General Terry drummed his fingers on the table for a moment as he contemplated Brisbin's remark. Finally, he looked over at Custer. "Well, what about it, Armstrong? Do you want an additional battalion? If so, I, Major Brisbin, and the officers and the men of his battalion will be happy to take service with you."

"Under your command?"

"As it would then be a combined command, yes. I feel Major Brisbin is correct on this."

Slowly, and with exacting detail, Custer buttered a roll before he answered. "Then I thank you, sir, but, as I explained earlier, I'm quite sure the Seventh is capable of handling anything it meets," he replied.

After dinner, while the officers talked about the implementation of the plan, Quinn invited Kate outside for some fresh air.

They walked forward onto the hurricane deck, then stood just below the jack staff. Looking down into the water, they could see a small collection of twigs and other surface accumulation floating trapped between the hull of the boat and the muddy riverbank a few feet away. From ashore, somewhere in the darkness, came the melody of a song being sung in four-part harmony.

"Oh, listen to the soldiers singing. It's beautiful, isn't it?" Kate said.

"Yes, it is," Quinn agreed. "I used to leave the window open in my B.O.Q. room at night sometimes, and I would be literally serenaded to sleep by the singing from the barracks."

"They are like children in a way, aren't they?" Kate asked. "The enlisted men, I mean. Happy-go-lucky, no cares or worries."

"I suppose one could be lulled into thinking that," Quinn replied. "And perhaps some of the more patronizing officers truly believe it. But the truth is far different."

"What is the truth?"

"An army regiment is like a city. The officers are the city officials and the employers. The enlisted men are the citizens of the city, and like the citizens of any city, they are a diverse bunch. We have heroes and villains, courageous and cowardly, virtuous and evil, the brilliant and the dim-witted living side by side, each with his own individual history."

"Do you think General Custer sees the men in that way?"

Quinn was silent for a long moment.

"He doesn't, does he?" Kate asked.

"I believe General Custer has an enormous pride in the Seventh," Quinn answered.

"Yes, in the Seventh Cavalry as a collective unit. But he doesn't feel about them as individual soldiers, the way you do, does he?"

Quinn sighed. "To be fair, he cannot think of

them in the same way. He can only think of the Seventh as it can be utilized tactically. If he starts thinking of the soldiers as individuals, he will lose his effectiveness of command."

From his pocket, Quinn pulled a piece of yellow ribbon. He handed it to Kate.

"Oh, thank you, how lovely. For me?"

"Yes. I'd like for you to wear it in your hair until I return," Quinn said. "There is a tradition in the cavalry that if a soldier has someone to wear his yellow ribbon, he will always return. And though I am, for the moment, a civilian, I subscribe to the theory that once you are a cavalryman you are always a cavalryman. Therefore, I believe the tradition holds for me as well."

"Of course I will wear it," Kate said, tying the ribbon in her hair. "But what can I give you in return?"

Quinn looked at her, her face radiantly beautiful in the moonlight, and as if moved by some outside force, he brought his lips to hers.

At first his kiss was hesitant, a cautious testing of the waters. But Kate didn't resist him. In fact, her lips were soft and receptive, even eager. She opened her mouth on his, then put her arms around him and pulled him to her.

Quinn could feel her body pressing against his. Through the silk of her dress, every curve and mound was made known to him by their close contact. He felt a heat in his body, then the immodest pressure of his growing need for her. He tried to pull away, but Kate plied herself to him even more tightly, not shying away from his condition, but seeming to take pleasure in being its cause. Finally they separated, and Quinn looked into her face.

"I . . . I'm sorry," he sputtered. "I had no right to force myself upon you in such a fashion. Please forgive me."

"No," Kate answered. "Once before you apologized to me for kissing me, and I let you because I was afraid that you were looking for Miss Parkinson in me. I don't think that is true now, is it?"

"No!" Quinn replied quickly. "I assure you, Kate, Miss Parkinson is the furthest thing from my mind."

"I believe you." Kate leaned into him for another kiss.

"Mr. Pendarrow! Mr. Pendarrow, are you out here?" Quinn recognized Custer's voice calling him and, quickly he stepped away from Kate so that a small distance separated them.

"Up here, General, on the hurricane deck," he called.

"Ah, then you are out here." Custer came forward on the boat, then seeing Kate, he touched the brim of his hat in a casual salute. "Miss McKenzie," he said.

"General."

"Did you hear Brisbin's caveat on the offer to

send an additional battalion with me?" Custer asked.

"Yes, sir, I did."

Custer snorted. "It was very clever of him to make such an offer, but you know, Pendarrow, this is to be a Seventh Cavalry battle, and I want all the honor for Seventh there is in it."

Quinn was a little surprised by Custer's remark. He had often heard Custer referred to as a vain man, and one who sought glory. But this was the first time he had ever heard Custer actually admit it.

"You look surprised to hear me say that," Custer said.

"Yes, sir, I suppose I am."

"Don't be. There's nothing wrong with seeking glory, my boy, as long as it is for the right cause. And, unlike material possessions, glory is something you can take with you when you shuffle off the mortal coil."

"I suppose that's right."

"No supposing to it. It *is* right. Now tell me, Quinn, can you carry fifteen days' rations, using only mules and horses?"

"Yes, sir."

"Good. I'll be counting on you. We will get under way at noon tomorrow."

"Can you really carry so much, using only pack mules?" Kate asked after Custer had left.

"To be sure, we could carry much more using

wagons," Quinn replied. "But Custer has already turned down the offer of artillery and Gatling guns by claiming that wheeled vehicles would slow his march. He can't turn down the guns by saying wheels will impede his advance, then turn around and use wagons, can he?"

"No, I suppose not. It's just that I would think he would want every advantage."

"Oh, don't worry about that. Custer is going to take every advantage he can. You heard him yourself. He has no plans on sharing the glory of this victory with anyone."

"It will be, won't it?" Kate asked.

"It will be what?"

"A victory?"

Quinn smiled. "Don't worry about that, either. General Terry's hammer-and-anvil plan is a good one. Gibbon is the anvil, Custer the hammer. When he brings the Seventh down in a smashing blow, the Indians will be crushed."

"What if the anvil isn't there?"

"What do you mean?"

"Custer has made a big point of being first. What if he gets there before the anvil is in place? If that is so, would that not dilute the force of the hammer blow, and give the advantage to the Indians?"

Quinn chuckled nervously. He would never admit it, but Kate had just put into words his own thoughts. "You worry too much," he said, dismissing her concerns without answering her question. "I'd better see to my men and animals. They have quite a task in front of them."

As the Seventh Cavalry prepared to depart the next day, Custer turned command over to Reno, then joined General Terry and the other officers, as well as Captain Marsh, on the hurricane deck of the *Far West*. Kate was there as well.

"With your permission, sir," Custer said, saluting General Terry. "I would like for the regiment to pay its respects."

"It would be my honor," General Terry replied, returning Custer's salute.

"Major Reno! Pass in review!" Custer called.

Reno gave the order, and the supplemental commands rippled through the ranks. The band began to play, and to the strains of "Garry Owen," the Seventh Cavalry moved sharply along the bank of the river, flags and pennants snapping in the breeze, each troop commander calling "eyes right," as his troop passed

"Nearly as thrilling as the victory parade in Washington, eh, Custer?" Terry said.

"Oh, I have heard of that parade. I would like to have seen it," Kate said.

Gibbon chuckled. "You would have seen Custer breaking ranks, dashing up Pennsylvania Avenue

on a spirited horse in front of thousands of spectators."

"I didn't break ranks," Custer replied. "My horse
was made nervous by the crowd, and it bolted."

"A horse trained to be obedient in the midst of
gunfire grew nervous over a crowd of adoring citizens?" Gibbon challenged. He laughed. "Well,
Custer, you were able to convince Sheridan and
Grant, so I suppose that's all that matters. And it
did make a fine show. All the papers wrote about it,
and a few of the artists even made woodcuts of the
event."

"Yes," Custer said, smiling almost triumphantly
at the others. "It did make a fine show, didn't it?"

Terry laughed out loud. "Custer, you are an absolutely hopeless prima donna."

As the final rank of soldiers passed in review, the
pack horses and mules started by. Kate saw Quinn
riding to one side of these beasts of burden, inspecting them carefully and examining the packs on the
loading frames. For a moment she feared he wasn't
going to look up in time to see her. Then as he drew
even he did look up.

"Good-bye, Quinn!" she called to him. "Stay
safe!"

Quinn nodded and waved, but made no answer.

"Well, it's time I joined my command," Custer
said. He saluted Terry, then bounded down the

gangplank. As he climbed into the saddle, Gibbon called out to him.

"Now, don't be greedy, Custer! Save some Indians for us!"

"No, I won't!" Custer replied with a wave. He slapped his legs against Vic's side and the horse bolted forward as Custer and his orderly rode at a gallop to reach the front of the column.

"My word," Gibbon said to the others. "What do you suppose Custer meant by that? I won't be greedy? Or I won't save you any Indians?"

Terry laughed. "That's Custer for you—enigmatic until the end."

Chapter Sixteen

For the march, Custer had divided his command into four battalions, plus Trains: Major Reno's battalion composed of companies A, G, and M; Captain Benteen's battalion of D, H, and K; Custer's two battalions from C, E, J, I, and L companies.

Less than two miles from the camp, the regiment reached the mouth of the Rosebud. There, the water was forty feet wide and three feet deep—deep enough that the horses balked and the men had to dismount and lead their animals across. That worked well with the cavalry mounts, but when Quinn tried to bring the pack animals across, they refused to go into the water.

With horses whinnying, mules braying, and skinners turning the air blue with their curses, a cacophony of sound erupted at the water's edge. The animals began twisting around in circles, first ducking their heads, then rearing up to pull against their leads. The packers jerked on their lines and grabbed halters as they tried to bring the animals under control. Several of the packs were loosened by the antics of the animals; some even fell off and had to be repacked.

"Mr. Pendarrow, some of the animals in the rear aren't causing us any trouble," Scott said. "Should we go ahead and take them over?"

"Yes, by all means," Quinn answered. "Don't worry about position in line. Let's just get as many over as we can, as quickly as we can, any way we can."

"Yes, sir."

Scott moved back along the line, tapping the skinners who had their animals under control. Several of them crossed the river without difficulty, though a few got halfway across before they started balking.

"Pendarrow, what the hell is going on here?" Captain Benteen yelled angrily. Quinn looked up to see the white-haired officer riding back across the river toward him.

"Well, as you can see, Captain, we are having some difficulty getting the animals to take the water," Quinn said.

"Because of you, the rest of the regiment has had to come to a complete halt on the other side," Benteen said. "We can't proceed another foot until the last of your animals has made the crossing."

"I'm aware of that."

"Well, hurry it up, man! You've been at this for over an hour already," Benteen said, his frustration clearly showing. He turned and rode his horse back across the river. As he hadn't dismounted either time he crossed the river, his horse had a difficult time of it and at one point nearly lost its footing. Quinn found himself wishing the horse had stumbled and thrown Benteen into the river.

"Too bad the sonofabitch didn't get tossed," Scott mumbled, saying aloud what Quinn was only thinking. Despite himself, Quinn laughed.

It took another half hour to get all the pack animals across. Then, with the loads checked and secured, they resumed the march.

After making only twelve miles, they went into camp at the base of a steep bluff on the left bank of the river. The campsite was well chosen for the abundance of wood, grass, and water that was available.

Quinn was checking the loading frames when Custer's orderly appeared.

"Mr. Pendarrow, General Custer has called all his officers together."

"Fine," Quinn said without stopping what he was doing. "I'm not an officer."

"I know you ain't, sir. But the general, he told me to ask you personally if you wouldn't care to come, too."

"Well, now, how can you refuse an invitation like that?" Scott asked. "You go ahead, Mr. Pendarrow. I'll finish checking the loads."

"Thanks," Quinn said.

Most of the officers were already there by the time Quinn arrived, though some were still materializing from the fading twilight. General Custer stood by a small mulberry tree, watching the assembly grow until it was completed. He had pulled a twig from the tree and was sucking on it. Cooke had his hand down inside the canvas part of his trousers, shamelessly scratching his crotch.

Tom Custer took a pull of whiskey from a bottle, then passed it over to his brother-in-law, Jimmi Calhoun.

"Here's Pendarrow, late as usual," Captain Weir said. The others laughed.

"Did all the animals come up all right?" Custer asked.

Quinn nodded.

"What was the problem today?"

"The ford was too deep," Quinn said. "The animals didn't want to take it."

Custer ran his hand through his hair and sighed. "I expected that with wagons. Didn't think we'd have a problem with just pack animals."

"Once we got them across, we had no problem with them."

"I'll try and find more shallow fords from now on," he said.

"Thank you, sir. That will help."

Satisfied that all the officers were present, Custer began addressing them.

"Gentlemen, until this point, we have been on our way. But from now on, we will consider ourselves in the Indians' back yard. I would like to keep our presence here a secret for as long as possible. That means no more trumpet calls. From now on, I want all orders to be issued verbally or by hand signals. Also, have your men secure all loose equipment. An approaching cavalry regiment makes as much noise as a band on parade."

The officers all nodded.

"As you know, we have a schedule to keep, so it is up to each of you to see to it that the men respond quickly to all orders. Mr. Pendarrow, that goes especially for Trains, since the sad fact is we can't proceed at a pace any faster than you can maintain."

"We'll do our best to stay up, General."

Custer continued. "I want the men up and breakfasted in time to be on the march the moment I give the word. Do not let anyone straggle behind. We are, as I explained, in Sioux country. The hostiles would like nothing better than to catch one or two of our men by themselves. Death wouldn't be easy, gentlemen, and you might use that as an incentive to keep the men moving to orders."

Again, the officers nodded.

"Mr. Pendarrow, I'm afraid they would find any stragglers among your men particularly attractive, as they would be able to help themselves to whatever supplies the straggler might be packing."

Quinn nodded.

"And now," Custer said, "I have something I would like to get off my chest. It has come to my knowledge that my official actions have been criticized by some of the officers of the regiment at department headquarters. Gentlemen, I am willing to accept recommendations from the most junior second lieutenant of the regiment, should that recommendation be given to me in a proper manner. But the regulations are quite clear concerning criticisms of commanding officers, and I will take all necessary steps to punish whoever might be guilty of such an offense, should there be a recurrence."

"General, may I speak?" Benteen asked.

"Go ahead."

"It seems to me that you are lashing the shoulders of all to get at some. Now, as we are all here, wouldn't it be better to specify which officer or officers you are accusing?"

"Colonel Benteen," Custer said, using Benteen's brevet rank, "I am not here to be chastised by you.

But, for your own information, I will say that none of my remarks have been directed toward you. Now, gentlemen, reveille is at three a.m. To horse at five. Any questions?"

There were none.

"That will be all."

As one, the officers saluted, then everyone started back toward their own unit.

"Mr. Pendarrow," Custer called. "Wait a moment, won't you?"

Quinn stopped.

"The boys . . . Boston and young Autie . . . how are they doing?"

"They are doing quite well, actually. They work well with the others, and they seem to be well liked by everyone. And I'm sure you realize getting along with the others isn't all that easy when you are so closely related to the commanding officer."

"True, true," Custer said. "Well, I'm glad to hear they are doing well. Uh, Quinn?"

"Yes, General?"

"If it looks as if we are about to encounter the Indians, I would appreciate it if you would let them join me."

"Let them join you, General? But won't you be in more danger than Trains?"

Custer sighed. "Who is to say? You know how it is with Indians. There is no rhyme or reason to when, where, or how they will react. It could be that the boys would be safer with me than with you. And, at any rate, I promised my sisters I would look after them. I would feel more comfortable if, when danger struck, I had them close enough to me to be able to fulfill that obligation."

"Very good, General. At the first sign of trouble I will release them to join you."

"Thank you," Custer said.

June 23

Although Custer was true to his promise to find somewhat easier fords, the route of advance for the regiment on the second day caused them to have to cross the river five times in the first three miles. It wasn't quite so difficult to get the animals across as it had been on the previous day, but they still didn't like it and, twice during the march, the entire regiment had to halt to allow Trains to catch up.

It was necessary to cross the stream two more times before making camp on the right bank of the river at 4:30 that afternoon. In eleven and a half hours of hard marching, they had covered a distance of thirty-five miles.

Although the initial element of the regiment arrived at the campsite by 4:30, it was nearly 7:00 P.M. by the time the final pack mule arrived. Quinn stayed busy for that entire two and one-half hours, riding from the encampment back along the trail to check on the status of his stragglers, and then back to camp to oversee the bivouac.

He was famished by the time he finally got into the camp but he believed he was more tired than hungry. He unsaddled his horse, then found a rock to lean against and, sitting down beside it, pushed his back against it, seeking some respite from the ache and soreness.

Scott came toward him, carrying a plate and a cup.

"What's that?" Quinn asked.

"While you were out bringing in the last of our stray sheep, I was fixing supper," he said. "Here are some beans and cornbread."

"Thanks." Quinn took a bite, then looked up at Scott in pleasant surprise. "Hey, this is very good. Where did you find the ham you used for flavoring?"

"Isn't that what you fellas had on the boat the other night?"

"Yes."

"I bribed the cook for the bone and hock."

"I'm glad you did. The beans are delicious," Quinn said, eating with obvious gusto.

It was nearly midnight before the last problem was taken care of. Only then was Quinn satisfied that he could turn in. He couldn't allow himself the luxury of taking off his clothes, but he was able to slip out of his boots. Then, wriggling his toes in the grass, he slept the sleep of the exhausted.

June 24

Although there had been indications of Indians nearby ever since they left the mouth of the Powder River, on this day even the most green recruit was able to read the signs. At first, Quinn was puzzled as to why the Indians were making no attempt to cover their trail, then he realized that they weren't covering their trail because they couldn't. There were just too many of them. It was obvious, also, that they didn't care whether their trail was covered or not.

Scott came up to ride alongside Quinn. "You ever know the Indians to be so confident?"

"No," Quinn replied.

At that moment Isaiah Dorman, a big black man who was one of the scouts, rode up to them. Dorman was the only black man in the entire expedition. He had been a scout for two years and was considered particularly valuable because of his ability to speak Sioux. He had lived with the Sioux for two years, knew Sitting Bull and Crazy Horse personally, and had married a Santee woman.

"Varnum sent me back for a box of pistol ammunition," Dorman said.

"Posey!" Scott called. "Bring up a box of pistol shells."

Dorman rode alongside Scott and Quinn while he waited.

"Tell me, Dorman, what do you make of the sign we've been seeing?" Quinn asked.

"Not hard to read, Mr. Pendarrow," Dorman replied. "All the grass has been eaten by their ponies, the ground is left ploughed up by lodge poles, littered with horse turds, buffalo hides, bones, and carcasses. We're not following a village. Hell, we're trailing a city."

"How many do you think there are?" Scott asked.

"Hard to say how many total," Dorman answered. "But I'd say there are at least two to three thousand warriors."

"My God!" Quinn said. "Does Custer know this?"

At that moment Posey arrived with the shells. Dorman took them, put them in his saddlebag, then looked up at Quinn to answer his question.

"Custer? Hell, Mr. Pendarrow, he knows. He just don't give a shit." Dorman jerked his horse around, then galloped back to the front of the line of march.

Some time later, the column halted for a water break. Quinn walked down to the river to fill his canteen alongside Custer and several of the other officers. As he did so, he overheard Jimmi Calhoun talking to Custer.

"General, you been paying attention to the sign?" Calhoun asked as he dipped his own canteen into the stream. "There could be two or three thousand warriors ahead of us."

"Oh, that might be stretching it a bit," Custer replied.

"Not according to all the scouts. I've never seen them so nervous. I don't mind telling you, General, I, for one, will be glad when we join up with Terry again."

Custer took a drink of his water. When he lowered the canteen, little droplets of water were clinging to his mustache. He wiped his mouth with the back of his hand, then corked the canteen. "We aren't going to join Terry," he said resolutely.

"I beg your pardon?"

"Think about it, Jimmi," Custer said, taking his hat off and running his hand over his uncharacteristically short hair. "If we join forces with Terry, who will be commander in the field?"

"Why, General Terry, I suppose," Calhoun answered.

"Oh, there is no 'suppose' to it. Since General Terry is senior officer, the command would be his. As would be the glory, even though it would be the Seventh who would bear the brunt of battle."

Custer put his hat back on. "I don't intend to let that happen."

"General, may I raise a point?" Benteen asked.

"Certainly. As I said the other night, I am not unwilling to listen to my officers."

"Consider this. Perhaps the Seventh Cavalry is strong enough to handle the Indians—"

"No perhaps about it. We are strong enough," Custer insisted.

"Yes, sir, but is Gibbon's regiment?"

"What do you mean?"

"What I'm getting at, is that General Terry and Colonel Gibbon will be proceeding down the Little Bighorn secure in the belief that they can depend upon the Seventh to be in a certain place at a certain time. If they run into the Indians and we aren't there to help them, I fear they may be wiped out."

"Benteen, I must admit that you do have a point," he said. "All right, suppose we do this. Suppose we don't go all the way to the mouth of the Tongue. It must be obvious by now, even to the most obtuse, that the Indians aren't south of us. They are to our west. I think we should turn west, and increase our rate of march so that we make contact tomorrow. That way we will be certain that Gibbon and his men will be out of harm's way. And if, for some reason, we don't make contact tomorrow, then we will return to the plan as drawn up by Terry. Will that take care of your worry?"

"About Colonel Gibbon? Yes, sir," Benteen said.

"But you still have some concern."

"If the scouts are correct, we will be outnumbered by a ratio of twenty to one, maybe more."

"Boldness, Captain Benteen. What we lack in numbers, we shall make up with boldness."

"Boldness?" Benteen repeated.

"Boldness, Captain. It is a tactic that has always served me well."

"Autie," Tom Custer called, coming down the steep riverbank with his boots dislodging the loose rocks. "Take a look at this." He held out a stick from which hung two scalps, obviously from white men.

"There!" Custer said, pointing to the scalps. "I ask you, gentlemen. Do we need any more justification than that for what we are doing here? No doubt these men were poor prospectors, doing no more harm than poking around in the rocks and dirt. I only wish we could identify them so we could let their families know of their fate. Have someone bury the scalps, Tom. It's the closest thing to a Christian burial we can give to the poor creatures who once wore them."

"Right," Tom said.

"General Custer," Major Reno called from a short

distance up the stream. "Bloody Knife has found something that I think you ought to see."

Quinn followed the others up the bank of the river, then down into a little ravine, where they found a sweat lodge.

"A sweat lodge, Reno? Why the big interest?" Custer turned and started to leave.

"Take a look inside."

Custer turned back, then pulled aside the flap to look in. There he saw three red stones in a row, then a circle of rocks with the skull of a buffalo bull on one side and the skull of a cow on the other. A stick was aimed at the cow.

"What does it mean?" he asked

"It means the Indians will fight like bulls and the white men will run like women," Bloody Knife explained.

Custer grunted. "Does it now? Big talk from a race of people who have done nothing but run from me my entire life."

"General, you don't seem to be getting the point," one of the civilian scouts, Mitch Bouyer, said. "These here Indians ain't runnin'."

"Well, then we will settle it, won't we?"

The Seventh made camp and started supper. Custer's striker erected his tent, and then Custer planted his flag in the alkali dirt out front. A sudden gust of wind blew it down. Lieutenant Godfrey picked it up and replanted it, but it blew over a second time. When he put it up a third time, he had to use a heavy stone to support it.

The Indian scouts, seeing the flag blow over, exchanged long, silent glances. Quinn watched them, and though they said nothing to each other, he knew that the symbolism of Custer's flag blowing over wasn't lost on them.

Chapter Seventeen

Quinn threw his blanket out on the ground, then lay down, intending to get a little sleep. He was no sooner settled in than a rider materialized out of the darkness. "Pendarrow, get the animals packed and ready to go," he said.

Quinn sat up. "When are we leaving?"

"Within the hour," Benteen replied.

"What's the big hurry?" Quinn called to him. "I thought we weren't due to meet up with Terry and Gibbon until the twenty-sixth."

"Well, I guess Terry has his time table, and Custer has his own," Benteen said as he rode away, once again swallowed up by the darkness.

The regiment got away again at midnight. On through the night they went, with no lights permitted, not even the faintest glow of pipes or rolled cigarettes. They were able to keep their bearing by following the dust clouds that billowed up before them. Also, the rearmost men of each element had to violate Custer's edict of silence by pounding their tin cups on the saddle horns to guide the troop behind them.

As the night sky grew gray in the east, any hope of discovering the village before daylight faded. Since the opportunity was lost anyway, Custer finally called a halt. Word came down that they would rest for a while in a wooded ravine between two slopes. A few of the men unsaddled their mounts, but most simply lay down where they were.

They had not selected a very good campsite. What little grass there was for the horses had been cropped very close by the Indian ponies. Here, too, the water was so alkaline that the horses refused to drink it. Even the coffee the men made with the water was practically impossible to drink.

June 25

Quinn had gotten perhaps an hour's sleep when Sergeant Scott awakened him. "We've got a problem, sir."

Quinn sat up and rubbed his eyes. "What sort of problem?"

"We lost a couple of boxes off one of the pack mules during the night."

"What was in the boxes?"

"Field rations. A whole day's worth. The men aren't going to like going without eating for a day."

"Not only that, if the Indians find the boxes, they will know we are here."

"Yes, sir, that's what I was thinking too. I think I had better go back and bring the boxes in."

"I'll go with you," Quinn said, getting up.

"No, sir, no need in that. This is an army job," Scott said. Then, seeing Quinn's expression, he clarified his comment. "Not meaning you aren't army, Mr. Pendarrow. But you are in charge of Trains. It wouldn't be a good idea for you to risk your neck going back just to pick up a couple of boxes. I'll go."

"Take some men with you."

"Yes, sir, I will. Posey is out rounding up some men now."

"Posey?"

"He's turned into a good man since he came off the sauce," Scott said. "We've still got a corporal's slot open. I think he would make a good one."

At that moment, Posey came up to join them. "Sergeant, I have five men armed and mounted," he said. "And your horse is saddled."

"Thanks," Scott said. He looked at Quinn. "With your permission?"

"Yes, go retrieve the boxes. And be careful."

"Yes, sir."

"You, too, Corporal Posey."

Posey looked back at Quinn in surprise. "Corporal?"

"I'm sure you will be, as soon as I make my recommendation to Custer."

Posey smiled brightly. "Thank you, sir."

Scott and the others had been on the back trail for the better part of an hour. For the last several minutes they had been following Ash Creek. Scott held up his hand to bring the patrol to a halt. Posey was chewing tobacco, and he leaned over to expectorate, then wiped the back of his hand across his chin.

"Damn," Posey said. "How far back did those boxes fall off?"

"Maybe the Indians have already found them," one of the other men suggested.

Scott pulled a pair of field glasses from his saddlebag and began sweeping the terrain.

"Do you see something?" Posey asked.

"No," Scott answered. "But I've been chasing Indians ever since I came out here after the War of Yankee Aggression, and I know that you don't always see them. Sometimes you just feel them, and I've been feeling them now for the last several minutes."

Posey snorted. "War of Yankee Aggression my ass."

Scott grinned. Their service on opposite sides

during the war had become good-natured banter between them.

Suddenly, there was a singing swoosh of an arrow. It made a hollow thocking sound as it hit Posey's saddle. The arrow stuck, and the shaft quivered right in front of his leg. Posey, struck dumb for just an instant by the shock of the near miss, looked at it in surprise. His horse jumped nervously, though it had not been hurt.

"There they are!" one of the troopers shouted. A band of Sioux came swooping down over the crest of a hill, whooping and shouting at the top of their lungs. Scott didn't take time to count them, though he estimated there were about ten in the band, twice their own number.

"Let's get out of here!" Scott shouted, slapping his heels against the flanks of his horse, urging it on. They raced along the bank of Ash Creek, occasionally slipping down into the water itself and sending up sheets of spray.

Scott led the troopers out of the creekbed and onto flat terrain to an area large enough to allow him to swing his men around. At first it was unclear to the others what he was doing; then they realized that their sergeant had, by describing a large circle, turned the rout into an attack. The Indians realized it at about the same time. They wheeled about in confusion and started to retreat themselves.

"Let's go get them!" Scott shouted. He charged after the confused, retreating Indians, urging his horse on faster and faster. He rapidly drew closer to the Indians, though he was also pulling away from his own men. Within a short time he was abreast with the rear ranks of the Indians.

The Indians had abandoned all thought of attack and were now fleeing for their lives. They turned their rifles on Scott and fired, the bullets buzzing by his head. Scott pulled his pistol, took slow and deliberate aim, fired, then watched as his target tumbled from the saddle. The Indians broke up, scattering in every direction like a covey of quail. After that it was no longer possible to pursue them as a body, so Scott broke off the charge and regrouped his men.

"Sergeant Scott," Posey said, pointing, "there are our boxes."

"Let's get them back," Scott said.

A couple of the men rode forward and retrieved the rations.

"It's all right, Sergeant," one of them called back. "They just got one of the boxes open and looks like they didn't have time to get anything from it."

"Good," Scott said.

As the men rode back, Scott noticed they were talking and laughing among themselves.

"What is it?" he asked. "What's wrong?"

"Ain't nothin' wrong, Sergeant," one of the men

said. "'Ceptin' that you are one kind of fightin' fool."

When Scott and the others returned with the two boxes, he recommended to Quinn that they tell Custer he had been spotted by the Indians.

Quinn nodded in agreement. "It's not something he's going to want to hear," he said. "But he needs to know about it."

"Yes, sir."

"Maybe you had better come with me when I tell him," Quinn suggested. "He may want to ask you a few questions."

Scott grinned wryly. "I was afraid you would suggest that."

Custer listened attentively while Sergeant Scott made his report. Oddly, he showed no displeasure over the incident. "So the fat is in the fire. Well, I have felt for some time now that they knew we were here. This just confirms it."

"I'm sorry about the boxes, General," Quinn said.

Custer put his hand on Quinn's shoulder. "Not to worry, my boy. You did the right thing by sending back for them. And Sergeant Scott, I commend you for undertaking the detail."

At that moment, Lieutenant Varnum, chief of scouts, and Isaiah Dorman arrived.

"Ah, here's Varnum and Dorman," Custer said.

"I sent them ahead last night to see what they could find."

"We'll be getting back to Trains then, General," Quinn said.

"No, no, you may as well stay here and hear their report. You've got a right to know what we have ahead of us," Custer said. "All right, Varnum, let's hear it. What did you see? Did you find the village? Or have they skedaddled like they always do?"

Before Varnum answered, he pulled a bottle of whiskey from his back pocket and took a long, Adam's apple–bobbing pull from it. He wiped the back of his hand across his mouth and looked at Custer with flat, expressionless eyes.

"Drinking so early in the morning?" Custer said. "Varnum, what is it? What have you seen?"

"General, if you want my advice, you will halt this march right now and wait until General Terry's column reaches us. With both columns combined, we might be able to escape."

"Escape?" Custer barked with a little laugh. "Escape what?"

"Annihilation," Varnum replied.

Custer snorted. "Oh, come now, Varnum. Annihilation? Aren't you being a bit overly dramatic?"

"General, it looks to me like every Indian in the whole country is gathered down there. The entire valley on the other side of Crow's Nest is covered with tepees. It's white with the damn things, and there are so many campfires that smoke covers the whole basin. You tell him, Dorman."

Varnum passed his bottle to Dorman, sharing it as easily with the black scout he had come to respect as he would share it with any of his fellow officers. Dorman took a deep swallow before he spoke.

"General, there are more warriors ahead than there are bullets in all the belts of all the soldiers in this command."

For just an instant Custer looked shocked. Then he smiled at all the officers who, upon seeing Varnum and Dorman return, had gathered around to hear the report.

"Well, I guess we shall get through them in one day," Custer said.

"If we hit them in the morning, just before daybreak, the shock effect may carry the day for us," Benteen suggested.

"Yes," Custer said. "And that was my plan. Unfortunately, that is no longer an option."

"What do you mean?" Benteen asked, surprised by Custer's statement.

"We've been seen, Benteen," Custer said. "Tell him, Mr. Pendarrow."

Quinn told of losing two of the boxes during the night, and of his retrieval party exchanging fire with the Indians.

"Well, that tears it," Benteen said angrily. "Pendarrow, you have been nothing but trouble ever since you were given that job. You've delayed the column, you've had accidents, no doubt you have lost half our supplies, and now this."

"On the contrary, Captain Benteen," Custer said. "I believe Mr. Pendarrow has done a remarkable job under the most trying of circumstances. At any rate, there is no sense now in crying over spilt milk . . . or spilled crates, for that matter. We've only one thing to do, and that is proceed at once to attack the Indians."

"General, the men and horses are exhausted," Benteen protested. "We should give them time to recruit."

"There is no time, Benteen. We have been seen."

"That may be true, sir, but attacking the Indians today will not make them unsee us. We will gain nothing by attacking today, whereas if we hit them tomorrow morning before dawn, they will be no better prepared to repel us than they are now."

"I am not concerned about them repelling us, for I do not believe that to be a possibility," Custer replied. "What concerns me is the possibility that the entire village may slip away during the night."

"Well, if you believe what Lieutenant Varnum says, and as he is our scout, I see no reason not to believe him, these Indians aren't going anywhere. You've seen all the signs, same as I have. These Indians are just spoiling for a fight."

"Yes, and I'm going to give it to them," Custer said.

"Under their conditions, General? That defies all the tactics of warfare."

Custer reacted with an expression of indignation. "Tactics of warfare? Captain Benteen, I have fought successful engagements against such men as Lee, Longstreet, Jackson, and Jeb Stuart. Those men understood the tactics of warfare. How can you even compare these savages to men of their stature?"

"I wouldn't dream of making such a comparison, General," Benteen said dryly.

"I would think not," Custer replied. "Gentlemen, get your men mounted. We are pressing on. Mr. Pendarrow, I have a request of you. I would like for you to release Sergeant Scott to me, to be assigned as I see fit."

Quinn hesitated.

"Can you not get along without him?"

"Yes, of course I can," Quinn said. "It's just that I value his service highly, and hate to lose him."

"I understand that, Mr. Pendarrow. And it is precisely because of the value of his service that I am now asking that you release him to me."

"Well, of course, General, you are the commander. It is your decision."

"Good, thank you. Colonel Scott, you are hereby detached from Trains."

Not only Scott, but the officers who were there

assembled, looked up in surprise at hearing Scott being addressed as colonel.

Custer chuckled. "You were a colonel during the late war, were you not?"

"Yes, sir," Scott said.

"And you commanded a battalion of cavalry at Saylors' Creek?"

"A regiment, sir."

"The Confederate cavalry fought well there, as well as any cavalry unit has ever fought anywhere," Custer said. "I hate to see that kind of experience wasted on Trains. If you don't mind, I am going to assign you to Major Reno's battalion as his acting sergeant major. Reno, do you have any objections to that?"

"No objections, General," Reno replied.

"Good. I want you to keep acting Sergeant Major Scott by your side at all times. Not only was he a gallant and courageous officer during the war, he also has a great deal of experience fighting the Indians. I'm giving him to you instead of Benteen because of the two of you, you are less experienced."

"Yes, sir," Reno said.

"All right, gentlemen, return to your units and make all preparations to move out."

"General," Quinn called.

"Yes?"

"I'll need a new sergeant."

Custer stroked his chin. "Under the circumstances, I don't see how I can take a sergeant from any of the line companies."

"That won't be necessary, General. With your permission, I'll appoint a new sergeant from within Trains ranks."

"You have someone in mind?"

"Yes, sir. Buford Posey."

Custer looked at Quinn for a moment, then laughed. "Correct me if I'm wrong, Pendarrow, but isn't Buford Posey the very man you just had me break from sergeant?"

"He is."

"And you want him back?"

"He is experienced, knowledgeable, and I believe he has learned his lesson."

Custer looked over at his adjutant. "Have the orders drawn up, promoting Buford Posey to sergeant."

"Yes, sir," Cooke replied.

"You've got your wish, Pendarrow. I hope you can live with it," Custer said.

Quinn returned alone. "Sergeant Posey!" he called as soon as he was back in his bivouac area.

Upon hearing Posey addressed as sergeant once more, several of the men looked at Quinn in surprise. Posey, who had just been promoted to corporal, didn't even question Quinn this time.

"Yes, sir?"

"Scott has gone back to a line company. You are

my new Trains sergeant. We'll be moving out within the hour, so get the animals loaded."

"Yes, sir!" Posey said with a huge smile. "All right, men, off your asses, on your feet . . . out of the shade and into the heat! Let's strap it on!"

The animals were loaded more easily that day than on previous days, but, whether it was because they had grown use to the procedure or were just too exhausted to resist, Quinn didn't know. For whatever reason, the result was that when word came down to move out, Trains was ready.

Custer set a fast pace, moving the regiment at a trot. Because Reno and Benteen were riding in front of the column with Custer, Sergeant Scott was there as well, trailing the regimental guidon of the leading troop commanders.

Scott had ambivalent feelings about his new assignment. On the one hand, he was pleased to be back in a line company. On the other hand, he knew the importance of Trains company and he felt a sense of obligation to Quinn Pendarrow to help get them through. However, he was a soldier, and he had no recourse but to follow orders, and his orders had made him acting sergeant major to Major Reno.

Custer held up his hand, and the column, which had been proceeding at a trot, slowed to a walk. After allowing the horses a few minutes to pace themselves out, Custer halted the column.

"Benteen," he called.

Scott saw Benteen move to him.

"Colonel Benteen, do you see those hills over there?" Custer pointed to the low-lying rolling ridge, stark against the bright sky. The flank riders had already brought back a description of the country just on the other side—an endless procession of jagged draws and long, narrow coulees.

"I see them, sir."

"Good. I want you to take your battalion over there. You will parallel our course, continuously feeling to your left, to make certain that the hostiles don't try to run. Pitch into anything you find. If you find nothing in the first valley, proceed to the next and pitch into anything you might find there. Beyond that, you may use your own judgment as to any action you need to take."

"General, no self-respecting Indian would be over there. There is nothing there but barren hills. The Indians are in front of us."

"Yes, and we want to make certain they stay in front of us. That will be your job, Benteen, to keep them from getting away."

Scott could tell by Benteen's expression that he clearly did not like the orders Custer had just given him.

"General, hadn't we better keep the regiment together? If this is as big a camp as they say, we'll need every man we have."

"You have your orders, Colonel," Custer said curtly.

"Very good, sir," Benteen replied, duly chastised. Standing in his stirrups, he looked down the left side of the trailing column. "Battalion!" he called. "Left oblique!"

The left file of the column turned their horses away at an angle.

"Form column of twos!"

The element, consisting of three companies, moved into two columns and, with Benteen at its head, started toward the nearby hills.

The rest of the regiment, minus Benteen's battalion, continued to march down Ash Creek, Custer and his two battalions on the right side of the creek, Reno with his one battalion on the left. Scott saw that the men were riding like zombies, exhausted from twenty hours of marching in the previous twenty-four. Nevertheless, Custer maintained a pace that was so rapid that when Scott moved out of line to look back toward the rear, he saw that Trains was gradually falling behind.

The column reached the point where the south fork of Ash Creek joined the main branch. This had clearly been the site of a village, though now only one teepee remained standing. Custer signaled to Reno to come to him, and Reno, accompanied by Sergeant Scott, crossed the creek to Custer's side.

"Let's take a look at the teepee." Custer pointed.

The three men walked over to look inside, where they saw the body of a slain warrior.

"Heathen bastards can't bury their dead like everyone else," Reno muttered.

Custer signaled his scouts to set fire to the teepee, and they did.

A yell from the top of a hill just north of where they had stopped caused the men to look up. There Fred Gerard, one of the civilian scouts, was waving his hat and yelling. "Here are your Indians, General, running like devils!"

Gerard pointed down the creek, where in the distance they could see a party of warriors racing their ponies toward the river.

"Reno, return to your battalion!" Custer ordered. "Move forward at a trot!"

Reno and Scott started back across the creek.

"Move, man, move!" Custer called to him, causing Reno to spur his horse into a quick sprint.

Once Reno and Scott were back in position, Reno ordered his battalion forward. Some distance ahead they could see dust boiling up from behind the high bluffs that hid the Little Bighorn Valley.

They moved down the creek for another three miles, then Custer brought the two columns together again. By now, both horses and men were on the verge of exhaustion, and Custer called a halt. He allowed the men to water their horses.

The Indian scouts began singing.

"What are they doing?" Custer asked.

"They are singing their death songs, General," Mitch Bouyer said.

"Death songs?" Custer signaled to Bloody Knife, asking the Indian to come to him. "Are you afraid, Bloody Knife?"

"Custer, today you and I go down a road that we do not know."

It was hot, and Custer took off his buckskin jacket, folded it, and tied it to his saddle roll. He was now wearing a dark blue shirt, poked down into buckskin trousers. Using his handkerchief, he wiped the sweat from his face, then put it away. "Look," he said. "You don't have to go with us." He pointed to the other Indian scouts. "None of you Indian scouts have to go. This isn't your war. You have done your duty."

"I have already told the sun that I will not see it go behind the hills tonight," Bloody Knife replied. "I cannot turn back now."

Chapter Eighteen

Back with Trains Company, Quinn watched dispiritedly as the column moved away from him. He tried to keep up, and he moved up and down the line, urging the pack horses and mules to a quicker pace, but they were even more exhausted than the cavalry mounts. As a result, the body of men in front of them got smaller and smaller until, finally, only the billowing clouds of dust gave evidence to the presence of a regiment of cavalry.

Boston and Autie Reed rode up to him.

"Mr. Pendarrow, can't we go faster?" Autie Reed asked. "They are getting away from us!"

With an exasperated sigh, Quinn waved his arm toward the pack animals. "If you know a way to make these beasts go any faster, Mr. Reed, I wish you would share it with me."

"There is no way to make them go faster."

"Well, there you go. We're sort of stuck with it, aren't we?"

"No, sir," Boston said.

"What do you mean?"

Boston cleared his throat. "I know my brother told you that when it looked like we were going to see action, you were to let us go."

"You know that, do you?"

"Yes, he told us," Autie Reed said. "And it looks like we are going to see action, doesn't it?"

"It looks that way," Quinn admitted.

"Then we want to go forward."

Quinn was quiet for a long moment. "Boys, I don't think you really want to do that," he finally said, shaking his head. "I don't have a good feeling about this fight. I don't have a good feeling at all."

"But you have to let us go forward if we want, right? I mean, my brother said."

"If you want to go, I won't try to stop you," Quinn said.

"Yahoo!" Autie Reed shouted. "Come on, Bos, let's go!"

The two young men slapped their legs against the sides of their horses, urging them into a gallop. Quinn watched them ride away, waving their hats and yelling in excitement. The distance made them diminish in size until, finally, they could no longer be seen.

Sergeant Posey came up a few minutes later. "You let them two boys go forward?"

"Yes," Quinn said. "I really didn't have any

choice. Custer gave me strict orders that if action was imminent, I was to release them so they could go to him."

"Uh-huh," Posey said. "Well, what Custer done was, he just got them two boys kilt. That's what he done."

Sergeant Scott saw Boston and Autie Reed riding up at a gallop. The horses were covered with lather as the animals foamed from their exertion. The two boys dismounted, then led them down to the creek to drink.

"Hold them back a little if you can," Scott said. "Don't let them drink too fast, not after running like that."

The two boys began fighting with their horses, trying to prevent them from drinking too fast.

"How far back is Trains?" Scott asked.

"I'm not sure," Boston replied. "Maybe two, two and half miles."

"They having any problems?"

Autie Reed laughed. "Just in keeping up is all. With nothing but a bunch of stumble-footed mules and IC horses, there's no way they can keep up with the regiment advancing at a trot."

"What are you doing up here?"

"We're going with the general," Boston said.

"Yes, we're going with the general," Autie Reed

mimicked. With their horses watered, they rode over to join the ranks of Tom Custer's company.

When Scott returned to the formation, Custer came over to talk to Reno. "Major Reno, I want you to take your battalion across the river and engage the Indians."

Reno blinked in surprise, then looked squarely at Custer. "General, do you mean make a feint?"

"No, Major. I want you to fully engage the Indians. Charge right through. You attack the village at the south end of the valley, and I will support you."

"You will support me?"

"Yes."

"Very well, sir."

As Benteen had done earlier, Reno ordered his battalion oblique left, pulling them away from the others. When the battalion reached the top of the hill, they saw the Indian village below them for the first time. The valley was one solid mass of tepees, starting, by coincidence, at almost the exact point where Reno crested the hill and stretching for at least three miles up the valley.

"My God!" Reno said. "Look at that! It's like attacking St. Louis! I've never seen a village so large."

Many of the men had dismounted and walked to the edge of the hill to get a better look. Some were so tired that they didn't care what was in front of them. A few of these men lay down.

Reno sat in his saddle for a long moment, as if mesmerized by what he was seeing.

"Major?" Scott said.

Reno showed no sign of having even heard Scott.

"Major, we have to attack, sir. General Custer is about to commit his forces. We must attack."

Reno pointed to the valley below. "Sergeant, I am not going to take three companies against a force that large," he said. "To do so would be pure folly."

"Major, you must. If you don't attack and carry it through, General Custer and every man with him could be killed. Don't you understand? They will be wiped out to the last man. We must attack!"

"Sergeant Scott is right," Captain Weir said. "We must attack."

"Very well," Reno said reluctantly. "I will make a demonstration against the village . . . but it will be a demonstration only. Trumpeter, sound boots and saddles."

The trumpeter sounded his call and the men, realizing then that they were about to go into action, let out a cheer. Reno cut them short at once. "Stop that cheering!" he ordered. "You are no better than wild Indians when you do that!"

"Major, let them yell!" Scott said. "It is good for the morale."

"Screaming like wild banshees may have been all right in the Confederate army, Sergeant, but these men are soldiers in the U.S. Cavalry and, by God, they will act like soldiers!"

The troops mounted and formed a skirmish line of 112 men, spread out in front of the ridge where Ash Creek emptied into the Little Bighorn River. Scott saw Dorman move up alongside Bloody Knife. The two men exchanged a few words, then Dorman pulled out his rifle. It wasn't the government-issue Springfield carbine the solders were carrying, but a customized Winchester. He operated the lever, jacking a round into the chamber. Then he spit on the site and rubbed it with his thumb. The men waited for a long moment, and the tension built.

"Major?" Scott said. Reno looked at Scott, and Scott could see fear in his commander's eyes. Then, summoning his courage, Reno stood in his stirrups.

"Trumpeter, sound the charge!" Reno shouted.

The trumpet blew its thrilling clarion call, and the men swept down the ridge, across the river, and into the trees.

The wife of Sitting Bull, Walks Alongside, was scraping the hide of a freshly killed antelope. Scores of other antelope hides dotted the prairie, pegged out to dry in the sun. As she stood up, she could see several horses hobbled within the camp itself, while to the west, on a plateau that rose some two hundred feet above the river, thousands of ponies grazed, attended by young boys from all the tribes of the camp.

In all her forty winter counts, this was the largest gathering of Indians she had ever seen. Thousands of tanned buffalo-hide tepees were pitched in seven great camp circles, each circle more than a half mile in diameter. Dogs of all sizes and types slunk around the tepees, protecting their staked-out territory from all intruders by bared fangs and low growls.

To the uninitiated, the arrangement of the village might appear to be haphazard, but Walks Alongside knew that the ancient customs governing the placement of each camp circle allotted a place for each band within the circle, and established the location of every lodge and tepee within each band. This gave every Indian a definite address that was known to all so that, though the camp had just been erected, a friend could call upon a friend without having to ask directions.

At the northernmost end of the village were three hundred lodges of the Cheyenne. At the south end was the largest camp circle of all, the three thousand Hunkpapa Sioux. Looking up, Walks Alongside saw her husband walking slowly and painfully through the camp. Sitting Bull's weakened condition was the result of a Sun Dance ceremony he had undergone three days earlier.

Sitting Bull had spent the previous night upon

the ridge overlooking the camp, praying and meditating. Walks Alongside was very proud of her husband and she thought he made a very imposing figure. Today he was wearing a tanned buckskin shirt that she had decorated with green porcupine quill work and tassels of human hair. His leggings and moccasins were also smoke tanned, though his long breechclout was deep red. He was wearing a single feather at the back of his head, and his face was painted red.

Walks Alongside was nearly finished with her task when she heard shooting coming from the south end of the camp. Looking in that direction, she saw dust rising, then she saw a warrior emerge from his tepee and run for his horse. The warrior's wife and child stood just outside the tepee, watching as the warrior galloped toward the sound of the guns.

"Soldiers are coming! Soldiers are coming!" someone yelled as he ran through the camp. His warning was totally unnecessary though, as everyone in the camp already knew they were being attacked. Walks Alongside hurried over to the tepee of her sister to help tend to the children.

"Look," one of the women said, "the soldiers making the attack are few. Why would so few attack so many?"

"Who can understand the ways of the white man?" Walks Alongside replied anxiously.

As the soldiers approached the village, the battle came much closer, and the bullets began whizzing through the camp, rattling off the tepee poles and peppering the lodge skins with holes.

Though many ran to look for shelter from the bullets, Walks Alongside saw her husband showing absolutely no fear as he walked unhurriedly through the camp. "Be brave!" Sitting Bull shouted. "We have much to fight for. If we lose the battle, we have nothing to live for! Fight like brave men!"

Two children, wet from swimming in the river, ran by. A crippled old man, supporting himself on a crutch, came hobbling along. A bullet cut his crutch in two and he fell. Walks Alongside ran out to help him to his feet, then pulled him over to the relative safety of a small depression.

Warriors—by the few, then by the dozens, then by the scores—rushed to join the battle.

"Hoka hay!"

"It is a good day to die!"

"My God!" Reno shouted as he led his battalion toward the village. "My God, they aren't running away! They're charging us! Bugler! Sound the dismount!"

"Reno, no!" Scott screamed, so shocked by Reno's intention to dismount that he left out the man's rank. "You can't dismount! We must push through!"

Despite Sergeant Scott's shout, Reno discontinued the attack and dismounted in a clump of trees in a gully. "Take cover!" he shouted. "Take cover and fire from the ditch!"

At that very moment Scott had his horse shot out from under him and, afoot he had no recourse but to take cover with the others. Already he saw soldiers struggling to remove the swollen copper cartridges from the breeches of their weapons, and he realized that not only were they outnumbered by the Indians, many of the Indians possessed Henry and Winchester repeating rifles.

"Major, we can't stay here!" Scott yelled. "We've got to get mounted! We have to push ahead!"

Even as Scott spoke, he knew he would have to catch a mount somewhere to replace his own mortally wounded animal. A hailstorm of arrows dropped into the ditch then, and a half dozen men shouted out in pain as the arrows found their marks.

"You're right!" Reno shouted. "Mount up! We're going to move back. Move back! Go back across the river!"

"Look! Sioux warriors leave now!" Bloody Knife said, pointing toward the village. Just as he had said, the Sioux were leaving, heading toward the north end of the village. Scott believed that by now Custer must have attacked and the Sioux were going to join the battle with him.

"Major, Custer's plan is working!" Scott yelled. "We've got to press the attack!"

Suddenly, a bullet plunged into Bloody Knife's head, causing his skull to explode. As a result, blood and brain tissue splattered onto Reno's face. Some of it got into his mouth, and he gagged and began spitting.

"Ahh!! Ahh!! Dismount! Dismount!" he shouted, and half the troopers who had mounted on his first command, dismounted again, though Reno did not.

"Withdraw to the river!" he ordered, then led the retreat, leaving behind several of his men, now totally disoriented by the confusing and contradictory orders. They stayed behind in the gully and watched as their comrades and all the horses left.

They were trapped.

Because his horse had been shot from under him, Scott was one of those left behind when Reno retreated. He watched Reno's men hit the river. The bank was several feet above the water, and the men had to urge their horses over. Once in the water, the horses started across, while the Indians continued to work the levers of their repeating rifles, pouring a high volume of fire at the fleeing soldiers. The climb up the other side of the river was as steep as the jump down had been. Scott saw Lieutenant Hodgson being pulled across the river, holding on to the stirrup of a trooper's horse. As the horse started climbing up the other side, Hodgson was hit by several bullets and he let go, then slid back into the water.

Scott looked around the thicket at the small group of frightened, trapped soldiers. "Sergeant Scott, what will we do?" one of them asked.

"First, everyone check your weapon to make sure it is loaded."

The troopers did as they were told.

"Now, lay low here in the thicket," Scott said. "Don't fire unless you are fired on. Perhaps the Indians will overlook us, and, when they pull back, we can get the hell out of here."

Scott and the others took cover in the little thicket of trees and waited. The Indians who had swooped by in pursuit of Reno's retreating soldiers now returned, laughing and shouting. Several of them were brandishing freshly taken scalps.

"The heathen devils," one of the men sobbed and started to stand up. Scott reached for him and pulled him back down.

"Be quiet," he cautioned.

"We are all going to be killed!" one of the others said fearfully.

"Yes," Scott said. "We probably are. But we all have to die sometime. If it is to be here and now, let us at least die as brave men."

As they lay there, they saw several Indian women coming out from the village. They began picking up their own dead and wounded. The women were crying over the bodies of their men and, for a moment, Scott could almost feel sorry for their grief. The pity he felt was soon dispelled, however, for the bodies of the soldiers were stripped of their clothes and severely mutilated. Then one of the women discovered Isaiah Dorman, and she shouted at the others. Though badly wounded, the black scout was not yet dead when the women raised him to a sitting position.

At first Scott thought the women were going to help him, but then, to his horrified surprise, one of them slit his throat. Another stuck Dorman's own tin mug under the jugular vein, filling it to overflowing with the blood. Another took a sharpened stake and drove it through Dorman's testicles. Dorman opened his mouth to scream, but the slice across his throat prevented any sound from coming out. Scott watched the silent scream, fighting hard to keep from screaming out his own rage.

The Indians moved around the thicket all afternoon, riding back and forth, running, shouting at one another, and sometimes even crashing through the thicket. Fortunately, they had no idea that Scott and the others were still there, for they didn't appear to be searching for anyone. In the meantime, Scott realized that Reno had probably taken a position on the far side of the river in the bluffs, for he could hear sporadic firing from that direction.

*   *   *

Custer's biggest concern had been that the Indians would run when they learned of his presence. But when he crested the hill and saw the village on the other side of the river, he realized that the Indians were not going to run from him as expected, but would stand and fight. Looking back toward the column, he took his hat off and waved it over his head. "We've got them, boys," he called out happily. "We've got them!"

At first Custer couldn't see the entire village because the view of the section farthest downstream was obscured by the bends in the river and the timber growing along the banks. As they moved along the crest of the hill, however, more and more of the village became visible, and Custer realized for the first time what truly lay in front of them. Tom, who was riding alongside Custer, saw the village as well.

"Do we have them, or do they have us?" Tom asked.

"It's pretty big, isn't it?" Custer replied.

"We'd better get Benteen up here fast," Tom suggested.

"Orderly!" Custer called. A young rider came up to him.

"Orderly, I want you to take a message to Colonel Benteen. Ride as fast as you can and tell him to hurry. Tell him it's a big village, and I want him to be quick and to bring all the ammunition packs."

Nodding, the orderly pulled his horse around.

"Wait, Orderly, I'll give you a message," Lieutenant Cooke called out.

The orderly checked his horse as Cooke wrote something very quickly, then tore the page out of his message book and handed it over.

"Now, Orderly, ride as fast as you can to Colonel Benteen," Custer said. "Take the same trail we came down. If you have time and there is no danger, come back, but otherwise stay with your company."

Nodding again, the orderly left at a gallop.

A few minutes after the orderly left, Boston and Autie Reed rode up to the front of the column. "Did we find them?" Boston asked.

Custer stared at the two young men for a moment as if pained by their presence. "I forgot that you were here. I should've sent you back with the orderly."

"You said you wanted us to be near you if we were about to get into a fight," Boston said.

"Did I?"

"Yes, you know you did."

"Well, I've changed my mind."

Boston giggled. "It's a little late now, isn't it?"

"Maybe not. Lieutenant Calhoun, post," Custer called.

"Yes, sir!" Calhoun answered, leaving his company and riding over as directed.

"Jimmi, I want you to take Boston and Autie

Reed to the rear, out of harm's way. You stay there too. With Tom and me, Maggie's going to have a hard enough time as it is. No sense in taking you away from her, too."

Calhoun looked dumbstruck. "General, you can't mean that! I'd rather stay with my men."

"That is an order, Lieutenant!" Custer yelled sharply.

Calhoun sighed. "Autie, of course I'll do anything you ask," he said. "But do you really think we would make it more than a quarter of a mile from here?"

"We have no chance here, Jimmi, and you know it," Custer said.

"What if we didn't attack?" Tom asked. "What if we stayed right here and kept an eye on them until Terry and Gibbon arrived?"

Gunfire erupted from the southern end of the village.

"It's too late. Listen, do you hear that?" Custer asked. "Reno is committed. We have no choice now. We have to attack. Otherwise, he'll be wiped out."

"What do you want of me, General?" Calhoun asked. "Do I stay with you? Or do I run with the boys?"

"Autie, we aren't going anywhere," Boston insisted. "We are going to stay."

Custer looked over at Tom.

Tom shrugged his shoulders. "Hell, let 'em stay,

Autie," he said. "We're all going to die anyway. We may as well die together."

Custer nodded grimly, his face grown ashen, then stood in his stirrups and looked back over his command. "Trumpeter!" he called.

"Y-yes, sir?"

"Sound the charge!"

The trumpeter lifted the instrument, but he was so frightened he couldn't make a sound. Custer rode over to him.

"Blow your horn, son," he said gently.

"I . . . I can't, General. I'm too scared!"

"Don't be afraid, Billy. Whatever happens to one of us is going to happen to us all," Custer said.

"You . . . you know my first name?"

"Of course I do. You're a good man. I'll be proud to have you at my side when we ride into Fiddler's Green to kick the devil in the ass."

The young trumpeter smiled, then raised his horn. The notes of the call to battle took wing.

Chapter Nineteen

When the notes of the bugle call drifted down across the stream and into the village, Red Eagle hurried to the north end of the camp. He arrived there just in time to see the soldiers charging down the hill toward the village. At first he could hear only the beat of shod hooves. Then came the jangle of gear and the rattle of bits. Finally, he heard the soldiers themselves, shouting and screaming at the top of their lungs as they approached. Closer and closer they came, until the great blue mass became distinguishable.

But the charge of the soldiers would not carry into the village, for Red Eagle knew that there were hundreds of Indians waiting in ambush, holding their fire until the moment the soldiers hit the stream. When the first horse entered the river, the Indians rose up and fired. A soldier on a gray horse was hit, and he tumbled from the saddle, his blood making a dark stain spread out in the swirling water.

Red Eagle recognized Custer, who was firing as he advanced. He was particularly well mounted, and in the shallow water his horse kicked up a sparkling silver spray with its gamboling, arrogant gate. By now all the soldiers were firing, and the air was thick with smoke as shot after shot rang out.

Then, incredibly, Red Eagle saw Custer jerk back in his saddle. He dropped his rifle and put his hand to his chest, trying to stop the blood that spilled through his fingers. When Red Eagle looked around, he saw that the shot had been fired by a young girl who couldn't have counted more than sixteen winters. Custer reeled, then fell from the saddle.

"My God, Custer!" one of the soldiers yelled, and he jumped down to grab the general to keep him from going under. Another soldier jumped down as well, and they managed to get Custer back onto his horse. In the meantime the Indians were still firing, and the soldier carrying the flag went down. One of the other troopers grabbed the flag to keep it from falling.

"Back! Fall back!" someone shouted.

The soldiers turned their horses and started riding hard back up the hill they had just descended. When they reached the top of the hill, they dismounted and began firing at the Indians, who were by now surging up the hill toward them.

As the warriors charged, the troopers opened such a heavy fire that the Indians had to fall back. Though hard pressed from all sides, the troopers were standing their ground. Custer, still alive, was holding one hand over the wound in his chest, sitting on the ground and firing his pistol at his attackers.

During the retreat back up the hill from Medicine Tail Coulee, the soldiers had separated into two distinct groups. Now they were making an attempt to reach the highest point on the hill, where they could rejoin and take up a strong defensive position. But even as they moved, more Indians came to join the fight, running hard from the south end of the village, where they had been engaged with Reno's battalion. As an increasing number of Indians poured over the hapless soldiers, it reminded Red Eagle of a swiftly flowing stream eddying around rocks. As the soldiers lost more and more of their men, the volume of their fire began to slacken.

Red Eagle advanced up the hill with the others, exposing himself to the same danger as the others, though fulfilling his promise to Sitting Bull to not take part in the battle. As the battle progressed, though, he realized that he would have made no contribution as a leader anyway, for there were no war chiefs on the field. Instead, every warrior fought independently of their bands and leaders, moving as they pleased. They were guided only by their desire to defend their village, strike the enemy, capture the enemy's horse or weapon, or rescue a friend in danger. They carried the battle not by strategy, but by the sheer weight of numbers.

As firing from the handful of remaining soldiers fell off into a few, isolated shots, even the old women and young children could cross the stream in safety. They climbed up the hill to witness the final stage of the battle. One by one the last soldiers were gunned or clubbed down, until finally there was absolute and total silence.

The Indians merely stood around for several minutes, too shocked by what had happened. There was no celebration of victory, nor wailing for the dead. No one spoke a word as they began methodically stripping the bodies, mutilating them so that they would be marked when they entered the next life.

Quinn Pendarrow had ridden ahead of his packers and was approximately six miles southeast of Custer's position. Rejoining the trail just ahead, Benteen's troops were coming back across Ash Creek, having finished their scout through the hills. When Benteen saw Quinn coming up the trail behind them, he turned his horse and rode back.

"Where's Custer?" Benteen asked.

"Up ahead, as far as I know," Quinn replied.

"Have you heard anything from him?"

"No. What about you?"

Benteen took a drink from his canteen before he answered. "Nothing. Not one word since he sent me off on that wild-goose chase." Benteen took in the hills to the south with an impatient wave of his hand. "There were no Indians out there, and Custer knew there wouldn't be any. If you ask me, he just wanted me out of the way." Benteen looked around. "Where is Trains?"

"About a mile back," Quinn answered.

"Odd that we have heard nothing at all from our gallant leader. You would think we would have by now."

Over a rise, approximately one thousand yards ahead of them, a soldier appeared on horseback, riding back toward them as fast as he could. The rider was bent low over the head of the animal, slapping the reins back and forth on either side of the neck as he urged the horse to its maximum effort.

"Here comes a galloper," Quinn said.

Benteen twisted around, then raised his field glasses for a closer look. "It's Trooper Martini, Custer's orderly for the day."

"Martini? I don't think I know him."

"He calls himself John Martin now," Benteen

said, lowering the glasses. "But his real name is Giovanni Martini. He is a thick-headed, dull-witted Italian who barely speaks English and is about as fit to be a cavalryman as he is to be a king."

"Well, whatever message he's bringing from Custer must be important. He's riding hard, and whether he's fit to be a cavalryman or not, the boy can ride."

It took nearly a full minute for Martin to close the distance between them, though Quinn couldn't help but think it would have taken less time had Benteen ridden out to meet him. Instead, the captain just sat quietly in his saddle until Martin arrived.

Martin saluted. *"Il capitano Benteen, il General Custer dice, villaggio grande, viene rapidamente, porta i pacchetti."*

"What?" Benteen asked. "What did you say?"

Martin looked confused.

"Villaggio grande," Quinn said. "Village? Big village?"

"Sí, big village. Much Indian," Martin said. "He say come quick, bring . . . *pachetti* . . ." Through hand signals, Martin described the packs.

"Bring packs?" Benteen asked.

"Sí. Bring packs."

"Is that it? Is that all the general had to say?"

"He say, 'We got them, boys.' " Martin laughed. "We got them, boys," he repeated.

"All right," Benteen said, "rejoin the troop."

"Here troop? Il General Custer say I come back."

"You are going back. We're all going," Benteen said. "Now, rejoin the troop."

"*Sí, Capitano.*" Martin started to rejoin the troops, then almost as an afterthought he pulled out a piece of paper. "Message for you," he said.

"Well, when were you going to give it to me?" Benteen asked gruffly, taking the message. He read it, then handed it to Quinn. "You may as well read it, too," he said. "It pertains to you."

BENTEEN
COME ON. BIG VILLAGE. BE QUICK. BRING PACKS. W. W. COOKE. PS. BRING PACS.

"Looks like he scribbled it in a hurry," Quinn said, pointing to the omitted "k" in the last word.

"Yes. Listen, how long would it take you to bring the packs up?"

"Ten minutes to get them to this point, I suppose," Quinn said. "I can put them into a trot, speed it up a bit. The problem is, the animals aren't in that good a condition to begin with. And if I run and if I run them too long, they may just drop in place . . . then where will we be?"

"All right, bring them up as fast as you think possible."

Quinn jerked his horse around, then started toward the rear at a gallop. Behind him Benteen advanced his battalion no faster than a trot.

The moon came out, but there was a heavy overcast of clouds so it wasn't too bright. Scott knew that if they were ever going to escape, they would have to do so then.

"Let's go," he ordered, and in a crouch he led his little group of men out of the woods. They were about halfway to the river when they saw a mounted band of Indians. Scott signaled the others, and they all dropped to the ground, remaining very still. The Indians, laughing and talking, rode right past them but didn't see them in the dark.

Finally, they reached the river's edge, and one by one they slid down the bank, then dropped their heads into the water and drank deeply, satisfying the thirst that had bedeviled them during the long, hot, terrifying afternoon.

They were able to drink from the river, but they couldn't cross there because the water was too deep and the current too swift.

Upriver, Scott could see and hear great circles of the Indians holding a war dance around burning piles of wood and brush. The flames lighted the village with an eerie, flickering glow, and in that light Scott could see that the Indians were grotesquely painted. In addition, many were carrying the severed heads of the slain soldiers.

"Sergeant, hold it!" one of the men whispered harshly. "There's someone ahead!"

Scott signaled for the others to be quiet, and he moved forward silently on his stomach. In the dark ahead he could make out four men and two horses, but it was too dark for him to identify them as friend or foe. Then he heard one of them talk.

"Lieutenant, my boots is all full of water. I need to take a minute to empty 'em," the voice said.

Scott nearly laughed out loud. The voice belonged to Trooper O'Neill.

"All right, but be quick about it," another voice answered. "We've been wandering around out here half the night. We don't want to still be here when the sun comes up." That voice belonged to Lieutenant De Rudio.

"Lieutenant De Rudio," Scott whispered harshly.

"Shh!" Scott heard one of the men say. "I heard something."

"Lieutenant De Rudio, it's me, Sergeant Scott. I have three men with me."

"It's Sergeant Scott!" O'Neill said happily.

"Quiet," De Rudio hissed. "Want every Indian in the village to know we're here?"

"Sorry, sir," O'Neill said.

"Scott, bring your men in, but be as quiet as you can."

"Yes, sir," Scott said. Still on his belly, he wriggled back through the weeds and tall grass until he reached the others. "Come on. I found some of our own."

With De Rudio now in command, the little band of survivors explored numerous places along the river until they finally found a place to cross. De Rudio led them over, then just as they emerged on the other side, a small group of mounted riders approached the bluff. All wore blue uniform jackets except for the leader. The leader was wearing a very familiar buckskin jacket.

"It's Captain Custer," O'Neill said. "Thank God, boys, we're back among our own."

"Tom!" De Rudio called. "Boy, are we glad to see you! You don't know what we've been through, and you . . . wait a minute, how did you escape the—"

"It's not Captain Custer!" Scott shouted. "It's an Indian!" The Indian raised his pistol and fired. Scott fired back. The Indian in Custer's uniform tumbled from the saddle, and the others rode away quickly.

"Let's get out of this river before they come back!" De Rudio ordered, and the soldiers followed him as he climbed up the bluff away from the river.

Crouched low, the men ran for several hundred yards until they heard voices speaking English. De Rudio held up his hand to halt the troopers.

"That's Corporal McAfee's voice," one of the troopers said. "I know that for sure, he's done chewed me out enough times."

"Call out to him," De Rudio said.

"McAfee! Corporal McAfee!"

"Who's that?" McAfee called back.

"Mac, it's me, Dockins. Lieutenant De Rudio, Sergeant Scott, and some others are with me. Tell the boys not to shoot. We're comin' in."

"All right, come on."

When Scott and the others came through, they were welcomed by the combined battalions of Benteen and Reno. Trains had also come up during the afternoon, and soldier and civilian alike had constructed hasty fortifications in the hillside, in some cases using the boxes and crates from the pack animals to build ramparts. They couldn't attack the Indians, but their combined positions were strong enough that they could defend themselves against any attack the Indians might make.

"Where is the general?" Scott asked as he drank a cup of coffee Quinn offered him.

"So far we haven't heard from him."

"Has anyone tried to go to him?"

"Captain Weir did late this afternoon," Quinn replied. "He got only to the next hill, then he was driven back."

"Nobody has tried since then?"

"Sergeant Scott, Custer is the commander," Reno said. "It is his responsibility to find us. Why didn't he come to my aid as he promised me? And why doesn't he come now? Doesn't he realize we are trapped here?"

"I'm sure he does realize it, Major," Benteen said. "He's probably just as trapped. If he is still alive," he added ominously.

"Major, there may be more stragglers trapped on the other side of the river," Scott suggested. "With your permission, I'll take some men over to look for them."

"Permission denied," Reno replied. "If anyone is left over there, they are going to have to return on their own."

"What if they're wounded?" Scott asked.

"It can't be helped."

"But we can't leave wounded over there," Scott insisted.

"Why not? Our courageous major would have left our wounded here if Benteen hadn't stopped him."

Scott stood up. "Then I request permission to return on my own."

"What can you do?"

"If I find them, I'll show them the best way to get back," Scott said.

"Don't be foolish. You'll get yourself killed."

"I did it once and got away with it. And now that I know where the best ford is, I can do it again."

"I'll go with you," Quinn offered.

"No, I won't let both of you go," Reno said.

"I'm a civilian, Reno, remember? You can't stop me."

"Hell, Marcus, leave them alone," Benteen said. "None of us may get out of here alive anyway. Go ahead, Sergeant, Mr. Pendarrow, see who else you can find over there. Good luck to the both of you."

"Thanks," Quinn replied.

Quinn and Scott later made five more trips across the river, right into the heart of the Indian camp. They brought seventeen more soldiers to safety, the last group just after daybreak.

Although there was some continued fighting on the morning of the 26th of June, by early afternoon it was apparent to everyone that the Indians were leaving. Striking their tepees, they began pouring out of the valley in the hundreds, then in the thousands, heading west toward the Big Horn Mountains.

"Major, the Indians are leaving," Quinn said.

"The village is leaving," Reno replied. "We don't know if the warriors are with them."

"Of course the warriors are with them. Look at all the men. They're leaving, lock, stock and barrel."

"We'll wait a little longer," Reno said.

"I think we should try and make contact with General Custer now."

Reno glared at Quinn. "You are a civilian, Mr. Pendarrow. Civilians have nothing to do with this."

"Well, now, is that a fact?" Quinn challenged. He pointed to his civilian mule skinners, all of whom had faces blackened with gunpowder from their participation in the fight.

"You want to tell those men that they had nothing to do with this fight? When we arrived yesterday, just in time to keep you from being overrun, I didn't hear you suggest that our firepower wasn't wanted because we were civilians. When my men risked their lives building ramparts out of the boxes and crates we brought in on the mules, you didn't say they needn't bother because they are civilians.

"Under the most arduous conditions you can imagine, much more difficult than anything any trooper went through, these *civilians* brought up the food, ammunition, and forage that made this entire expedition possible. They weren't bound by any oath of enlistment—they were bound only by their code of honor. They could have turned around at any time, but they didn't.

"And, by the way, Dr. Porter, who has been tirelessly tending to the wounded, is also a civilian. Now, are you really prepared to say that no civilian has any stake in this?"

"I don't deny the contribution made by civilians," Reno said. "I am merely stating that in the matter of tactics, the army is in charge."

"Well, you be in charge of all the tactics you want. I'm going to see if I can find Custer." Wearily, Quinn started toward his horse. Behind him he heard the deadly, metallic click of a pistol being cocked.

"You're going nowhere, mister," Reno said.

Quinn turned to see that Reno had actually leveled a gun at him. "You're going to shoot me?"

"If I have to."

"As you pointed out, Reno, I'm a civilian. You have no authority over me except that pistol. So if you're going to use it, use it now. Otherwise, put it away and stop making a damn fool of yourself."

Reno hesitated for second, then lowered his gun, and put it away. It wasn't until then Quinn realized that, unseen by anyone else, both Scott and Posey had quietly taken aim at Reno. Now they lowered their guns as well.

"Go ahead," Reno said. "Get yourself scalped. It's all the same to me."

With a nod toward Scott and Posey, Quinn mounted his horse and started toward the last place anyone had seen Custer.

He could see the buzzards circling overhead as soon as he crossed Medicine Tail Coulee. Preparing himself for what he would see on the other side of the ridge, he urged his horse into a canter and rode to the top of the hill.

He was overwhelmed by what he saw. There in the valley below him were the remains of Custer's command.

Every last man was dead.

Slowly, Quinn rode down the gentle slope into the valley of death. The bodies were white, so terribly white. At first he didn't understand why, then he realized it was because most were naked, stripped of the last trappings of their mortal life.

A few were still in uniform. Quinn saw that the reporter, Mark Kellogg, was also clothed. Quinn dismounted and leading his horse began walking through the grisly area. Already buzzards were feasting on the remains, and he turned away and retched when he saw one bird pull the brain out of the scalped cranium of one of the soldiers. The soldier was lying with his back to Quinn, and Quinn didn't want to look into his face because he didn't want to recognize him. The bodies were somewhat more spread out than he would have thought, as if there had been several defensive positions rather than one large consolidated position. But given the fluidity of battle and no availability of cover, such as that found by the Reno and Benteen battalions, Quinn assumed the soldiers had done the best they could.

As he passed by the bodies, one after another, his presence caused the nearest buzzards to take to the air with a dry, blood-chilling flap of wings. They would circle once, then return as soon as he was by.

"Why did the soldiers come?" a voice asked.

Startled, Quinn whirled around, reaching for his pistol as he did so. He found himself facing a half dozen Indians, all armed and all pointing their weapons at him.

"Do not shoot at us and we will not shoot at you," the Indian said.

"You are Red Eagle," Quinn said.

"Yes. Picture Woman. She is safe?"

"Picture Woman?"

"Woman who makes pictures," Red Eagle said. He made a motion as if painting. "I take her to river."

"Oh, Miss McKenzie," Quinn said. "Yes, she is safe."

"It is good that she is safe."

Quinn shook his head. "You told her you want peace. Is this how you show that you want peace?" He held an arm out, taking in the carnage.

"Soldiers come to our village, kill women, children, old people, so we kill them. If my people go to white man's town and kill your women and your children, then you would kill them because a man who fights for his home has strong medicine."

Quinn nodded. "I'm afraid I have to agree with you on that."

Red Eagle made a motion with his hand over his head, then he pointed at Quinn. At first Quinn didn't understand, then he realized that Red Eagle was duplicating the bullet that Quinn once fired at him, ruffling the feathers of his headdress.

"You shoot gun that makes bullet do this?" Red Eagle asked, demonstrating again.

"Yes, that was me."

To Quinn's surprise, Red Eagle smiled. "It was a good fight that day," he said. "Warrior fighting warrior. Not like this."

"Yes, it was a good fight."

"You do not wear soldier clothes. You are soldier no more?"

"That's right. I am no longer a soldier."

"But you were with soldiers on the hill?" He pointed south, where Reno and Benteen were.

"Yes."

"Even there, we could have killed all of you," Red Eagle said. "But we did not, because now we want peace. Go back to your people. Tell them we do not want war anymore. We have beaten you. We have beaten the soldiers of Crook, and now of Custer. Do not come here again. You scare the buffalo. We want to hunt. We want to live in peace."

Quinn shook his head. "It's too late for that. There are many more soldiers coming, and they will not stop until all the Sioux have returned to their reservations."

"Then many more soldiers will die."

"And many more Indians. Why will you not return to your reservations? It is good for you there. You are given beef and clothing. You are given blankets and rifles for hunting. You can live there in peace, and we can live in peace."

Red Eagle shook his head. "We are not like cattle, to be kept in pens. We are like buffalo, to go where we wish."

"I wish it could be like that for you," Quinn said sadly. "I truly do."

The Indians turned to leave, but as they did so, Red Eagle turned back toward Quinn, gesturing toward the corpses of the soldiers. "There were no cowards here. All died bravely."

Chapter Twenty

Kate was taking a nap in her cabin with the window open to allow a breeze to circulate. She was used to the normal noises of the boat and the banter of the soldiers who were camped on the side of the river for their protection. She was even used to loud conversations that would sometimes take place right outside her window. Most of the time, though, the conversations passed unnoticed as she slept.

But the words she heard spoken this day struck like a dagger in her heart, awakening her immediately.

"Surely you must be mistaken. It simply isn't possible that Custer's entire command has been killed to a man?"

In a flash, Kate had the casement thrown open, and she leaned out the cabin window. "What is that?" she asked. "What are you saying?"

"It's Curly, ma'am," one of the deckhands said.

"He says that General Custer has been killed, and every man with him."

"Oh, no!" Kate gasped in horror.

Captain Marsh happened by then, and seeing how upset Kate was, sought to comfort her. "I wouldn't pay much attention to what the Indian says. He was supposed to be with Custer but, as you can see, he plainly isn't. If you want my opinion, he just skedaddled sometime before any of the fighting started, and this is his excuse."

Twenty-four hours later, Kate learned that there was much more truth in the Indian guide's dire news than anyone was initially willing to believe. While the battalions of Reno and Benteen had suffered heavy casualties in the fight, the majority of the officers and men in those two commands had survived. However, the two battalions that had gone into battle under Custer's immediate command had been wiped out to a man.

Kate's immediate concern was over Quinn Pendarrow's safety. Had he survived the fight? She was assured by everyone that there was no chance Trains had been up with Custer, so she shouldn't worry that he would be among those killed with Custer. But many had been killed with Reno and Benteen, and they were told that a little over fifty wounded men were being brought back to the boat, some of whom had grievous wounds. Could Quinn be among the wounded?

The earliest report of civilian casualties to reach them included Mark Kellogg, Boston Custer, Autie Reed, and one civilian packer. Three civilian packers were wounded. Kate was glad that Quinn's name was not on that list, but the news that one civilian packer was killed and three were wounded caused her to worry until she saw the troops arrive. Among them, uninjured, was Quinn Pendarrow.

From the time he learned of the arriving wounded, Captain Marsh had been preparing the boat to transport them back. He did this by fabricating mattresses of grass and canvas, then spreading the beds out on the boiler deck. There were fifty-two wounded, and minutes after the last wounded man was brought aboard, Captain Marsh, with steam pressure at the maximum, pulled away from the bank and started on the thousand-mile trip back to Fort Lincoln.

The two military surgeons assigned to the Seventh Cavalry had been killed. Only the civilian surgeon, Dr. Porter, survived the battle, and he had been tending the wounded without rest for five nights. Concerned for the doctor's health, General Terry asked Quinn if he would go back on the boat with the wounded to provide whatever assistance he could. Quinn agreed. Kate volunteered as well, and Quinn and Kate worked with Dr. Porter, changing dressings and feeding and caring for the more seriously wounded.

It was fifty-three miles to where the Bighorn emptied into the Yellowstone. For that entire fifty-three miles, the Bighorn was little more than a stream.

"Why, I've seen more water from a heavy dew," George Foulk, the engineer, told Quinn, "but that didn't stop Captain Marsh from coming upriver, and you better believe it won't stop him going down."

The first part of the trip was the most hazardous, as they had to dodge around numerous islands, an even more difficult feat because no one had ever brought a boat up that far except Captain Marsh himself, and he had done it only once, moving slowly and carefully.

No chance for that now. Marsh kept the boat going as fast as he could under the circumstances, fighting hard to keep the boat in what channel there was in the narrow stream.

By the time they reached the mouth of the Yellowstone, fourteen of the wounded had recovered sufficiently to be off-loaded. Here they joined Colonel Gibbon's command for the march back home. At five o'clock on the afternoon of July 3, the steamboat started down the Yellowstone.

Even on the more well-traveled rivers, many steamboats would not travel at night. But this was an emergency, and despite the snags and sandbars, as well as the ever-shifting channel, Captain Marsh did not put in at night.

With Captain Marsh and his chief pilot, Dave Campbell, taking turns at the wheel in four-hour shifts, the boat rushed on at full steam, many times topping twenty miles per hour. From time to time the bottom of the boat came into contact with a rock just below the surface of the water, or strike a snag with enough force to throw deckhands off their feet and cause the wounded to slide about. Often, as the pilot whipped the boat to and fro to follow the twisting channel, the boat came dangerously close to burying itself in the bank. Every time though, a skillful turn of the wheel swung the boat back into the channel, escaping any serious damage, but sometimes scraping her sides along the bank of the stream.

Finally the *Far West* moved out of the Yellowstone and into the broad Missouri River. Now Captain Marsh was in familiar territory, and he called for full speed ahead. Down in the engine room, exhausted firemen, their hands and faces blackened with soot, fed wood into the roaring, insatiable fireboxes until the steady thump of the engines became like the heartbeat of all who were on board.

"Hey, Mr. Pendarrow," one of the wounded soldiers said as Quinn was feeding him his lunch. Two broken arms prohibited the man from feeding himself, otherwise he was quite healthy.

"Yes?"

"That Miss McKenzie, she's something, isn't she?"

Quinn looked across the deck and saw Kate smiling warmly at a much more seriously wounded soldier as she gently bathed his head. "Yes, Madden, she is something."

"You know what I think?" Madden asked.

"No, but I'm sure you are about to tell me," Quinn answered with a long suffering sigh. He had already learned that Madden was a talker. In the twenty-four hours that they had been under way, Madden had come up with at least three get-rich-quick schemes, all three of which required a rather sizable investment from Quinn.

"I never seen that girl who dumped you . . . you know, the one you quit the army for? But, I'm tellin' you, she can't hold a candle to this one."

Quinn laughed. "If you've never seen the other one, how do you know?"

"I don't need to see her," Madden said. "I've seen this one. That's enough."

Quinn looked over at Kate. "You may have a point there, Madden."

It was nearly midnight on the night of July 4. Kate had finished her walk through the sleeping patients who were spread out along the boiler deck. Then, satisfying herself that none of them needed her attention, she went down the ladderway to the main deck. Here she stood by one of the support pillars, watching the starboard engine in its labor. Her neck and shoulders were tense, and she reached around and tried to massage the aching muscles. The cool air made her shiver.

"Here." Quinn's voice came from the darkness behind her. "Let me do that."

Before Kate could protest, strong hands and gentle fingers went to her neck and shoulders and began kneading her flesh expertly, skillfully, spreading a soothing sensation throughout the pounding soreness that had started there.

"You . . . shouldn't . . . be . . . doing . . . this." Kate tried to protest, but his hands were having such an amazing, relaxing effect that she found it impossible to resist strenuously.

Quinn laughed softly. "You really want me to stop?" He pulled his hand away.

"No, no, don't stop, please!" she said, grabbing his hand and putting it back on her neck. "It feels wonderful."

"I thought you might like it." Quinn resumed the massage.

"Quinn, do you think we will get the rest of these men back safely? We've lost one, you know."

"I know, but according to Dr. Porter his chances

weren't very good when we started. I don't think we'll lose any more."

"I pray that we don't."

"Here, turn this way and hold still," Quinn said.

"What are you going to do?"

"You'll see." From the back, Quinn put his arms around Kate, locking his hands just beneath her breasts. He pulled her against him, then leaned back and lifted her feet from the floor. Miraculously, it seemed, her muscles quit hurting.

"How did you do that?"

"It's just an old trick I learned," Quinn replied. He turned her toward him and looked into her face for a long moment, then put his arms on her shoulders. "And this," he added, "is a trick of my own."

Quinn pulled Kate to him, and before she realized what was happening, or could react in any way, he pressed her lips against his. His hands left her shoulders, and his arms wound around her tightly, pulling her soft body to his. Kate let herself go limp in his arms.

Quinn knew at that moment that she had just turned herself over to him, placing her future in his hands. If he wanted, he knew he could have her, right here, right now, in the dark on this deck. She wouldn't resist him, and there was little likelihood that they would be seen.

But he knew, too, that in giving herself over to

him, she had placed him on his honor. It was not a responsibility he intended to fail.

She pulled away from his lips and looked into his eyes. "Quinn, you *are* over Miss Parkinson, aren't you?"

"Who is Miss Parkinson?" Quinn replied.

At eleven o' clock at night on the fifth of July, the *Far West* put in to Bismarck. Captain Marsh had made the trip back in the amazing time of fifty-eight hours, crashing through growths of water grass, sparring over sand bars, plunging through whirlpools, passing under high bluffs, and dodging islands. As soon as the boat docked, Captain Marsh went into town to awaken the telegraph operator, J. M. Carnahan. With Carnahan's skilled fingers operating the telegraph key, word of Custer's disastrous defeat went out to the rest of the world.

At dawn on the sixth of July, Dr. Middleton, the post surgeon, asked Quinn if he would mind accompanying him while he broke the news to Libbie Custer. "You were there, you saw his body. I think your presence will help her accept what she surely will want to deny."

"All right," Quinn agreed. "It isn't something I relish, but if you think it will help."

As he walked across the quadrangle on that bright, early morning, Quinn looked at the house of the commanding officer, standing big and white, the windows on the many cupolas shining gold in the early morning sun. Always until this moment, Quinn had regarded this house as the Custer home. He thought it odd how he was thinking of it at this moment, not as the Custer home, but as the house of the commanding officer.

They started to go to the front door, then as an afterthought, decided to go around to the back door instead. That way they could wake the maid and let her summon Libbie.

The maid showed them to the parlor, then a few moments later Libbie joined them. Quinn could tell by the haunted look in Libbie's eyes that she already knew why they were there, and he would have traded anything in the world to not to be there at this moment. Maggie Calhoun, looking just as distressed, came in behind her.

"My husband?" Libbie asked.

Dr. Middleton didn't say anything. He just nodded.

"Tom, Boston, the others?"

"I'm sorry, Mrs. Custer," Quinn said. "It's all of them. The general, Tom, Boston, Autie Reed"—he looked at Maggie— "and Lieutenant Calhoun."

"Oh, Libbie," Maggie said, burying her face in her hands as she sobbed. "What are we going to do?"

"I'm going to get my wrap, Maggie, then I'm

going to comfort the other wives. That's what I'm going to do. I'm sure Autie would want it that way."

New York, one year later

The showing at the New York Art League Gallery drew an overflow crowd. All the city's newspapers had front page stories about it, and there were even some representatives from other art museums attending the viewing to make arrangements for their own shows.

Although it was originally to be called "Plains Indians in their Habitat," the title of the show had changed, due to recent history. It was now being called "The Great Plains Morality Play." There were lamentations by one and all that P. G. McKenzie had been forced to sacrifice himself in the pursuit of his art.

According to the *New York World*:

> There is little difference between the supreme oblation paid by Mr. McKenzie and that of the noble soldiers who, in the true spirit of their calling, followed their leader into the valley of death.
>
> We are fortunate that Mr. McKenzie's daughter did not suffer the same fate, for indeed she braved the same dangers as her noble father. That she survived, and will be the special guest of the New York Art League, is a gift of Divine Providence to all who love art and want a living connection by which we can pay homage to the talent of P. G. McKenzie.

The newspaper went on to list the paintings that would be displayed: *Mother and Child Outside Teepee, Old Man with Bow, Children at Play, Woman with Blanket, Three Young Boys,* and *A Sioux Brave.*

One of the paintings was so controversial that there was some discussion in light of recent events as to whether or not so show it. The painting was entitled *Peacemaker,* and it was of a rather ferocious, but undeniably handsome warrior in full regalia. The warrior was Red Eagle, and he was known to have participated in the fight against General Crook and suspected to have taken part in the Custer fight.

Kate had insisted that this work be shown with the others, and reluctantly the Art League acquiesced to her demands.

One more painting was to be unveiled by a special guest on the night of the showing. There was much speculation as to what the painting might be and who would present it. The secret was so closely guarded that only a few of the Art League curators actually knew. The anticipation of that unveiling had drawn the large crowd on that night.

Those standing in front of the gallery saw a carriage pull to the curb and stop. A young man in the dress uniform of a captain of the cavalry stepped down from the carriage, then turned to offer his hand to the beautiful young woman with him.

"Allow me," the captain offered.

"Why, thank you, Captain Pendarrow, sir," Kate replied, smiling broadly as she exited the carriage.

Arm in arm, the two climbed the polished concrete steps to enter the gallery. Once inside, they were cheered by the guests in attendance, for it was now well known that Captain Pendarrow had marched with Custer to the very gates of Valhalla, while Kate McKenzie had waited on board the steamer *Far West*, closer to the battle than any other non-Indian female.

As a band played in the background, Kate and Quinn joined the others who were viewing the paintings. Then they walked to the middle of the rotunda of the gallery, where on a stand covered by a black silk cloth was the painting that the curators had decided to make the crown jewel of the show. As yet, no one knew what the painting was, for none but the curators had seen it.

At a signal from the director of the gallery, the band quieted. With the halt in the music, the gallery visitors knew that the unveiling was about to take place, and they moved closer to the draped painting.

The director introduced Kate Pendarrow, and the crowd waited expectantly for her to remove the cloth.

"Ladies and gentlemen," Kate said, "as you know, I am here representing my father, and many of you may have thought that I would be the one who would unveil the principal painting of this show. I had been asked to do so, and indeed, it would have been a great honor. But there is someone else who deserves the honor even more than I, and I prevailed upon that person to be here tonight. And so now it is my great privilege to present to you one of the bravest women I know, the widow of a great American hero, Mrs. George Armstrong Custer."

Libbie Custer's presence was a complete surprise to everyone, and the ovation for her was thunderous. Coming from a small anteroom at the side of the rotunda, she stood in the middle of the throngs of admirers for a long moment until the applause died. Then she began to speak in a quiet, well-modulated voice that ensured absolute attention from her listeners.

"Ladies and gentlemen, throughout my months of sorrow, your willingness to share my grief has sustained me. Your appreciation of my husband's service to his country has lifted me. Your recognition of his valor has honored me. From the bottom of my heart, I thank you, one and all."

Again, the audience applauded.

"And now, thanks to the artistic talent of a wonderful and courageous artist, Mr. P. G. McKenzie, I am proud to say that the memories of my husband and family will live in the hearts of Americans forever."

Libbie pulled on a velvet cord, and the black silk drapery fell away. Now exposed to view for the very first time, the painting was greeted by several enthusiastic "oohs" and "ahs."

There in one group portrait was the family Custer, the brothers, George, Thomas, and Boston, the nephew, Autie Reed, and the brother-in-law, Jimmi Calhoun. In a ghostly background image was the regimental flag of the Seventh Cavalry. The title of the painting was "Following the Guidon."

As the crowd filed by for closer examination, many paused in front, just long enough to wipe tears from their eyes.

Kate and Quinn stood back, just out of the circle, watching the crowd's reaction.

"Are you going to tell them?" Quinn asked quietly.

"Tell them what?"

"That it was you who painted *Peacemaker* and *Following the Guideon*."

"No."

"Why not?"

"For one thing it was all we could do to get them to show *Peacemaker*," Kate said. "If the curators knew that I painted it, they wouldn't even consider showing it. And since they decided to make *Following the Guideon* the centerpiece of the entire show, it could put an indelible blemish on my father's entire career if word got out that I painted it. I can't allow that to happen."

"I can understand that," Quinn said. "But what about your own career?"

Smiling, Kate looked into Quinn's eyes. "I have a career. I am Mrs. Quinn Pendarrow."